BIRTH PLACE

A Collection of Recollections

Lindiwe Dhlakama

Published in 2019

Cover art by Eugene Ramirez Mapondera

Printed and bound in Zimbabwe

ISBN: 9781779064783

For my parents, Rebecca Dhlakama
and Lazarus Dhlakama.

Sapuya!

Jembe!

CONTENTS

Title Page 1
Copyright 2
Dedication 3
Chisipite 7
Who's the Witch? 37
Miseducation 77
What Happened to Rodney 111
The Promised Land 143
DNA 209
Chaos and Confusion 212
Trenches 243
How Daddy Happened 282
God of Man 306
The Interview 350
ACKNOWLEDGEMENTS 389

CHISIPITE

A cool breeze moved through the dry Savanna as the pink sun rose slowly above the distant hills. The imposter sun, waving to his idol, floated out further into the deep, green waters of the lake which also served as a waterhole. On the horizon one could make out the lone baobab tree because of its wide trunk which was scarred with the memories of those who had carved silent messages in it, used it to scratch their tough hides or simply to satiate misdirected aggression. Closer than the Baobab were the umbrella shaped Acacia trees which the animals loved to shelter under during the rainy season owing to their leafy canopies, but now was not that season and the hungry giraffes had aided in the trees' annual shedding. Dotted on the landscape were raison bushes, buffalo thorns and even cacti. Only the Savanna could shed her green garb and still look enchanting in her dusty, yellow-brown undergarments.

It was a chilly Autumn morning but by midday it would be scorching hot as the raging sun hung in a cloudless sky and the thorn trees would fail to give even the loneliest rock hyrax sufficient protection from the heat.

The rains were a few weeks gone but the morning dew never failed to give the illusion that it had drizzled during the night. The pied kingfisher screamed its war cry as it folded its dappled wings to swoop into the warm lake waters and grab an unsuspecting barred minnow. Besides the pied kingfisher all was still quiet, save for the wind whistling as it chased itself through the tall grass and, of course, a prolonged grunt from one of the bad-tempered black rhinos who were just awakening.

Steam rose from Itai's enamel cup. As a sentimental person, Itai had had his enamel cup for several years now. When his mother packed it for him just before he left home to come to Mutupo for work, it was a bright baby blue, but now it was a dull blue with silver-black patches where the paint had peeled off from friction with other crockery or from being dropped on the hard ground. Besides its sentimental value, to Itai it was a perfectly functional cup. You see Itai, an environmentalist, never threw anything away that could be recycled. He often waited until something broke down from old age or over-use before replacing it, and even then, it could be several weeks of mourning before then. That blue enamel cup would probably be recycled into a piggy bank should it let him down and spring a leak.

Itai looked down at the hot water with a sprinkle of tea leaves floating at its surface. He remembered that he needed to buy or borrow more tea leaves. His blood was probably well saturated with strong Tanganda tea as he never failed to have at least three cups a day regardless of the weather, but obviously more in winter and on rainy days. Tea was his cure for hunger when food was running low, loneliness when even the majesty of nature and Zama herself could not get his mind out of the dreary clouds and even served as his celebratory drink when all around him the other rangers were drinking home-made beer and spirits. It thus went without saying that he hated weak tea. Nevertheless, half a loaf was better than none and so he brought the warm enamel cup to his lips and stared out into his personal haven, keeping a close and loving eye on Zama, the love of his life and his sole purpose as far as he was concerned.

Itai loved tea and nature more than anything. This was because he was the fifth of six children to parents who used to be farm hands on a tea farm in Chipinge. He spent most of his life outdoors either helping his father with the farming or playing with his siblings and friends just outside the workers' compound. Sadly, these utopian days came to an abrupt end when Mr.

Bekker and his family the owners of the farm which he, his family and about two hundred other farm hands and their families were intimidated off their land by a large crowd of chanting political activists. Mr. Bekker's family had not put up much of a fight for fear of losing their lives because everyone was aware of the farm evasions which had started a year prior where several white farmers, particularly those who had tried to put up a fight legal or otherwise, had lost their lives. Itai suspected that Mr. Bekker's large farm had not been targeted earlier because he was a local favourite. Mr. Bekker, born and raised in Chipinge, could speak fluent Ndau and was always on good terms with everyone. Furthermore, he was always willing to help his community and he had built two public wells in his district, plus opened a free clinic on his property which his wife- a nurse, and mother- a retired doctor, worked at. When the community heard about the farm invasions, they swore -in the privacy of their own homes of course- that they would protect Mr. Bekker and his family to the death but that of course, was easier said than done.

Itai vividly remembered the day of the farm invasion. He was fourteen or fifteen years old. On that particular day he was playing a large game of soccer with his siblings and dozens of other children just outside the compound at dusk. All the farm work was finished for the day and his father no longer required his assistance. He heard the chanting and felt the stomping at first from very far away. Always having had very good hearing and always having been in touch with his senses he was the first to hear it. He stopped the game and asked the other children if they could hear it too or feel the earth vibrate but they, in their enthusiasm for the game, ignored him.

The chanting and stomping got louder and harder and soon on the horizon, all could see a large crowd surrounded by angry red dust approaching. No one knew what to think of it and so some of the children went back to call their parents. Itai knew what it meant, and the adults knew what it was as everyone had been anticipating it. Mr. Bekker and his family had been immediately cautioned and they fearfully locked themselves in the main house and told the workers to do the same in their own homes.

The large crowd grew louder like a swarm of disturbed locusts descending from the sky. Some of the brave or less obedient children waited until the very last possible moment, when the crowd was forcing its way through the gates, to run and hide in their parents' living quarters. That was the day Itai knew that life would never be the same.

From the day of the invasion he had expected life to turn bad, and it did. The Bekkers having left, the new owner of the farm told all the workers and their families to stay on and continue working. Out of desperation many did, but months passed and no salaries came from the new owner who was in fact a book keeper in Gweru so was seldom ever on the farm. The new owner moved half the workers out of their little homes and attempted to rent out the vacated houses. The machinery broke down and the well ran dry. Within a year, most of the workers had looted what they could off the farm to try and sell on their desperate journeys to find better working and living conditions. Itai's family was one of the last to leave because every day Itai's mother, strong in faith, convinced his father that Mr. Bekker would return, that he would put up a fight to get his farm back because he loved his farm family and would not let them struggle on like that. Itai's father, always a gentle man with his passionate wife, tolerated her fancies and stayed on, but secretly Itai knew that it was because they had nowhere else to go. Itai's father had grown up an orphan and had been lucky enough to get a job on that very farm at a young age. He excelled at his job, got married, brought his wife to the farm and got promoted to manager of farm equipment. When old Granddad Bekker became ill and needed round the clock supervision it was Itai's mother who was called upon to look after his every need and this provided an extra income for his family. Life was good for Itai's family and the farm was all Itai knew and wanted.

After a year the last of the farm workers were forced off the farm as the new owner decided to build lodges on the property to try and lure tourists despite there being no tourist attractions nearby. Itai's father, perhaps due to his sentimental attachment to the farm and having nowhere else to go, tried one night to convince the new owner to let him stay on and turn over a good crop yield for him. Itai's mother and the children held their breaths as they waited for their father to return. On his return the family took one look at his face and knew they needed to pack up their belongings and be ready to leave the following morning.

From there his family went to live in the rural areas for many months with their mother's second cousin. Itai's father went first to Chipinge town and then on to Harare to look for employment. Against all odds, the family flourished in rural Chipinge. They cultivated their aunt's land and the children played outdoors all day. Itai even enjoyed his role as chief cowherd more than going to school- which he and his siblings no longer did as there was no money for school fees.

Nearly a year had gone by when the family received word from their father that he had secured a job and lodging in Harare and was eager for his family to finally join him. They were all excited for the change except for Itai who had grown to despise change and who had a feeling that he was going to hate city life. Upon arrival in the capital he discovered that there was hardly any grass at all. He had never seen so many buildings and pavements and cars. His father tried to assure the family that the small cottage that they lived in at the end of the garden he worked as a gardener in was a step up the ladder, but a few cramped weeks later proved otherwise. The parents bickered more and more and tensions were always high as everyone lived on top of each other. There was still no money for school so instead the children walked to town every day except for Sundays to entertain themselves or to try and look for a livelihood and, for the two older girls, to increase their chances of being sought by suiters. Their daily walks to town worked in their favour. Several months into their move Itai's oldest sister got married to the man who she had just fallen pregnant by and who also convinced her to go and live in Mazowe with his mother. She happily obliged and took her younger sister with her. The two older brothers told their parents a vague story about how they had made a deal to procure a plot in Mutare and were off. Itai got a job in a store that sold farming equipment in town as a sales clerk and Itai's youngest brother stayed home to help his father with the gardening and his mother, who was discovered to be four months pregnant with her seventh child but being of a mature age was advised not to put too much strain on herself, around the cottage.

Even though Itai was excellent at his job he hated it with a passion. Even more than that, he hated the cramped cottage and the dirty city of Harare. He was not used to being trapped in a building all day and all night and he so missed running with the wind and being roused with the sun by the purple crested louries during the rainy summer months.

Then one day, Itai helped a customer who was particularly chatty. "I'm going to volunteer at Mutupo with the Rhino's this week so I need this list of equipment, you know, so I don't go empty handed," the customer informed him as he pushed her trolley around the store collecting everything on her list. That evening, he used one of his precious dollars in an internet café in town. He had learnt the power of the internet on one of his daily walks with his siblings in the past, and him and his brothers had taken the time to learn how to Google information. He sat at a computer and stared blankly at the screen holding the piece of paper with login details in his hand trying to remember what to do.

"You punch in that code into that space," an impatient lab assistant called out from across the room. He did so, clicked on the Google Chrome icon and typed in the words 'Mutupo' and '*Chipembere*'. He clicked on the first link that showed up and gasped at the image of a vast wilderness with rhinos, elephants, buffalos and giraffes that popped up. His gut told him that this is where he needed to be. He tore off a page from the user manual next to his keyboard, wrote down the nature reserve's address and hurried home.

That evening he told his parents that he was going to go to Marondera to look after Rhinos. His mother said that that would not be a lucrative business decision as rhinos were not as far as she knew, edible. His father said that he would rather Itai stayed put at his current job, especially since volunteers did not get paid, and that he needed Itai's earnings to help with the new baby that was on the way. Itai said nothing and the topic was soon closed. However, early the next morning Itai packed up a few belongings, took his money from under his mattress, put half in his pocket and the other half next to his sleeping father's head and left to go figure out where he could find transport that headed in the direction of Marondera and Mutupo Nature Reserve.

Two days later a dirty, tired and penniless Itai walked confidently into Alice's office and declared that he was there to volunteer to look after the rhinos. Alice sat him down, offered him a strong cup of tea, apologising for the lack of milk, and called her husband Kristopher in from outside where he was flying his drone and recording aerial shots of the land.

"Unfortunately, our volunteer program is not all the way running at the moment what with the poaching tragedy," Kris said apologetically. Itai nodded, gulped down the last of his tea and stood up to leave. "We, we are looking for full time game rangers though, if... if you are qualified. The rhinos and elephants now need round the clock surveillance and protection of course. We may need two rangers per rhino. Do you have a CV or reference I could get in contact with?" Itai smiled, sat back down and told the apologetic couple all about his life, from the Bekker Farm to cow herding in rural Chipinge. The couple looked at each other a while when he had finished and seemed to communicate silently. "I, I mean, I guess we can get Advance to train you on what you need to know. He's the lead game ranger," Kris added, "Look, we've been hit hard, as Mutupo and as a country economically, so I mean, your salary won't be that great, more of an allowance really until we get back to our former glory."

"But," Alice chimed in, pink in the face, "of course you do get accommodation since it is an around the clock job and we do provide one meal a day. Sadza or rice in the evenings. Right Kris?" she looked up at her husband who nodded. Itai nodded too and then all three where nodding all at each other. Itai stood up extended his hand to Kris who shook it and asked Alice where Advance could be found. The rest was history.

Itai moved his blue enamel cup in a circular motion before taking his final gulp of now cold tea. He watched Zama struggle to get up for a few seconds before her stocky legs finally managed to balance her rotund body. She grunted a warning when the two male white rhinos, Nhowe and Hasha, sauntered over to the bush she intended to make her breakfast and the two bachelors took the hint and moved of sullenly in the opposite direction, stopping to munch on some grass as they did so. Itai saw Advance and Sam climb onto the low boughs of a nearby acacia tree from where they could keep an eye on their wards until their bachelors decided to move further off and they would have to leave their comfortable sentry points and follow them.

Itai got a call on his radio informing him that Kris needed him to ride on one of the safari trucks for the morning tour. "But Zama..." he tried to interject. Kris assured him that Zama would be well taken care of by Shingirirai and although Itai did not trust Zama with anybody, let alone Shingirirai as he was only a new ranger, he conceded and made his way to Sable Lodge where the tours began. Itai knew Mutupo inside out and could fill any job at the nature reserve, but his most important job was taking care of and protecting Zama. Not only was this because he felt, of course, sentimental to the rhino he single-handedly raised from a traumatised calf, but also because this once timid and clumsy calf was now pregnant with the reserve's first calf since the poaching incident which had set the rhino breeding program way back. If all went well Zama would not only give birth to a calf, but to new hope.

As Kris drove one of the two tour trucks Itai sat with the passengers explaining the reserve's history and telling them facts about the various animals they came across. Kris stopped the truck and a tower of giraffes appeared to float gracefully towards the truck. As they neared, Itai stopped dolling out his facts on giraffes and retrieved a sack from under his seat. He emptied the sacks contents- dry vegetable pellets- into several small heaps only a couple of meters from the truck and the passengers oohed and aahed as one by one the giraffes spread wide their long forelegs and lowered their graceful necks to the ground far below them to feed on Itai's offerings. A baby began to cry as a young giraffe smacked his powerful neck into that of a giraffe eating near the truck. The assaulted giraffe bolted and the aggressor took over the abandoned pile of food.

The oohs and aahs turned into groans and gasps as at Happy the Crocodile's large enclosure, Itai concluded his information session by jumping nimbly over the low walls of his enclosure to deliver to Happy the thigh and leg of a Zebra. Itai casually dropped the thigh and leg a meter away to the left of the sullen looking Happy and stood slightly to the right of him. Happy, whose tail alone was in the swampy waters, opened is yellow lizard eyes and saw the meat. "*Hesi,* Happy," Itai greeted him. The crowd gasped as the obese crocodile elevated himself on his stubby legs. Itai knew that the gasp was less in awe of his majesty and more shock that such an unapologetically portly creature could move at all. The judgemental gasp must not have affected Happy at all because he made his way slowly to the meat and took it in his powerful jaws. The crowd gasped again when Happy turned and made his way at lightning speed into the water, disappearing with his easy earned meal. Itai knew that this time they were impressed. "Happy and I know and respect each other," Itai explained when one of the elderly passengers chided him for playing with his life. Kris drove on as Itai answered the numerous questions that were being fired in his direction.

They drove past a sounder of warthogs. They stopped briefly for Itai to dole out his facts. The warthogs, which before the disturbance seemed to be on an urgent family mission, stopped too and looked on at them as if wondering what such ugly creatures which walked on only two legs could possibly be doing in the wilderness. Itai secretly thought that the adult warthog looked like a displeased British man from the Elizabethan era, complete with the moustache and only lacking a single eye glass from which to pass judgement through. He was however, advised not to voice this observation to the tourists early on in his career as someone had taken offence to the comparison. The warthogs finished passing their judgement and then trotted off followed but their five little piglets who, though cute, looked like smaller versions of Itai's displeased British gentleman.

Kris drove the truck on, past an open gate and stopped briefly for Itai to open another gate which they drove through and waited for Itai to hop back on the truck after closing it. They drove into a sort of clearing surrounded by trees with scratched bark and broken branches. This unsettled some of the passengers as they thought that whatever had left such a huge scar on the vegetation must be large and angry. In the stationary truck they all looked around wondering what it was they were going to see. They all nearly jumped when they saw the three large elephants only a short distance from the truck. Itai chuckled and explained that despite being the largest land mammal elephants were very quiet animals. He explained too that the massacred wildlife around them was simply due to one of the bulls scratching his back. Itai hopped out the truck and emptied a sack of vegetable pellets into three neat piles for the elephants. The mighty beasts used their trunks to pick up the food and feed it into their mouths. Itai made small talk with the elephants' rangers as the passengers took pictures and took in the amazing animals. After a while, from the distance came trotting the biggest elephant that any of the passengers had ever seen. He had enormous ears which he used to cool his body and two large, strong tusks. One of his tusks was slightly shorter than the other but despite this he was the most handsome of them all. "*Hesi*, Toto, hello," Itai greeted him affectionately as he came to a holt next to the other elephants near the truck. Samson, his ranger, came jogging just behind Toto. The other elephants had already finished their treats and there was nothing for Toto left. Toto looked around and used his trunk to fidget with his tusks like a shy child too timid to admit that he really wanted some treats too. After some time Itai got back into the truck as Kris started up the engine.

"*Iwe* Itai," Samson called after him, "*Ipawo* Toto *chikafu*. Give Toto some treats!"

"*Ah iye anga arikupi Toto wacho*? Where was he all this time? His loss" Itai admonished.

Samson pleaded his ward's case. Kris killed the engine whilst Itai jumped off the truck and grabbed a new sack off the truck and opened it.

"*Arikutopedzera dzimwe mhuka*. He's taking other animals' share," Itai tutted as Samson bent down to scoop up as many pellets as he could from the sack. Toto was grateful that Samson had advocated for him and he moved his great head up and down in gratitude. Samson, food in hand, stood in front of Toto and the giant beast opened its mouth and Samson threw the pellets in. The passengers were mesmerized by Toto's charm. One passenger reached out his hand from where he sat to try and touch Toto but Itai quickly explained that although charming, Toto and all the animals at Mutupo were still in fact wild animals and should be respected as such. It was only the rangers that spent their lives with their specific animal that were allowed near them as they knew how to interact with the animals with love and respect. As the truck drove away the passengers smiled at the image of Samson and Toto together, Samson hanging on to Toto's tusks and Toto lifting him off the ground.

They drove on for a while until they reached a herd of buffalo which was grazing peacefully. Amidst the buffalo, towards the front of the herd was an elephant- the self-proclaimed matriarch of the herd. Sindi the Confused Elephant, Itai explained, was the first elephant to arrive at the reserve and having no other family, they made the decision to put the young elephant with the buffalo. It was a long two years before the reserve got more elephants and, in that time, it was ingrained in Sindi's mind that she was a buffalo so much so that now when the other elephants tried to communicate with her, she could not respond to the foreign creatures, and had no desire to. The situation did not stop there. Itai explained that Sindi in the past caused the Buffalo population to dwindle because every time a bull mounted a cow, Sindi would see it as a challenge to her authority and get into such a fit of rage that she would often kill the bull, thus stopping the reproductive process whilst also culling the herd. Now, he continued to explain, they had to separate Sindi from her family at night and at times even ball chain her to give the herd a chance to reproduce. Goodness knew, Itai added, what Sindi thought when a calf was born.

Thoroughly amused, they drove on, back the way they came and towards the area which they knew they would find the reserves most important tenants – the Rhinos – two white and four black. The truck parked near Zama, with two other black rhinos in the near distance. Zama was picking at a shrub for her second breakfast, undisturbed by the fascinated humans.

"If you are brave enough you can come out of the truck," Itai announced, winking. A scrawny but rowdy orange-headed boy jumped out without hesitation. "How fast can you run young man?" Itai asked him. The boy told a story about how he was the fastest sprinter in his class and Itai smiled down at him. "Zama can run up to 55km per hour, especially when she is irritated. Can you run that fast?" The boy promptly climbed back into the truck. Itai stood up in front of the crowd and straightened his back so that he was as tall and present as possible. Behind him the two black rhinos moved on from the bushes they were foraging and their rangers followed them at a respectable distance. Zama, only several meters from Itai and the truck of gawking onlookers, turned so that she had her eye on the humans. Itai recited all his facts about rhinos, only stopping when Kris hopped out the driver's seat and suggested that he make the big announcement already. "Here," Itai cleared his throat, "here at Mutupo Nature Reserve, we run a black rhino breeding program. Times have been tough and we are still recovering from a devastating poaching incident. But we are very proud to announce, here at Mutupo Nature Reserve, that, we are expecting our very first baby from Zama that you see here." Much to Itai's delight and expectation the crowd clapped and cheered. Zama, however, was not too happy about the celebration because she gave a prolonged grunt and turned to face the truck head on. Heeding the warning Itai and Kris got back into the truck and drove on, leaving the expectant mother to be in peace.

"She's fifteen months pregnant, meaning baby should be arriving any time now. That is why we keep a close eye on her. I was the one that discovered the pregnancy. How? You test her udder to see if she is lactating and I saw that yes, she was. I do not advise that anyone do this, only someone who that particular rhino trusts. I have been with Zama since she herself was just a baby," Itai said responding to a question. He turned to see if Shingirirai's eyes were indeed on Zama. Shingirirai yawned from his low bough on his tree perch. When he noticed Itai looking at him he grinned and waved at him enthusiastically. Itai nodded back. He was an okay boy, Itai thought, but he had much to learn. Itai was not altogether comfortable leaving Zama under his drowsy supervision. Upon questioning, Itai explained why none of the Rhinos had horns. He explained that after the poaching incident nature reserves had concluded that it was safest for the rhinos if they sawed off their horns. That way, poachers would have little to no incentive. He explained that government officials would come and saw off the horns, what the government did with the horns, he was not willing to speculate, nor could he say why the reserve did not often receive the subsidies they were meant to receive in the exchange.

"What happened with the poaching incident?" asked a coloured woman with a baby on her hip and a pale ginger next to her. Itai turned back to the passengers, reluctantly peeling his eyes from the grazing Zama.

Itai managed to divert the crowd's attention away from the question by dolling out information about the wildebeest and zebra as one particular wildebeest, having been separated from most of the other wildebeest and zebras raced the truck and ran in front of it, instead of crossing the path behind the truck. "As you can see," Itai said, "the wildebeest is not a smart animal.

The only way it gets by is by following and copying the zebra. The great migration- it will be the zebra that is migrating and the wildebeest simply following. Even when there is a predator, say, a hungry lion, the wildebeest only run away because the smart zebras are running away, otherwise it would just run in circles. That is why you will always find zebras close to where wildebeests are!" The crowd chuckled and looked on at the silly wildebeest as it rejoined the rest of its family. The truck came to an abrupt stop and waited as a tortoise crossed the dusty road. Halfway across the road the tortoise decided that it was shy and retreated into its shell. Itai stopped his tortoise facts and jumped out the truck to move the tortoise out of the road. He held it up to the crowd before setting it down in the shrubbery beside the road. Itai hopped back into the truck and they continued to the Eastern reservoir where lunch would be served. There everyone settled down to a light lunch and relaxation. It was then that someone raised the question about the poaching incident again.

Itai had not been there personally otherwise, he likes to believe, the incident would not have happened at all. He had however, heard enough to put two and two together and build his memory of the happenings of that day.

It must have been early morning, perhaps a couple of hours before the light of day. A truck-load of men came with powerful ammunition which would deliver fatal blows to even the biggest rhino. Some came in a helicopter and landed in the tall grass. The noise startled the sleeping rhinos awake and they ran away from the commotion, but the poachers were excellent marksmen- they aimed and fired, almost always killing the rhino. They made sure not to damage the precious horns when killing the animals. Once the marksmen killed each rhino, two men would run up to the diseased creature and saw off its horns, in some cases even the smaller horn. They sawed at the flesh, blood splattering everywhere. Some of the rhinos did not die instantly from the bullets, they must have died from blood loss after half their face was sawed off. The poachers chuckled and joked as they worked. Itai had seen the pictures of the devastation. He could not look at those pictures without feeling sick to his stomach. He flipped through the album with the pictures in but by the eleventh picture he had excused himself and went outside and thrown up against a tree. The poachers worked as fast and as efficiently as any professional villains could. Shooting, and hacking, and sawing and dragging. They hunted down all the rhinos, killing Kaya last, Kaya was pregnant with what would have been the reserves eleventh black rhino. Her baby died in her stomach as she bled to death as the men hacked at her face. They finished up and loaded the horns into their truck and helicopter. By the time the Mutupo family got to the scene it was much too late. All there was left was a field of rhino cadavers, trails of blood, bullet shells and shrapnel. Blood seeped into the black soil slowly and thickly like honey on bread, but more bitter than sweet. As the blood sunk deeper into the dark earth, so did the nation's only rhino breeding program, hope for endangered wildlife conservation and hope for the nation in general. All were devastated. All was devastated. All was ruined.

A young white rhino which had not yet horned was badly injured, but had escaped the worst of it and Kris and his team had managed to save Hasha. It was Zama though, who stole everyone's hearts. She was a very young calf and her mother, Nandi, had been killed. In fear and confusion she had managed to run, crashing through a fence, into the buffalo's territory and in amongst large bales of hay she hid. It was after the body count did not add up that Alice knew that Zama was missing. They searched for her for two days and when she was found she was in very poor health. Her wounds were infected and she was weak from hunger and thirst. She did not walk, even after she was put on medication and fed. For months she did not walk due to the trauma of what had happened and no one knew what to do with her. When Itai started working there Zama still would not walk. Itai went into the enclosure where they kept her and knelt beside her. She turned her head and the two eyed each other. Her with suspicion and him with determination. For several minutes man and beast remained that way, staring at each other. From that day on Itai made Zama his personal responsibility and less than two weeks thereafter Zama was walking, not very well at first, but within the month she would trot timidly after Itai as he did his chores around the reserve. That was several years ago and now she was grown and confident and man and beast maintained a relationship built on trust and respect, and though Itai kept this to himself, love.

The crowd was quiet. Some were sad, some angry, some both, but that all turned to confusion and a feeling of betrayal when Itai answered one of their questions.

"No, it wasn't men from Mozambique who poached. The poachers, they were in our nation's army uniform," he said, looking out across the water.

There was nothing left to say after that.

Itai was glad when the day was done. He did not stay to chat and play checkers or draughts with the others after dinner. He was feeling anxious and on edge and he concluded that it was because of the painful memory that he had to dig up that afternoon. He went into his room. He opened his cabinet and poured the last of his Tanganda tea leaves into his blue enamel cup. The tea leaves would not have filled even half a teaspoon and he knew that drinking tea that weak would be the equivalent to just drinking hot water. Nonetheless he poured some boiling water into the cup because he knew that he needed any amount of tea to calm his nerves. The tea leaves hardly stained the water so he added an extra teaspoon of his brown honey to compensate. The hot liquid did indeed calm his nerves as it ran down his throat and warmed him. From a small leather purse in his clothes drawer he counted out some money. He took half of it and put it in an envelope which also contained a page length letter to his parents. On the front of the envelope he wrote their address and licked the envelope shut. He sat for a moment longer to finish and savour his tea. Just as he got up to leave the room Itai got a call on his radio. His heart began to beat fast when he recognised Shingirirai's breathless voice.

"What is it?" Itai demanded, his own voice rising

to unnatural levels in panic.

"I've, I've phoned Kris," Shingirirai managed to reply, not quite answering the question.

"*Chii ko?* What is it please?" Itai pleaded.

"Za, Zama," was the response, "Oh I see Kris arriving..."

Itai was out the door, running toward where he knew Zama would be at that time of day. He arrived to find a restless Zama, a wide eyed Shingirirai and Kris and Dr Chan a respectable distance from her.

Shingirirai clutched his arm, "*Mukoma*, big brother, I had my eye on her the whole time. I don't know what's wrong with her she just started acting strange and making these sounds. I swear I had my eye on her the entire day, *naMwari*, by God!"

Itai shook him off, sighed and offered up a brief prayer to the heavens above. He patted Shingirirai's back and nodded at Kris and the doctor. "It's alright. Take it easy brother, she is in labour." The doctor nodded and explained to Shingirirai what was happening. The young ranger grinned sheepishly, relieved that it was not owing to his carelessness that Zama would soon be a mother.

It was another three hours before the calf began

to make an appearance. Zama was restless but strong and determined, and after a while the calf began to very slowly slide out. Dr Chan saw no need for any intervention and from her warning grunts when anyone got too close to her, neither did Zama. However, as the calf came slipping out Itai places a blanket on the ground just behind Zama so that the calf would not land on the hard ground.

The calf had finally arrived. Mutupo's fifth black rhino and seventh rhino. The first calf to be born after the tragedy. Itai was beside himself with joy. He hid his tears from the others by bending his head to look down at the calf as he rubbed it dry with a rough blanket. Zama grunted and pushed him away from her new calf with her heavy head. Still, she did not mind too much that he knelt close by, staring at the new born whilst she fussed over it. Kris stood behind Itai with his hand on Itai's shoulder. Shingirirai and the vet stood just behind them.

"Name her," Kris said gently to Itai,
"Youname her Itai. You name her."

Itai tried to speak but his voice
croaked. He cleared his throat.
"Chisipite. I will name her Chisipite
because she is a spring, a fountain
that brings new hope to a parched

land."

Zama gave a long, low grunt of approval. Her breath forming steam that rose from her nostrils and into the cool night air.

WHO'S THE WITCH?

There is a small town and rural area called Chipinge. That is, for the most part, where this story takes place. It is a small town to the South of South East of Zimbabwe's capital Harare, and about eight hours away- depending on who is driving. Chipinge lies on the boarder of Zimbabwe and Mozambique and is so undisturbed by infrastructure that one has simply to walk past a couple of bushes and around a few trees to pass between the two countries. Whilst crossing between the two countries, one has also to believe that the landmines that the Portuguese colonizers planted along the outermost parts of Mozambique before they left were either all removed, have long since detonated, or are simply too old to be set off. In any case, no horrors of landmines have yet been told.

There was a tribe led by Soshangane and so called, that migrated from the Zulu Kingdom within present day South Africa, fleeing the blood thirsty and brutal rule of Shaka kaSenzangakhona, more contemporarily known as Shaka Zulu, some years prior to the year 1828. This was the breaking up and the separation of the Nguni. I am not certain of what came of the other Nguni families, many of whom undoubtedly fled the south of Africa moving up Northward, but I do know what happened to my Nguni people, the Soshangane. My ancestors travelled North until they came to the edge of present-day Zimbabwe and settled in modern day Chipinge, spilling over somewhat into the neighbouring Mozambique region. Their Zulu tongues took on the Shona melody of the indigenous people yet stopped just past half way, thus forming the Ndau dialect that we are ridiculed for today. The Shona say we sound funny when we speak. Many of us also speak Zulu which is why we blend well with Zimbabwe's Ndebele people and a lot of us are mistaken for Ndebele people because of our names which sound like, or are, Ndebele. However, many of us neglect our dialect daily to be better understood by the Shona people who make up most of the country. In the end, we fit in everywhere, and nowhere.

To my recollection Chipinge is hot and dusty. Its landscape has only sparse patches of green and the rest has scarred and broken pieces of trees that were once alive but whose spirits have long since left the land where desperation has driven out the respectful fear of nature. You see, wood is the only form of fuel there is there, and the trees are dead or dying and all sorts of erosion is rampant. The rivers and streams- their water levels are low for no reasons that are apparent, but the little water there is is still used daily for baths and for laundry and recreational purposes.

The Ndau people, if I am to make a sweeping statement, are not as scarred and barren as the landscape. On the contrary, they are a welcoming people with rich histories and a culture so deep that globalisation has not yet managed to dilute it to nothingness. Their histories are written in tales of old, clay pots painted bright with different types of soil and the names they call each other by. The best thing to do, if you are Ndau, is to marry another Ndau so that you do not dilute the richness of your culture with the liquidities of the other types of Shona or

Ndebele people and so that any offspring had are not confused and ultimately led astray from what they truly are.

Ndau people are often made fun of for the

way they speak, but they speak with pride and often a little bit too loudly and emphatically. Still, most of what they speak is of ancient wisdom passed down from generation to generation. Some of these wisdoms, the ones that can be explained in laymen's terms, consist of which herbs are effective for contraception, which words to speak to an enemy to destroy him without seeming to, which crops do best in which season and which essential oils will make your hair grow thicker.

One thing that I have failed to mention until now is that this area Chipinge, for a reason I will refrain from speculating about, is most notoriously known for witchcraft. It is the town and rural area in Zimbabwe people go to when they need supernatural assistance. Like I mentioned earlier, the Ndau are teased for the way they speak, but they that tease them do so quietly so that the one speaking does not hear them lest they take offense and cast a spell on them. The people of Zimbabwe are still very much in touch with their essence and so they know and are weary of the effects of spells and potions. I heard of a man from a high-density suburb who made the mistake, once, of stealing a chicken from his neighbour who he did not know – surely, he did not know beforehand – was actually from Chipinge. The neighbour did not see him or know who it was that had stolen from her, all she knew was that her chicken was no longer there. She shook her head and casually went about her business as usual. However, it is said that the next day after a long restful night of sleep after the thief had killed, cooked and eaten the chicken, it is said that he woke up with no mouth. He had no mouth and instead, where his lips should have been, he had a beak. You can imagine the shock and the fear and even the ridicule he had to endure as he walked through the neighbourhood as surely, he eventually had to. I do not know what became of this man, bird, thief or even where he is today after the story was splashed on the front page of every newspaper in Harare. I do wonder though from time to time, if he ever stole again.

For ease of reference, but mainly for entertainment purposes, I have compiled a short and brief list of the most popular supernatural things, for lack of a better word, that have come out of or are said about Chipinge and its witchcraft:

Tokoloshi: the tokoloshi is a small trinket or being that one procures for personal benefits usually affiliated with wealth. It is usually something given to you by a witchdoctor or herbalist which is not easily described to others and should not be seen by anyone aside from the person that procured it. It is said- because I have never knowingly seen it with my own eyes-that its most common form is one that resembles the African equivalent of a Leprechaun. A small little man with a bad and mysterious temperament that runs from shade to shade in fear of being discovered. I believe that it is a small man just as I've described who goes about doing his masters bidding and casting black magic on those that anger his master. In my mind, he is much like J.K Rowling's house elf except unapologetic and powerful. There are reportedly numerous encounters that holy men have had with these tokoloshis after they have been summoned to rid the area of one that a nosey neighbour has reported their dubious neighbour of having. In these encounters, which are reported in newspapers and sometimes on national news, the tokoloshi is photographed or shown having already been destroyed and burnt to only a pile of ashes very different in resemblance to the description that the holy man and a few lucky neighbours describe it to have been in originally to the journalist. Sometimes, however, the audience gets to see it before the holy man destroys it but in these underwhelming cases it has usually magicked itself into a form more accommodating to the human eye which is usually that of a nondescript old rolled up rag or an eerie basket or clay pot of some sorts. Some say tokoloshis can also take the form of cats or owls.

Snakes: These snakes can be said to be in the

same family as a tokoloshi. They are acquired the same way and often they grow constantly to the size, some have been reported, of a very large python or anaconda. These snakes are not to be mistaken for the common scientifically recorded types of snakes that anyone can find in the wild, no, these snakes are nameless but one thing that differentiates them from other snakes is not that they are venomous, it is that they can talk. Not only can they talk, but these snakes are procured from wherever talking snakes are procured from because they vomit money. They are gotten for the sole purpose of them vomiting money- and US dollars at that, not bond notes- for their masters. I should also like to think that they would also have a companionship advantage since they can talk. It would be a waste to feel lonely with a talking snake in the house. I also believe from the experience of others, that these snakes differ from tokoloshis in temperament as they can be quite amiable. My brother's wife told me of a story about one such snake which stood at the edge of the road trying to hitch a ride. Frustrated it moved further into the road and with, I assume, its tail end, it managed to hail a kombi which stopped. It climbed into the kombi, shot-gun seat, before anyone knew what to do. I don't imagine that anyone ran out of the vehicle screaming. I think perhaps curiosity got the better of the driver, the conductor and the passengers, and also, I suspect that no one wanted to offend the gentleman snake by running away from it whilst it, like everyone else, was just trying to get from point A to point B in the quickest way possible. So, the snake that had hailed the vehicle with what I would assume would be its tail end, climbed into the passenger seat and requested that the driver take him to a certain address where he and his owner lived. Whilst on the way the snake told the driver and the eavesdropping passengers the very sad story of how his master thought he had no more use for him and so had tied him up in a sack, driven several hours away from home into the wilderness, and there had thrown him into a river where he thought he would drown and be gone forever. The snake told his audience that he had, thank God, managed to escape the sack before he drowned and now he was on his way back to his owner whom he missed very much. The driver, to be polite, berated the owner's carelessness and selfishness and wished the snake well. The kombi driver uncharacteristically drove the snake right up to the gate of where he said he lived and just before the snake left the vehicle he thanked the driver for his kindness and offered to pay him. The driver declined emphatically saying that it was his prerogative to help a fellow countryman whenever he could without expecting payment. Whilst the driver was still talking the snake vomited right there and then on the seat that he was seated on. He opened his mouth vide, revealing his glittering fangs and from the depths of him he vomited hundreds upon hundreds of one hundred US dollar notes onto the seat and floor of the kombi. No one moved or made a sound until the snake, well spent, finished vomiting money. Anyone that has ever thrown up knows that it can take a lot out of you and so the snake was tired and panting by the time it had finished. It climbed out of the kombi and warned the driver to spend the money within twenty-four hours before the money expired. The driver was speechless and he and the passengers could only stare, rather rudely in my opinion, as the generous talking snake that vomited money slithered under the gate of his house towards the owner that had tried to dump and drown him.

Pot Plants: Plants, though not as extravagant as talking snakes that vomit money, are also useful and are the most subtle and modest form of supernatural items. These plants can also acquire wealth and other blessings. These plants are often displayed in the houses of the owner in plain view so one could never be sure if they have seen one such plant or any other potted plant. I heard of a woman who acquired one such magical plant for personal reasons after her husband left her for another woman. It is said that this woman would lovingly water her plant every day at sunrise with milk and that the plant, in return, was good to her. As the plant grew bigger and bigger, bringing bigger and bigger blessings into her home, it started to demand that it be watered at sunset instead of sunrise, and with blood instead of milk. The woman, rather shaken, tried to water it with the blood of a goat, but it told her that it could taste the difference and it emphatically demanded to be watered with human blood. I tried to find out what became of the woman and her plant but I found no leads.

Ghosts: Ghosts are not to be claimed as a product of Chipinge because there are ghosts in all countries and all cultures. However, there are different types of ghosts and ominous beings and unlike tokoloshis and snakes, they are not items one can claim for their own benefit as they do what they want and often go about their own biddings. The most common type of ghost is a *chidhoma*. A *chidhoma* has no describable form but it makes its presence known by appearing as a fire which bounces off the ground and disappears into the sky before anyone can make head and tail of it and whilst people run away. Some say that a *chidhoma* is the restless spirit of a dead person who has nowhere to go and whose sole purpose it to scare the living with its skeletal form- not to be confused with a *ngozi*. Another type of ghost is called a *dzangaradzimu*. This ghost is white and so tall that if you look up at it in an effort to see its face all you will see are legs that disappear into the sky. I asked someone who was born and raised in Chipinge whether they had ever seen a ghost and they said no, although they had on many occasions fled in the direction which peers where also fleeing in after someone had screamed that there was a ghost ahead of them.

I would, if I may, like to put dogs in this category as well, but not as an item of witchcraft or even an agent of evil, but as a sensor and seer of things not easily seen by man, and this I can testify to from personal experience. I have once been outside at night in the dark playing with my dog when suddenly the dog stopped playing and began barking at something in front of it. I, not easily spooked, looked in the direction in which it was barking as the barking got more incessant but I could not see anything. I walked forward a bit in an effort to make sure of the nothing that I was seeing and my dog pushed her body against my legs as if begging me not to be so foolish as to approach the invisibility. I told the dog that there was nothing there but after a while the dog began to back up, as if the nothingness was approaching us. My dog, intimidated, stopped barking, whined and then ran off, leaving me in the darkness alone with the thing. There are many stories of dogs barking at things that the

human eyes are not

privileged to see and one should always heed a dog's warning. It is also said that in a home where sickness is rife the home's dog, if it one day throws its head back and howls at the sky is announcing the approach of death and the ill person's family will know to prepare accordingly.

Avenging Spirits: Avenging spirits, known as *Ngozi*, are also not exclusively from Chipinge. They can be from anywhere and, simply explained, are the spirits of people that have been murdered that come back to haunt, torture, and kill off the family members and livestock of the person or people responsible for the person's death. I am most appreciative of this form of supernatural experience as it stops mindless murders and punishes perpetrators. There is a man from Gokwe allegedly, who was killed by a thug and his friends over a political dispute. The issue was supposed to be swept under the rug as it was of a political nature but when it came time for the coffin containing the young man's body to be moved from the morgue and taken to a burial ground, the coffin would not lift. For nearly a year the coffin refused to budge and, in the meantime, various sightings of the diseased young man were reported around the town. He was said to casually walk through the halls of hospitals, sit around graveyards or even stroll down busy highways. Various family members from the murderer's family began to die and all who had done an injustice to the young man in his death, be it the doctor who falsified his cause of death, the policemen who failed to arrest the murderer and those that aided in committing the murder, their loved ones began to die mysteriously, they themselves died or they lost their minds completely. The *Ngozi* only stopped and the coffin only allowed itself to be moved and buried when the family of the murderer agreed *kuripa,* that is, to pay several hundred heads of cattle and to admit to and apologise and turn themselves in for the crime that had been committed. Only then was the *Ngozi* appeased and the spirit of the young man no longer sighted.

Njuzu: *Njuzu* are mermaids and need no explanation save to say that they differ from the Western mermaids in that they are evil and not well meaning and docile like the likes of Ariel. What happens is that a person is taken from the shores of rivers and other water bodies by a mermaid. The mermaid takes this person for witchcraft purposes and if the mermaid likes the person the person will be somewhat inducted into their world and live underwater forever. The family and friends of the person that has been taken by a *njuzu* are not supposed to shed even one tear for their lost loved one. It they do, the mermaid will know and the person turns up washed up on the shore but with their head on backwards and obviously dead. I have only heard of one person, a young woman, who survived a mermaid, but I am undecided if survive is the right word for someone who has lost their mind.

N'anga: a *n'anga* is what is known in English as a witchdoctor. Some call themselves herbalists. *N'angas* are where people go to acquire such things as tokoloshis and talking snakes. *N'angas* are also the people to go to find out the truth about ominous occurrences and the likes. There are many *n'angas* in Chipinge.

Ceremonies: In Chipinge, and quite frankly all over the nation, there are several different ceremonies held whereby the ancestral spirit of a long dead relative possesses the body of a living person and speaks through them, often first demanding a beer to quench the thirst that is gotten, they admit, from coming from an extremely hot and burning climate. These ceremonies often involve several days of drinking and dancing and chanting before the host that the spirit has chosen to speak through begins to burp uncontrollably as the spirit makes its presence known before drinking and then announcing what it had arrived on earth to announce.

Lightning: Lightning is probably the most common form of witchcraft in Chipinge. So common is it that it is said to be sold in the market places of that area. Lightning is used by slighted people who seek to get revenge on the people who have hurt or offended them. You purchase your lightning and then send it to the person whom you want it to deal with. Where this lightning strikes, it leaves having laid eggs, perhaps for people to know that it is not the normal type of lightning.

Educational though this little glossary is, my personal advice would be for the public not to try and acquire or take part in these forms of witchcraft for something which people perceive to have such great benefit doesn't come without a great price to pay. In many cases, that price is often the sacrifice of a human life. Often, the family members of the owner of a tokoloshi or other item of witchcraft begin to die off mysteriously as the person becomes richer and richer. They sacrifice their family for riches which are undoubtedly only temporary. I cannot imagine what happens to the owners of witchcraft once they themselves die, often prematurely. However, I digress.

This story is about a victim of witchcraft in the absence of witchcraft. We will call our protagonist old lady, quite simply, Gogo.

Gogo lived in rural Chipinge. She had had her children and they were grown and had long since left the nest. Gogo was a widow and lived a quiet, inconspicuous life alone, working hard, working well, and enjoying the fruits of her many years of labour. Although she kept to herself, she was friendly when approached and always willing to lend a helping hand, an ear to listen and any spare clothes or food that she had. Her wrinkles had formed over the years and lay across the bottom half of her face giving her a permanent smile. Although she was old she was strong and happy. She had a modest home which she kept spotless at all times. Every morning she would wake up just before sunset and even before the birds that herald in the sun began their duty because, she had admonished her children when they were young, how could you let the birds beat you in worshiping the Lord. She would make herself a large cup of tea and sit outside her hut, watching the sunrise and worshipping her God in her own quiet and meditative way. When the sun was safely hung up in the sky she would get up and go about her daily chores. She would sweep her already pristine house and yard, then make herself a bowl of mealie meal porridge whilst her bath water warmed on the embers. After her breakfast, she would bath and dress and then, with a basket of goodies, visit an ailing friend or relative or church and community member, even if she did not know them. She made it a habit to uplift the spirits of those that were sick or grieving because she believed that healing began in one's own mind and often one needed help in turning a dark mind towards positive thoughts again. She knew this from experience because when her husband had died when their children were still young and she herself was just a young mother still figuring life out, her mind had turned very dark with grief and too often she considered harming herself or taking her own life. It was only with the help of well-meaning people in the very same community that she still to that day lived in that she managed to overcome her grief and raise her children into good and kind adults. In the afternoon, she would return to her home, feed her two goats and chickens and do a bit of gardening before making herself a meal from some of the produce she had grown herself in the garden. Again, she would sit outside staring up at the stars in the sky with her ever-smiling wrinkled face turned heavenward and a big enamel cup of tea in her hand. After a while she would go into her house and retire for the night in preparation to beat the birds and ready to do it all again the following day.

Sadly, in our culture, there are some who find the repair of a broken heart and the rebirth of an afflicted mind to be suspicious and many people watched her with disdain, hating her for no good reason other than for being a successful and content single mother and widow.

Widows, you see, are a community's soft spot. It is not uncommon, in this society where a girl is taught from a young age to rely on a man for everything and anything, for a widow to fall into a state of disarray and despair. A widow is not only expected to grieve unconsolably for many years thereafter, but she is also expected to be deemed unfit to raise children and to lose her home or any other assets her and her husband accumulated, whether out of negligence or to a male in-law taking ownership of them. This she is expected to continue until such and such a time that she is given as a wife to her husband's brother or other close relative or some desperate man agrees to marry her even though she has been had and has another man's children. However, Gogo had refused to be given away to one of her husband's relatives or any advances from other men because she knew that this would make her young children vulnerable, as no man whole heartedly agrees to be a father to children that are not his. She had, instead, gone from strength to strength and done it all by herself. For this reason, several low-quality human beings despised her for her success in the absence of a man. How could a woman, they wondered, survive so well without a husband or son to take care of her? Gogo had a son, her last born of three children, but he was very young when his father died and as he was growing up Gogo and the community noticed that he was very different and the community shunned him for his peculiarity but she loved him all the more for it and her love was always enough for him.

There came a time in the community where unexplained events- which could have been explained given a little more patience and skilful investigations- occurred. A two-year-old child who had been left to wander by its first-time mother who was more preoccupied with hearing the latest gossip from her neighbour than keeping an eye on her toddler, had gone missing and had the next day been found dead by a search party washed up on the bank of a nearby stream. A young man had left home after telling his family that he was going to look for a job in Harare but a week later the family had still not heard a word from him and relatives that lived along the way to and in Harare itself denied having seen or heard from him even though he had phoned ahead and told them to expect him. An entire family, mother, father and their two children who were originally from that community had perished, along with 39 others, in a bus accident that was termed a national disaster. And to top it all off, the rains were late that summer and a drought was expected.

People had had it with the tragedies in their home that came one after the other and one particular small group of men and women decided that the tragedies were too ominous and methodical to be mere coincidence, so they decided to go and consult a *n'anga*. They gathered up their meagre savings and travelled several hours to the village's outskirts where they were told by the *n'anga* that his consultation fee for what they were asking him to reveal had gone up to what they had brought plus a small goat. They travelled back the way they had come and managed to procure a small, ailing goat from a wealthy community member who was also curious about the cause of the devastations yet wanted nothing to do with witchdoctors. They went back again the way they had come and this time the witchdoctor agreed to communicate with the winds and find out what they wanted to know.

The *n'anga* wheezed and coughed and sniffed and convulsed and anointed himself with unspecified fluids until from the rotting purse of the skin of a cane rat, he produced various pieces of bark and bones and teeth- human and animal- which he threw on the mat before him. With his own walking stick he poked at the heap of debris whilst mumbling words the curious group were afraid to hear. After reading the bones he excused himself for an hour and when he came back he sat back on his mat, scratched at his protruding, malnourished belly and announced to the group that he had the answer that they were seeking. The small group leaned into him greedily, ready to get confirmation of the people they all individually suspected of killing people off. In short measured sentenced the *n'anga* revealed that the perpetrator who had the power and demonic assistance to cause deaths, disappearances and droughts was undoubted a witch that lived among them. The small group gasped, clung onto each other and the small, ailing goat gave its own feeble bleat of disbelief from where it was tied up to a nearby tree. When the initial shock had died down one of the group members, a man of thirty who thus far had had no notable life experiences, turned to the *n'anga* who was now silent but rocking himself gently where he sat and, putting a few crumpled notes before the *n'anga* before he was allowed to address him he asked, "Is the witch that mysterious widow that lives alone in that well swept little house?" All turned to the *n'anga* expectantly as all, at the mention of the word 'witch' had been secretly suspecting her and wanted to know if their witch-detecting sixth senses were correct.

The *n'anga* began to convulse. He fell backwards and frothed at the mouth, remaining this way until he sat back up and confirmed, "That very one, my children."

There was another gasp from the crowd and another bleat from the goat. Sara, a young woman who had had the pleasure of one of Gogo's visits when she was grieving the loss of her stillborn baby asked in disbelief, "Gogo?"

The *n'anga* was still and silent until she remembered that she needed to produce some money for her to be allowed to address him. She put a few crumpled notes on the mat in front of him and he immediately began to convulse, fell back and frothed at the mouth. When he was finished, he wiped his mouth and said, "Yes, that very one."

The small group thanked the *n'anga* and his winds in the necessary fashion and took their leave of him. Outraged at the witch's wickedness they plotted as they marched back the way they had come.

For days the group spread the word of the witch to accepting and unaccepting people. They fuelled their hate fires by adding on to the witch's list of crimes and added, to her death toll, their friends and relatives who at times didn't even live in the vicinity. Gogo, unsuspecting and unaware continued on with her everyday life but she did not miss the nasty stares she got from people wherever she went. She was surprised when one lady, on her way from church, spat at her and she was uncomfortable with the sudden attention where usually she was invisible and ignored accordingly. Nonetheless, she went on with her life in the hopes that she was simply being paranoid. One day on one of her visits with an elderly lady who was sick and bedridden she felt, for the first time, that she was not welcome. The patient's family did not offer her tea or a chair to sit beside the patient's bed. She was hurt because the elderly lady was someone she considered a friend and her family had been very loving towards her in the past. Nonetheless she visited with her friend and knelt by her bed. In a rare moment that the two were left alone the elderly patient opened her weak eyes and clung onto the sleeve of Gogo's dress. In a whisper so quiet that Gogo had to practically put her ear on her friend's mouth she told her friend that she had heard talk that people suspected Gogo was a witch and that she felt that Gogo's safety was in danger.

Gogo had reassured her friend that it was all nonsense and that nothing bad was going to happen to her because many people loved her in the community. On her walk home she repeated this reassurance to herself so that by the time she was home she herself began to believe it. That is, until she saw two large men standing by the entrance of her home. When they saw her approaching, they marched towards her and she instinctively shrunk back, making herself as small as possibly. They walked past her, both bumping into her hard as they did so. "We will kill you, witch," she heard the second one mutter as he walked away. That was when she finally saw the gravity of the situation and decided to get out of town, just until things died down, because, she thought, humans were rational creatures and they would soon come to their senses as time healed their grieving hearts.

Gogo decided to go and visit her daughter and her family in Mutare. She knew that she would be welcome there and that the break would do everyone good. She packed her bags and kept watch as she waited for the dawn. Before the birds ushered in the sun with their singing she was on a bus on the way to her daughter and to safety.

Gogo's forty-three-year-old son, the one I mentioned earlier and the one who was a little different was named Garikai Junior, after his father. Gogo had saved up many years ago to take him for tests when he was only excelling in one subject in school. The tests revealed that he was autistic and even though she did not fully know what that meant, she accepted it and made sure to nurture and encourage him in the subject that he was good at. He was excellent at art and so when he was expelled from school for failing, she sent him to Harare to learn at Peter Birch Art School. When he had completed his diploma there he moved on and he became a sculptor living in a community of other artists on a farm in Marondera. When he needed a little extra money, he would make custom made furniture. All in all, thanks to the efforts and wisdom of his mother, he had made something of himself despite himself which many people to this day in this country do not understand. He was happy and content and he loved his mother, she was his entire world and the two exchanged phone calls every two weeks.

Garikai decided to visit his mother who he had not seen for two months. He wanted to tell her in person that his sculpture of a vulture had been chosen as the national gallery's main exhibition piece. He got on a chicken bus from Marondera to Chipinge, and two tyre punctures and seven police road blocks later her was standing in his mother's kitchen. Upon his arrival, he found that his mother was not there and that the door was locked. He was not too disturbed by this because she had taught him the secret to unlocking the door with a couple of push and pulls and a thud in the right place. He let himself in but immediately got shivers down his spin. One of the superpowers that came with his autism was that he was highly analytical and could often sense situations that other people could not even, if he could not always easily interpret them. He ran his eyes over the house, inch by inch, and felt that it had been unlived in for some time. He was uneasy because his mother never left her house unattended for a day, and she would not go anywhere for an extended period of time without having informed him first. The half-folded doily on her coffee table and the open kitchen window also gave him a clue that his mother had left in a hurry. He knew that even in her old age there were things that she would never forget to do. Garikai felt one of his panic attacks approaching and instead of doing the breathing exercises the therapists his mother had hired for him had taught him, he let it wash over him and engulf him because, he felt, this panic attack was not in vain. As the room closed in on him and his breathing became shallow he allowed himself to black out, hoping that what he would find on the other end of the dark tunnel was his mother.

When Garikai came to, his body was exhausted and his mind foggy. He found that his mother had not returned but even then, he did not have the strength to worry any longer. He made sure that the kitchen door was secured and then climbed into his mother's warm bed and pretended that the sheets that enveloped him were her arms. Again, he blacked out.

Garikai was awakened by a large bang. He sat up as his heart thudded in his chest and tried to remember how to do the breathing exercises that he was taught would calm him down. He heard voices in the kitchen and immediately felt relieved that his mother was back. His heart skipped a beat only a few moments later when he heard that the voices were male voices in amongst banging cupboards and crashing crockery. Garikai was afraid and confused. The fog in his mind thickened so much so that when a group of nine men and a woman barged into his mother's room, he was still unsure as to the nature of the experience he was having. He needed a moment to analyse the events that had taken place to decipher whether it was a negative or positive situation but he had no time to do so as the event kept unfolding before him giving him no time, like his mother and fellow artists had learnt to do, to figure things out and get his bearings. The men were holding clubs and large sticks and the one woman, Sara, was holding a frying pan. The largest man, the one who was wearing brown bottoms and a leopard print vest asked Garikai what his name was and who he was to the woman known as Gogo. Garikai managed to answer these questions because they were simple questions which he had practised answering since he was in kindergarten. However, the next questions and accusations thickened the fog in his mind. They, all at once and confusingly so asked him where his mother was. He felt that he should let the small crowd know that he too was wondering where his mother was and give them piece by piece evidence of why he was worried about his mother's absence, but the words did not come out of his mouth in an order that was comprehensible, and besides, he felt another panic attack coming on as his senses finally told him that he was having a negative experience. The men and one woman began to demand that he reveal his mother to them and they called her all sorts of names. He could not, for the life of him, understand why they kept referring to his beloved mother as the witch. "Do, do not call her a witch!" he yelled with as much courage as he could muster. He was out of the bed now and on his feet. He decided that he would go back to Marondera there and then and inform the police there of his mother's disappearance. He had been taught from a young age that the police would help him if ever he felt like he was in trouble. "Excuse me," he said politely as he tried to walk past the small group and out of the door. As he did so, he suddenly felt the heavy blow of a frying pan coming down hard on the back of his head.

It would have been better if Garikai had blacked

out once again at this moment, for one who is unconscious seldom feels the pain of the torture that that group of people put him through in their efforts to find out where the witch was. They pocked him with sticks and clubbed his knees so that he could not escape, try as he may. When, in his panic and confusion, he stopped talking and instead rolled into a ball rocking himself and crying, they accused him of protecting the witch and also being a witch and helping his witch mother kill off their relatives, and so they saw it necessary to beat him to death, just as they had come to do to his mother. When Garikai cried out in pain and tried to protect his head from the blows with his arms two men pinned his arms down so the thugs had better access to his face and head. They beat him everywhere until his features were bloody and indistinguishable, they beat him until he could no longer cry out in pain, they beat him until they could hear his ribs snap, they beat him until he stopped whimpering and they only stopped beating him when they heard his gurgles as he choked on his own blood, and then they walked out of the house leaving him where he lay.

They kept an eye out for the return of the witch but she did not return home that night and they went to their respective homes where they washed the blood off their arms and faces and changed into their night clothes. All slept soundly that night, all except for Sara who, just before day break was woken by a nightmare in which she had replaced Garikai where he lay on the floor being beaten. The nightmare frightened her so much because she was a superstitious woman. In the protection of the still dark morning she crept back to Gogo's house and knelt over Garikai's body, unsure of what to do. She put a trembling hand to his bloody chest and jumped as he began to choke on his own blood once more. She ran out of Gogo's house and back to her own house.

Later, when the sun had risen Sara found a pay phone and called Gogo's daughter who she knew lived in Mutare. Anonymously she left a message for Gogo which informed her that her son lay on her dining room floor dying.

As soon as the message was conveyed to Gogo she knew what had happened and what had caused it. She got onto a bus back home and prayed every second of the way for her son to be saved. She tried all the phones of everyone she knew who lived near her home for them to help her son or take him to a hospital but there was no network and in the brief periods that there was no one would pick up their phone. Gogo arrived in time. She arrived in time to cradle her son into death. She rushed into her home, moving nimbly over the broken crockery and upturned furniture and knelt down where her son had lain for over a day in his own blood, sweat and urine. At first she though he was dead but then she heard his very faint gurgles. She lifted his head gently and placed it in her lap. He opened the only eye he had left and found that he could no longer see. Still, his mind had finally cleared of the fog and his heart was peaceful in his battered chest, he knew that he was finally in the arms of his beloved mother. “It’s okay my son, everything will be alright,” she whispered, careful that her voice did not betray her grief and anguish.

Garikai knew that all was well. For the first time in his life he felt a sense of calm and peace that encompassed his entire body. He was no longer in pain, pain of the body or of the mind. He felt an increasing warmth that he could not explain and began to feel like his soul was being gently carried. He was content as he knew where he was being taken. He knew that he was leaving the only person that mattered to him in the world behind, but somehow he also knew that they would be together again. In that moment the tables had turned and for the first time ever he was the one that needed to reassure her. Her warm tears were the only thing he could feel.

As he was taken, he looked up at her with his blind eye and smiled, with all the earthly strength he had left he said, "Mama." She saw her son mouth her name and then he was gone. All that night she sat there on the floor with him with his head on her lap and her small withered hand on his cheek. The sobs that came from her were the silent kind.

In the morning, she began the slow process of putting her life back in order as best she could. She washed the blood off her son's body, changed his torn and blood-stained clothes and then made the necessary arrangements for his body to be taken to a mortuary until she had arranged his burial. She called her daughters and told them that their brother was gone, and she cleaned her house. Even when she saw people scowling at her as she went about her errands she was not afraid. Grief has a way of numbing its host to all other emotions save itself. She walked with her head held high and willed anyone to try and come in between her and her son in her grief. Her daughters, their families and relatives from Mutare, Harare and Kwekwe came the next day to grieve with her. It was only when she was surrounded by all these people that she realized how alone she suddenly felt. It came over her like a wave crashing down as she felt the loneliness she had ignored for the past fifty years since her husband had died.

The funeral went as well as any funeral could.

Relatives stayed with her for as long as they all could, her younger daughter stayed with her longest but eventually she too had to get back to her own family and her own life. Left alone, Gogo would lay on her dining room floor, on the dark patch of carpet where her daughter had done her best to wash the blood out. There, she felt close to her son.

As she lay on the carpet in the dining room on her second night alone she heard them come in through the broken kitchen door. Part of her had put it far from her mind, but some part of her knew that the inevitable would still happen, even though the thugs had attended her son's funeral and even shaken her hand and said *nematambudziko,* sorry for your loss. She did not try to run away or defend herself, all she wished, as she saw a club swinging down towards her face in the darkness and heard the words, "we have found the witch," was that death would encompass her quickly.

They say that there is a white light at the painless end of death and that when you regain sight and see it as it grows and washes over you, you feel a sense of peace knowing that you are in the eternal land of the light. Gogo did not feel this peace. She felt excruciating pain. Still, she opened her eyes, allowing the light in, and searched eagerly for her son Garikai whom she was sure would be waiting for her. When her eyes adjusted to the glare she saw, to her disappointment, her daughter and her husband staring down at her. She realized with dismay, that she was not dead.

They bound her broken bones and stapled her torn skin. For the physical pain they gave her watered down painkillers that left her with enough pain for her to remember that she was still earth-bound. They hired a physical therapist to help her get her motor skills back. At first they had her on a drip, but after a few weeks they got her family to feed her watery baby food that she could suck in through her broken teeth with a plastic spoon and lukewarm tea from a styrofoam cup. They told her that she was lucky to be alive, that her daughter had forgotten something and had driven back the following day and found her laying in a pool of blood in the very spot that she had found her son. She did not feel lucky to be alive, in fact she wished she was not as she lay in bed day after day waiting for her old and frail body to heal enough for her to be able to be taken home.

It was near six months before she was allowed to leave the hospital. The visits that she got from her relatives had encouraged her to find renewed strength within herself and by the end of her hospitalisation she had healed enough to walk with a cane even though she had a never-ending dull pain that migrated from different parts of her body to the back of her head.

At first she was unsure about living in the old age home that her daughters put her in in Mutare. She missed the freedom of solitude and having her own space to cook, clean and grow things even though she knew that she no longer actually had this space as she had heard that a holy man had found her goblins in her house which he and the thugs had searched and subsequently burnt down. She mourned the loss of the only home she ever knew, the home she had raised her children in. At the old age home, she was given a tiny room with a warm bed. She found that it was not as she expected. The staff left her to her own devises, but after watching the other old folks she saw that they were not made to sit around watching birds fly by with unblinking eyes. They were strong despite their ages and they each had a routine that involved doing chores they enjoyed. The staff was part time and so the folks got the chance to do for themselves a lot of things. Gogo was inspired to improve and keep up her own strength, and when she felt strong enough, she developed a routine much like she had when she lived alone in Chipinge. Gogo woke up before dawn and swept the courtyard and the entrance to the home. She would stand looking up at the sky, in awe of how small she was compared to how great the universe was, and sometimes, she thought she heard her son's whispered greetings in the wind. With the sun up she would help with the distribution of breakfast and sit down to warm porridge and tea with the new friends she had never had and had been missing out on. At meal times they would share fond memories of the greatness of youth and tales of the roads they had travelled on in their lives. Sometimes, in winter, they would sit around a fire for warmth and mourn their losses and sing sad songs of sorrowful injustices and hard lives, showing each other their scars and allowing their friends to run weathered fingers to feel the scar tissue and lines that traced their faces and bodies. They understood each other, and loved each other and carried each other when need be and celebrated with each other a marriage or birth of a grand or great grandchild. In the afternoons Gogo would knit. She would knit blankets and scarves with the wool that her family brought her. She would give her creations away and when all the old folk and staff had at least one knitted item from her she began to knit warm clothes for the neighbouring orphanage which she took to visiting three times a week. On the afternoons that she was not at the orphanage her family would come to visit. Her daughter and her family dropped in at least once a week and so too her great nieces and nephews.

She loved and appreciated these visits greatly and cherished the fact that she lived close enough for her to see family and friends often. On holidays, she would leave the old folks' home and stay awhile with family, often going from one home to another where she was welcomed with the same warmth that she had welcomed people into her own home. She was happy, and with each passing day the scars that are invisible to the eye but not the heart began to heal.

Gogo enjoyed her life in the old folks' home for the greater part of six years, but as time has it, old age descended upon her like a bird of prey. It was as if she aged overnight and one morning she woke up in the body of a very old woman. She became slow and sluggish and at least once a week a fog filled her mind and made it hard to think. Nevertheless, she went about her routine, even when it took her several hours longer to complete.

One day as Gogo was taking her morning bath the fog visited her mind. For many minutes, she crouched in the bath tub, staring down at the bucket as the water in it got cold. A knock at the door startled her as a staff member checked if she was okay. The fog began to clear and she told him that she was. Shivering, she soaped herself up and as she lifted the bucket of luke-warm water above her head to rinse herself off she lost her grip and the bucket came crashing down, flooding the floor as it cracked on impact. Shaken she stepped out of the tub, scolding herself for her carelessness, but the water made the floor slippery and she fell on her hip and hit her head hard on the edge of the bath tub.

This time Gogo did not stay long in the hospital. They replaced her hip and gave her medication for the fog in her mind that started to come more frequently and sent her home to recover but the part-time staff at the old folks' home told her daughter that they were unable to give her the round the clock care that she needed. So, that is how, after six years of love and comfort, she found herself being driven back to the place that had rejected her so violently- Chipinge.

In Chipinge Gogo lived in the neighbouring village with her youngest daughter and her family who gave her the round the clock care that she needed. She never went back to see the ashes of her burnt home and she wouldn't have done so even if she had the strength to take herself. Her great niece brought her a wheelchair from Harare that her own husband had used before his death to make her life easier whilst she recovered, but her health never improved and every day she seemed to become weaker and weaker, her sight and senses leaving her not even nine months after returning to Chipinge.

A year later, the compound was woken up by the sound of all three of their dogs howling at the sky. In the afternoon when it was time for her lunch her daughter failed to rouse her from her midday nap. She held her mother's head in her lap as she herself howled to let everyone know that Gogo had finally departed. Her daughter closed the glassy eyes that stared up at her blindly. Gogo had died of a broken heart, having lived out the rest of her life in fear. They say that all is well that ends well, but I have come to understand that it is too few in this life that have the privilege of experiencing a happily ever after.

MISEDUCATION

Sarudzai was excited for civvies day but more so to tell her friends that she had obtained four unites in her grade seven exams. She knew that this guaranteed her a spot in a good secondary school. She was hoping she'd get to go to a boarding school in Mutare but she knew that it was likely that she would have to attend the same school as her twin brother, and with nine units, he hadn't done well enough to get into a good boarding school so they would probably go to their primary school's secondary school which was also nearly an hour's walk away from their homestead. Still, she was excited. She had woken up extra early today. She did not want to miss the final assembly and so by four thirty she was up, she had finished her chores by half past five, bathed and now at six she was slipping her Christmas dress over her head and lacing up her Sunday sandals. She picked up her school bag and walked to the hut that her brother shared with their father and older brother to see if he was ready for the long walk to school. The fact that they joined other children on the treck made it more bearable because Sarudzai was not at the age where she particularly enjoyed her brother's company. On their walk to school other children, boys and girls, would join them along the way and the group would split into two according to gender and by the time the two groups entered the school gates they were two chattering crowds. Sarudzai peeked her head into the hut impatiently and saw that her brother Samson, was still just putting on his shoes.

"*Hyeyi*!" father growled at her. "*Buda muno.* Get out!" Without needing to be told twice Sarudzai withdrew her little oiled up face from the men's hut. She walked a little way away and sat down on a bolder. She was impatient to get to school and so after only a couple of minutes she got up and decided to start the walk to school without her brother. However, before she took two steps away Father came out of the hut zipping up the zip on his old corduroy pants and scratching at his hairy chest. "Where are you going, *muskana*?"

Sarudzai lowered her eyes to the ground in respect. "To school," she replied in as placid a tone as possible. She knew her father was prone to fits of rage when the mood suited him. She was used to them but right now she had no time to entertain one such fit.

"School?" father roared with laughter. "*Ko,* have you finished helping your mother with the chores? Huh? Where's my porridge?" As Sarudzai turned to run to the kitchen to get Father his morning porridge before he found more things for her to do he trotted after her, hitting the back of her head every couple of steps until they entered the kitchen together where her mother was stirring the pot of porridge over the fire.

"*Ko muskana uyu*? She is still going to school?" father enquired of mother accusingly. Mother lowered her eyes in respect as Father towered over her. He continued, "Can she not read and write yet?" Mother was quiet and still with her eyes averted, so he turned and addressed Sarudzai who had taken over the stirring of the pot. "Can you read and write?"

"Yes, Baba," she acquiesced.

"So then why is the girl still going to school?" he addressed Mother again. Mother just shrugged and began to dish porridge into an aluminium bowl for father and the rest of the family.

As the family ate in silence, Sarudzai and her mother in the centre of the kitchen next to the fire pit and the father and the boys on stools against the wall, Father shook his head at himself before looking over at Sarudzai who was rushing to finish and make it to school on time. "Why do you still go to school?" he asked her quite suddenly jerking his upturned palm at her in question. "Huh? Why are you wasting my money to go to school instead of learning here at home how to be a good woman, huh? Will a man want a woman who can read but not cook? How much lobola will you bring us if you cannot sweep or bring in a good harvest of crops for your family?" Sarudzai kept as still as possible and tried to make herself smaller as she had learnt that mice did when they sensed a hungry predator above them. It did not work because father continued, "Next year is secondary school, yes? No! You no longer need to go. You will stay home from now on and learn from your mother." For Sarudzai this was the usual lecture from her father who took the opportunity to berate her thus every time she was unfortunate enough to not have left for school before he woke up. "Sarudzai?" father wanted some sort of response. Sarudzai dropped her aluminium bowl, picked up her school bag and raced out the kitchen leaving the wrath of her father to her mother. She would deal with whatever came her way in the evening after she had enjoyed her last day of primary school.

Father had started telling Sarudzai to focus on learning how to be a woman when she was in grade seven. Sarudzai could not understand why becoming a woman was mutually exclusive and could not be done whilst still getting an education. She was a good child and liked to obey her parents and avoid conflict, but in this she had made the decision to be rebellious and continued to go to secondary school with Samson as often as possible. She was adamant about furthering her education for the simple fact that she liked learning and she was good at it. So Sarudzai had continued to go to school for nearly two years after she obtained her four units at grade seven and dodge her father when he thought about her not going to school. She was an exemplary student, the teachers told her parents on the rare occasions they attended the scheduled parent-teacher interviews, and they were positive that she would excel and make it big in life.

One day as Sarudzai was sitting in her form two geography class learning the different causes of soil erosion, the deputy principal came into the class and asked to see her. Her friends smiled at her and patted her on the back, sure that it was for another academic accolade.

"Bring your books and your bag," he instructed her before turning and heading back to his office. Slightly puzzled, she packed up her books and almost missed the geography teacher's pitying glance as she walked out. She knocked on the deputy principal's door and was told to entre and take a seat on the chair in front of his desk. The deputy principal folded his arms neatly on his desk, looked at her over his thick glasses and smiled at her. "Sarudzai, you are hard working. One of our best pupils quite frankly. You represented our school well in the junior maths Olympiad last year and I was confident that you would continue to make our school proud." Sarudzai was smiling until she heard the tense of regret in the deputy principal's speech. The deputy principal lifted his chin and used his index finger to push his thick glassed as far up the bridge of his nose as possible. He continued, "Sarudzai I will not beat about the bush any longer. I called you into my office to inform you, with deep distress, that you will no longer be able to continue attending lessons with us."

Sarudzai had sensed this coming as soon as the deputy principal had started speaking. Still, her heart dropped and she felt a familiar lump build in her throat. "Why, Sir?" she croaked.

"Well, Sarudzai... Don't cry please. Be a big girl,"

he said, awkwardly averting his eyes as he was not used to tears and did not know what to do in their presence. "Don't cry Surudzai," as he continued to speak he made sure not to look in her direction any longer. "Simply put it is the issue of school fees. Your brother stopped coming with enough for the both of you two semesters back and when we sent word to your parents to enquire why, your father sent a message back saying that you are no longer to go to school."

Sarudzai let out a wail, like an injured animal, as she learnt that her father had finally won the ongoing battle between them. He had succeeded in stopping her schooling and would now proceed to make a woman out of her as he had been trying for the past several years to do. She thought about a life of chores and getting married and she let herself sob without holding anything back, not even her dignity, in front of the well-respected deputy principal.

"Don't cry Sarudzai, please, please, please. Yours in not the first family to fail to have enough school fees. Your parents will find the money and send you back here in no time. Just you wait and see."

Sarudzai, sobbing and shivering, picked up her bag and books and thanked the deputy principal for his time as he stood up and held the door open for her. She ran out, towards home where she would confront her father with all she had. The principal looked on after her as she ran out the school gates. He knew that it was not that Sarudzai's father could not afford the very low school fees that the school required. He had ignored him when he had brought up the merit-based scholarship that Sarudzai was illegible to apply for. Sarudzai was not the first girl to be snatched out of education for illogical reasons, especially in the rural areas. Still, he felt bad for Sarudzai as she was undoubtedly a very talented scholar. As his cell phone rang he made a mental note to visit with Sarudzai's father once more and remind him of the scholarship that Sarudzai could apply for. Maybe he'd talk to her mother instead and she could talk sense to her husband. "Nonsense," he muttered to himself as a commentary on the situation just before he answered his phone and Sarudzai disappeared into the distance.

* * *

Sarudzai was damp with her own sweat on the top half of her body, but on her legs, she was wet with a mixture of blood, urine and amniotic fluid. Her aunts had told her that as soon as the baby was delivered the joy of seeing her little one would make her forget the trauma her body had just been through, but she could still feel uncomfortable pain as her emptied uterus began to contract back into shape. In her weak and quivering arms, she held her baby. After twelve agonising hours of labour, she had delivered a baby boy whom her father's sister, her *tete,* had to rip the amniotic sack off of and who had, at first, refused to cry and let the air into his unused lungs. As she stared down at him blankly Tete came back into the room and said, "Your father says the baby is to be called Amos, after himself and your grandfather, of course." It was unfortunate. Sarudzai, as soon as her period had stopped, thought that whatever she bore out of herself would be called Godknows because only God knew the troubles she felt that she had been put through in her young life. Only God knew how she had tried to do the right thing, only God knew why she could not get what she felt she needed. She decided that she would call the boy Godknows every day of his life. In any case, his big forehead, she thought as she lowered her gaze from her aunt standing in the doorway down to the boy, resembled that of one who would be called by the nickname Godi, and not one called by the whimsical name of Amos. "Why have you not suckled him?" her aunt asked accusingly still standing in the doorway. "You need to get him fed so that you can clean yourself and this mess up." She pointed at the bloodied floor. "Your mother has gone to bury the placenta in the nearby forest but really Sarudzai, you are now irreversibly a woman by your own choosing, and you cannot expect your mother to continue to coddle you after the disgrace you have brought upon your father."

"Disgrace..." Sarudzai said down at the boy under her breath.

"Yes, disgrace! *Shuwa watinyadzisa mwana iwe, ah ah ah,*" Tete said as she clapped her hands with every syllable she spoke. She continued to berate her niece as she turned and walked away towards the gathering of men and notable women in the family. "And the way you screamed like it was the end of the world as you delivered that baby, I don't know. They want to make the baby, but are too weak and useless to push it out, *hede, huuri, hapeno.*" Turning briefly back towards the delivery hut she shouted, "Feed that Amos!"

The boy was awake but with his eyes closed. He was wrapped in a thick blanket and had a badly knitted hat on his head. Sarudzai looked at him, and then she looked at her swollen breasts with disgust and then back at the boy. She put him down on the mat beside her, shifted her own body forward until she was laid down and then closed her eyes and took deep breaths as she worked on overcoming the pain that she was still in. The baby began to fuss beside her, starting with a low whimpering that soon turned into a full-on cry. She covered the boy's open mouth with her head wrap so that his cries were muffled and with her hand still over his mouth she closed her eyes once again and tried to get some rest.

* * *

Sarudzai had not given up even when her father had stopped her from physically attending school. Although the relationship between her and her brother had become more and more strained as more and more their parents differentiated them, elevating her brother to a place of honour for no deserved reason, she had approached him on the weekend after she stopped attending secondary school with him. "You will teach me what you learn in class when you come home from school every day," she had informed him plainly.

Lazily he had opened his eyes and looked out into the near distance where the cows he had herded out were peacefully grazing. "What's in it for me?" he had wanted to know.

"What do you want?" she asked. She had known that her outlandish request would not easily be granted.

"You shall do my weekend chores," he said. Sarudzai was unsure how her father would feel about her herding their cows and goats on the weekend. All the same, her brother hardly had any chores as his father preferred him to study or visit with various specialists in the village on the weekends to learn a trade. Lately, he had taken to sculpting.

Sarudzai had agreed to do his weekend chores but when the following Monday came and she sat in front of him after he had come home from school expectantly he had irritably told her to go way. She was livid. She had gotten up an hour early that morning so that she would be ahead of time in doing her chores. In everything she had done that day she had made sure that she would have an undisturbed hour so her brother could teach her what he had learnt. She felt slighted and had tried to first argue her brother into teaching her and then plead with him but, he had told her, he had had a long day at school and did not want to be bothered. That night when she was serving him his *sadza*, she spat in his food without him knowing. The next day he again refused to tutor her and the day after that and, even though she did all his chores, he continued to refuse to teach her the following week.

One weekend when he had gone to a neighbour to sculpt with him, Sarudzai snuck into the room he shared with his father and older brother and slipped his school books off the shelf he kept them on. Hungrily she flipped through the pages, trying to capture everything she could before anyone could catch her in the act. Suddenly, she heard her mother's voice calling her from the kitchen. She hurriedly put all except the maths book back on the shelf and stuffed that one book into her shirt. She would read it when everyone had gone to bed at night. As she was turning to leave whilst clutching the book to her stomach under her shirt she jumped as she saw her brother's towering form blocking her escape route through the door. He was livid but she did not understand why. "I'll put it back!" she had said after they had stared at each other for a while in silence.

"Baba! Baba!" Samson called out for his father. "Come and see what Sarudzai is doing!" Sarudzai sunk to her knees and shot hatred at her brother out of her eyes. She knew the wrath that was accompanying her father's approaching form, so by the time he entered the hut she already had her arms raised to protect her from the blows he would deal her. He swung his open palms at her and invited her brother to join him in the discipline ritual. That night, when all were asleep, a bruised Sarudzai took the forgotten maths book out of her shirt and read its contents twice over by the dim light of a small candle.

* * *

Jonson had always been Sarudzai's friend. In nursery school they had played together and so too in the first few years of primary school before it became unfashionable for boys to play nicely with girls. However, even when Jonson had stopped playing with Sarudzai at school at break time, they always found time for each other's friendship, whether it was when they walked home together as they lived only ten minutes away from each other, or in the holidays or weekends. Even though Jonson had stopped playing with Sarudzai and the other girls at school, he did not play with the boys. The boys teased him out of playing with the girls but would not let him play with them because, they said, he was too soft and girly. Thus, Jonson played by himself at school.

Although Sarudzai continued to steal her brother's exercise books when she could and endure her father's beatings and her mother's scolding, she found that she could not learn much from her brother's books because besides the fact that a lot of his work was illegible, it did not do to stare at incorrect fractions which you had not been taught how to solve. She decided to ask Jonson, who she saw walked past her homestead every day on the way to school, to tutor her in secret, away from disapproving eyes. He had been, as far as she could remember, a below average student but she thought that that was better than nothing. She invited him to her little woodland on Sunday afternoons when she managed to slip away from her mother, or on Saturday mornings when she took thirty minutes out of her trip back home from fetching water to stop just outside his family compound and learnt all she could from him.

Her lessons with Jonson were not very fruitful. He was forgetful and unmotivated. On one occasion, they walked all the way to her little woodland only to discover that his satchel was empty, he had forgotten to put his books into his bag and he was not able to recount any useful information off by head. He was also prone to distraction. He wanted to tell her about everything that had happened at school and who had worn what on civvies day, but very seldom anything that had actually been taught in class. He would lean in towards her whilst they were seated on the ground, too close to her face, clutching her wrists and then proceeding to try and tell her the latest gossip. "*Hee,*" he would begin, his eyes glittering with excitement, "Mai Shura, you know the one from church? The mother of Tswarelo in form four? You remember *mhani*! Anyway, she was caught in Freddie's car. You know Freddie? Last year's head boy, you know him *mhani*. Anyway, and they say that he failed his A'levels and the school wouldn't let him repeat because apparently he had repeated his O'levels five times." All the while Sarudzai would be trying to escape his grip and the spittle that flew at her from the sides of his constantly moist lips.

Sarudzai was never one to be quick to judge but something about Jonson made her increasingly uncomfortable. She did not remember him being so gossipy or him being so obsessed with materialistic things, nor the way he constantly held his right arm in an upward arch, even when he was not supporting anything on it, nor the way he constantly wanted to high-five everyone. Sarudzai began to find their friendship to be very fickle and without benefit. On top of that, her parents had started to notice her prolonged absences and her various excuses had long since run out. She decided that she would arrange to meet him in her little woodland and thank him for his time. She was sure that they would continue to be friends, but the type of friends that need not see each other often and the type of friends that waved at each other from a distance.

Jonson agreed to her proposed meeting and brought his satchel with him. She was surprised to find that Jonson had arrived at their meeting place before she had as it was usually the other way around. She was, however, mostly surprised by his dejected look and demeanor. Without any coxing, he took a book out of his satchel and opened it, prepared to answer any questions she had about the content he placed in front of her.

As Sarudzai tried to make sense of Jonson's mumbling as he told her what he had learnt in math class whilst pointing at the various equations on the page she could not quite pretend that everything was alright with him. She looked at his face and only then did she notice that he had faint bruises that, she discovered when she ran a thumb over his skin, he had tried to cover up with what must have been his mother's cheap powder foundation. Sarudzai was no stranger to the marks of a thorough beating so she skipped the what happened question and asked him why it had happened. A single tear rolled down his cheek as he said, "The boys beat me up because my mother packed my sister's Barbie juice bottle in my lunch bag instead of my Transformers one." He could no longer hold back. He let out a sob and from that first one they kept rolling out. Sarudzai let him lay his head in her lap and rest, unsure of anything else she could do, but she knew that she'd no longer ask him to tutor her. She did not need the added emotional baggage, all she wanted to do was learn.

After her failure to learn from Jonson, Sarudzai had all but given up her plan to be tutored by anyone who was still in school. She tried her former girlfriends, those that lived close enough, but the few that were still in school had too many chores when they were not in school that they could not regularly meet up with her. They did, however, promise to find her in the holidays and give up some of their play time to catch her up with what they had learnt during the semester. Sarudzai knew that a promise not immediately carried out was usually never carried out, but she carried on with her everyday life in the hope that things would work themselves out.

Several months went past and Sarudzai had nearly adapted to being a woman rather than a scholar when on her walk home from fetching water she met Able. Sarudzai knew Able to be her friend Anashe's older brother who was in form four, two years older than them and, coincidentally, Jonson's cousin. Sarudzai met Able whilst he was leaning on a gate post with a piece of straw in his mouth talking to two grade seven girls who themselves were on their walk home from school. In a relaxed and all-knowing tone, he was asking them what they were learning in class and what each one of them were expecting to get for their grade seven exams. The girls each in turn blushed and admitted that they were, like everybody, aiming to pass with four units. When Able saw Sarudzai approaching, her told the little girls to get lost and when they had scuttled away he fell into step beside Sarudzai who was carrying a large pot filled with water on her head. "*Hesi*, Saru," he greeted her casually. His voice had broken, she noted.

Sarudzai was surprised that he had even seen her. She knew him as the smartest boy in secondary school, beating even the more senior boys to become the math Olympiad captain. There was no doubt in anybody's mind that he was going to be head boy in the next two years. He was popular among his peers and the staff, and he seemed to be destined for an easy but great life. People did not usually voluntarily talk to her so she was surprised enough at his greeting that she failed to answer in time and he was forced to greet her again. "I said *hesi*, Sarudzai," he reiterated. This time she managed to answer. After the usual formalities of small talk and discussing the recent weather patterns, the growth of crops and the family's health, Able said, "So I hear that you've been looking for a tutor since you are no longer in school. I heard Jonson telling my mother about how you'd fired him as your tutor over supper last week."

Sarudzai was surprised, but honestly, she though, what could she expect from Jonson. "I was failing to learn anything from him, to be honest," she confessed to the older boy.

"No doubt. I'm surprised you even tried. Listen, to learn you need to be taught by someone who finished and did well in that form. That means you need to learn from older people," Able said as he helped her unmount the water pot off her head just outside her family's compound.

"Well, I don't have any older people that I can ask to tutor me," she said plainly.

"I'll tutor you," he responded, equally as plainly.

Sarudzai looked at this boy that she had never even exchanged a greeting with dubiously.

"How would that benefit you? I can't pay you," she finally said.

Able laughed, "I don't need your money! Listen, we intelligent people need to stick together and keep the knowledge flowing. You know?"

"Yes, I know," she responded, answering a rhetorical question. She felt the old familiar hunger and excitement for learning in her chest. She could not believe that the smarted person she knew was offering to teach her. She took a couple of seconds to imagine herself excelling academically and even going to a college in the city. She thanked Able and agreed to have him tutor her on the weekends when he was free. He told her that on Sundays he usually took his father's livestock to the nearby fields to graze and that if she would meet him there he could teacher her all the subjects she wanted to learn whilst he was at it. This suited her perfectly and she did not care what her parents would say about her Sunday absences. For the first time in a while she began to feel more like a scholar than a woman again.

Able's lessons were organised and educational, even more so she dared believe, than those of some of the less motivated teachers at her secondary school. Not only did she enjoy Able's lessons, but she found that she enjoyed his company more and more. He always came well prepared with his form two exercise books in which he had neatly written in and on top of that he had a few text books which he said he had gotten from his uncle in Mutare who was himself a teacher. He made learning fun and easy and Sarudzai secretly admired him for his skill of passing on knowledge, she thought that if he ever became a teacher his pupils would be very lucky to be taught by him.

Able and Sarudzai's academic liaisons continued to take place for several months in the shade of various trees before an uninterested audience of cattle, sheep and goats. They were the highlight of Sarudzai's week and sometimes they were the only thing that kept her going when she felt that life had gotten dull and monotonous.

One day whilst the pair sat under the shade of an acacia tree whilst the animals grazed Able gave Sarudzai some simultaneous equations to solve. He looked at her whilst she worked. His eyes ran down the curve of her neck and he looked at the familiar way she pouted as she worked her way quickly and accurately through each equation. He leaned forward and put his mouth on the nape of her neck. Sarudzai got a fright when she felt wetness on her neck, she got even more of a fright when she realized that the wetness came from Able's moist lips. "What are you doing?" she demanded.

With his lips still on her neck he responded, "Teaching you biology."

"No, Able no!" she said sternly, pushing him away. She stared into his eyes and saw that he was hurt. Still, she reiterated, "No!" The two stared at each other for a while longer and as Able's eyes began to water Sarudzai went back to solving her equations. "I'm finished," she finally told Able. His face was turned away from her and he sniffed but did not answer. "Able," she said. Still, there was no response from him. Sarudzai threw the exercise book at him, got up and marched home with her teeth gritted and her fists balled up. She was livid that he had ruined her educational pursuits for her.

The next Sunday, however, Sarudzai decided to go back and see if the tension had defused between them. She had been thinking about the incident the whole week and her anger had subsided. She hoped that whatever he had felt had subsided too so that they could go back to learning amicably. Sure enough, when Sarudzai went back to Able she was relieved to find that things seemed to have gone back to normal. For two hours, the pair joked and learned and taught and explored the corners of each other's minds, until it was time for Sarudzai to go home, knowing that her mother would passively give her usual lecture about the role of a woman in the home. Just as Sarudzai got up to leave Able descended upon her. He held her down with his leg and placed his hand on her chest and his wet lips on her ear. He let her struggle until she was still and then he whispered into her ear, "Knowledge is power and power comes at a price, Saru."

"Able stop it! Leave me alone," she demanded. Able got off her and she sprung up and whipped around to face him. Her wide eyes signalled to him that she was shocked and hurt. Sarudzai had thought that they had, in their weeks together, built up a solid friendship and she did not think that friends treated each other like this. Able, on the other hand, was calm and collected. The tears of the previous week's rejection had long since dried up.

"Saru, life is give and take. Do not return here if you are not willing to do your part," he called after her as she ran away from him. She thought she heard his voice crack but she was not sure. She also thought that she would never return and that her education was over, but she was not sure.

Sarudzai did not return to Able for three weeks after that. Every Sunday around the time she usually met with him for tutoring she felt a pain in her chest. With disdain, she did her chores. Sometimes, when she was sure nobody was watching, she would allow herself to weep for the life she could have had, but lost. She felt that life had been unfair to her and that things were not meant to be that difficult.

One evening she overheard her mother standing up for her against her father. She was shocked that the silent woman who usually took whatever life handed to her had spoken words against her father. She was shocked until she realised that her mother had not stood up for her but, rather, for herself. "*Muskana uya,* that girl, is it not time for me to find her someone?

The extra money would be good for me." He had said casually during the rare occasions they were left alone in one of their bedrooms.

"*Aiwa*, no," her mother had said surprisingly firmly. "She is only fourteen or fifteen." "But still, that's a ripe age..." her father had responded after a moment of hesitation.

Mother had cut him off, "But still nothing *mhani imi,* who will help me out if she does?"

Sarudzai had walked away, opting not to hear anymore as two people who knew nothing about her argued over her future. She did decide that night that the following Sunday she would go back to Able and ask him to be reasonable and for him to continue to tutor her. That night as she was sleeping, she dreamt that she had a diploma and a job in Harare.

Sarudzai went back to learn from Able. She begged him to be reasonable and to tutor her. She was relieved that the old Able seemed to be back and she went back for three more Sundays. Sarudzai went back to learn from Able, even after the Sunday when he lay on her, crushing her under his weight, and told her that it was time for him to start receiving his payment. During the week she tried to fill her head with numbers and figures of speech and types of clouds. She tried to fill her mind with the things that he taught her ever Sunday before he took his payment whilst she lay still beneath him as stiff as a piece of wood. Even when she was on the ground like that with her fists balled up above her head where she was pinned, she would escape herself and ignore what was happening and instead do mental mathematics, count the different types of erosion there were, recount the effects of the Second World War, and form sentences using the word of the day. Sarudzai went back to learn from Able every Sunday despite herself because that was the price the girl had to pay for education.

* * *

As Sarudzai sunk into a reverie and as her baby's muffled cries died down, her mind took her back to the day the deputy principal had driven up to their homestead in his old beat up car an entire year and a half after her father had snatched her out of school and the future she had longed for and had worked so hard to achieve. This had been an unsuspected glimmer of hope for her for even though she knew by then that nothing would ever be the same again because of what was inside of her, she had faith in herself. Even so, she had once overheard- several years back before she was married to the chief- her mother's younger sister and her friends on the way to fetch water talking about a hermit of a woman in the neighbouring village who young, unwed women often visited if they needed to be unburdened. She would let nothing stand in her way if she was given the chance to learn again.

Her father initially had not been welcoming to

the principal, Mr Dzika's visit. The principal had asked to speak to the twin's mother but father would not allow her to be addressed by another man in his absence. The three of them sat under the shade of the mango tree in the yard, the two men facing each other on stools and mother sitting on the well swept ground beside father.

"I have come," began Mr Dzika after all the necessary greetings and reintroductions, "to address the issue of your daughter, err, Sarudzai, returning to school. We, the heads of the school, are able to offer her a merit-based scholarship as we feel that her representation of the school, especially in the up and coming maths Olympiad, is paramount to the school, and our town's continued success." He finished his opening remarks by cleaning his thick glasses with a handkerchief that he had fished out of his pocket.

Father leaned closer to the deputy principal with a glint in his eye. "You mean, if we send, err, the girl back to school, the school will pay us?" he asked in earnest.

"What? No!" Mr Dzika said in shock. "What I am saying is that it will cost you nothing to send her to school.

Father clicked his tongue in disbelief and looked

down at mother who lowered her eyes to the ground between the two men in respect for both of them. "Do you hear this *shura*?" he asked his wife who, in respect, did not respond. He turned back to the deputy principal and said, "What do you mean it will cost us nothing to send the girl to school. Who will cook and clean in this place? When it comes time to harvest, who will harvest? If she is at school and we have to hire help to stand in her place won't that be a cost to us for sending her to school?"

"It'll be a long-term investment is what I mean..."

But father cut Mr Dzika off. "A long-term investment when she is just going to go off and join another man's family when she gets married?" Father spat on the ground in disgust and then stared at the deputy principal square in the eye. No one said anything for a long time and then father asked in a low, deliberate voice, "Can a man eat education?" Mr Dzika did not respond so father asked another question, "Can a man take education to bed?"

"Mr Sadombo!" Mr Dzika exclaimed. "Look, times have changed and girls also need to get an education. In the towns nowadays, there are a lot of women in the workforce. My own neighbour and friend the Honourable Edith Maruta is a member of parliament, as I am sure you are aware of, and that is something she would not have been able to be if she had not gotten an education, Mr Sadombo!"

"Did you say Edith Maruta?"

"Yes..."

"Edith Maruta, Edith Maruta from Gokwe?"

"That very one," confirmed Mr Dzika, hoping he was finally getting through to Father.

Father looked down at mother, "*Nhai* Mama, don't you serve our visitor any refreshments? Go get us some *Chibuku* please!" Mother hurriedly got up and went to the kitchen to get the beer for the visitor and Father. Sarudzai had moved back further away from the entrance of the kitchen so that her mother would not see that she had been eavesdropping. Father grinned at Mr Dzika, shifted to the edge of his seat so that his face was close to the deputy principal's ear and then in a loud whisper he said, "I had Edith Maruta back in 1991 when we were both in secondary school." Mr Dzika stared wide-eyed at Father as Father flipped his wrist and clicked his tongue in a loud victorious chuckle. He hit the startled deputy principal's thigh. Mother returned with the Chibuku which she placed on a stool between the two men. "I bedded a member of parliament!" he reiterated. The deputy principal gave a nervous chuckle and took a sip of his Chibuku, unsure of how else to react. Mother, sensing that it was now men's talk, left the shade of the mango tree and went off to do her chores.

Forty minutes and more Chibuku later the two men, both happily drunk, were now deep into a conversation about which girls they had had back in their prime. "To, to be honest," stuttered the deputy principal, "I had Edith in 1988, it must had been. She was just coming into her womanhood and I was the first."

"No, no, I was first, she said so!" roared father.

"She told me the same thing! That slut!" slurred the deputy principal in disbelief.

Sarudzai had heard enough. Ignoring the calls of her mother who wanted her to go and collect more water for the kitchen she ran off to the little wooded area that she liked to sit in, and there she could not stop her bitter tears from falling as she finally accepted that her sex had long since sealed her fate long before she was born. Minutes later she watched as Mr Dzika's beat up car rolled off into the distance back the way it had come.

* * *

"What are you doing?" Tete's squeal brought Sarudzai back from her reverie. She calmly turned her head towards the boy and allowed her hand to drop to the floor as mother rushed into the room past Tete and picked up the baby to check that he was still breathing. "*Haya, mwana uyu,* Sarudzai you are too much. What do you think you are doing?" Tete asked. Mother tapped the boy on his back and he started to cry. "Do you know you can go to jail for that? And then when you have finished rotting in jail you will go on to rot in hell, I tell you, Muroora, your daughter is too much," she finished off by addressing mother.

"He was making noise," Sarudzai said weakly as her mother rocked the baby to sleep again.

As mother continued to rock the baby she looked down at her daughter. "Sarudzai," she said, equally as weakly, "Baba and the other men said you must tell them who the owner of this baby is so that he can be brought to pay damages."

"And lobola," Tete, having managed to calm her nerves, chimed in. "You are his wife know since he has taken you so he must pay lobola and take you to his home."

"Tete," mother said to stop her from talking. Mother looked down at her daughter pityingly. "It'll be fine Saru, this is how a lot of successful marriages start."

Sarudzai let the lazy tears roll slowly down the sides of her face from the corners of her eyes. "Mama. If I had been allowed to learn..."

"This child and her theatrics," said Tete as she left the room to go and report to the men and the notable women that Sarudzai did not know who the boy's father was and that she was trying to kill the baby.

"Sarudzai!" Mother said sternly when Tete had left. "Stop that now. You can't change the past, what has happened has happened. Now get up, clean this mess up, feed your son and be a woman."

Sarudzai wiped away her tears, allowed her body to continue to convulse with silent sobs, and then she began to clean up the evidence of her pain.

WHAT HAPPENED TO RODNEY

Jameson, 2015

"Would you like to join me in prayer?" This was the way she asked every night but there really was never an option- and rightfully so. We all filed into the room like we did every night, got on our knees and bent over our respective sofas.

"Let's all pray," again this was usual. We all prayed at the same time, Mum's voice- as the matriarch- always slightly louder than the rest of ours, perhaps because mothers have nothing to hide. I didn't have secrets either and my prayers were mostly a reverent worship session, but I know my teenage sister was at the stage in life where hormones and all things carnal began to enter her mind. Her prayers were usually silent.

There really is nothing that surpasses the love of God and I was put on this earth to praise him. Every action of mine is one in which I glorify Him so that I minister to those around me just by being alive. I feel praying gives me the strength and wisdom to do that so I pray as much as I can because the Bible says 'pray without ceasing.' Evening prayers are the best because, well, 'when two or more are gathered'. My family's prayers usually taper out before mine are done so I take the opportunity whilst they are all listening to pray for blessings upon their lives, it helps with their confidence and the faith they need to go through life. That's what usually happens, but that night was different.

I had been praying for my mother throughout the day because I noticed that something was affecting her spirit. It's hard to tell when someone is going through something spiritually but that is why I stay close to God, so He can give me such wisdom. My mother is a strong woman of God so she knows that a spiritual battle is fought through prayer. That is why hers went on longer than usual.

"God, I put Rodney in your hands mighty Father God. You are the all-knowing God. Mighty God, protect him. You are the one who knows if he is still alive Father God. Bring him back to us God. All things are possible with you God."

By the time my mother finished praying, my sister had fallen asleep, so it took a second to rouse her. We all rose from our positions and took our seats. Whilst Sara rubbed the sleep from her eyes my mother used her wrap-around to wipe the sweat from her face. Usually Sara would bid everyone a swift good night and rush back to her cell phone in her room or whatever it is teenage girls get up to at night, but like I noticed, that day was a different day from the crack of its dawn.

"Mama? Who is Rodney again?"

My mother's eyes shifted away from Sara as she unsuccessfully willed the tears that seemed to have stored up during her prayer not to spill. Spill they did.

"What do you mean who is Rodney? How can you fail to know Rodney?"

"I remember the name but-"

"Get out of here, go sleep. It's past your bedtime," and with that our mother left the room whilst dabbing at her eyes with her wrap again.

Sara turned to me in confusion. I understood my mother's outburst- what happened was painful for all of us- but I believe mothers have an extra heart for each of their children. However, I could also empathise with Sara because she was young when it happened, very young, what with being the last born by eight years.

“Jameson, who is Rodney again?”

Rodney wasn’t an openly discussed topic in the house anymore. We all thought about him privately and prayed for him separately. No longer did my mum utter ‘Rodney would love this’ whilst finishing off a freshly baked cheese cake and my father had long since removed his name from the list of his children’s names he called out before getting to mine when he was calling me- as seemed to be the habit with parents.

“Rodney was our brother,” my older brother answered before I could.

“Rodney *is* our brother,” I corrected.

“Jameson, it’s less painful for all of us if we just accept what happened and move on with our lives.”

“Only God knows what happened. Why should we throw him away just because-”

“What happened?” Sara interrupted Ryan and me before we could get into an argument. I do not like to argue, especially not with Ryan because he is my mentor especially when it comes to our faith. I must admit though that even though I look up to him he can be frustrating in the way he talks like he has lost faith sometimes, especially when it comes to Rodney. Yes, it hurts and confuses us all, but why lose the faith? We have got to keep the faith.

"What happened to Rodney?"

Rodney, 2007

One thing that does not make sense to me is why the old man moved us all back to Zimbabwe from England, especially at a time like this. He should have let me stay on and start up my hustle there. Shit, England was nice. I actually did well in school there and I enjoyed living there. Everything was easy even though we were foreigners. How messed up is that? It's easier to live in a foreign country than it is living in your own country- now that's messed up. I'm not saying everything was easy and breezy, but I'm saying it was comparatively easier. I'd probably have gone to university if we were still in England- I had the grades for it- but after we moved back home after I finished high school I just lost interest in school. A young man needs to pay his dues in this country you know, and school isn't going to help you do that. I know people with even master's degrees who are unemployed in this country. Learning will not put food on the table. So, I sat down with the parents and I told them that they need not worry about hustling college money because I wouldn't be going. They were quiet for a while and then the old man went on one of his speeches about how he expects me to be a torch light for my younger siblings and be the first of us all to graduate from college. That made me mad because I felt like they should have been more grateful that they needed to look for school fees money for one less child. My mum said selling used cars wasn't a real career when they asked what I planned to do. It's the grind Ma, it's called hustling. Respect the hustle.

It's so much harder to do my business here, especially using Zim dollars. The old man gave me start up capital for my business but that was a few months ago and this month, because of inflation I can no longer buy the used car I planned to buy. I have to settle for a cheaper used car.

What I do is I buy used cars which are imported from Japan. I don't really deal with the importing, not yet anyway. I just buy straight from the big boss, fix them up a little bit and then sell them at double the price and make a profit. It's hard in this economy, like I said. Because of inflation your profit may not be a profit anymore by the time you sell the car. Or you can tell a potential buyer the price today and have to call them just before they come to fetch the car to tell them to deposit an additional twenty five percent of the original price into your bank account and so sometimes you lose the client.

The old woman worries that I haven't been eating, but I do eat. If I only sold used cars then I probably wouldn't have the money for food, which brings me to my side hustle. I sell weed. I was last home six weeks ago because I get the weed from a distributer in Harare and then come and sell it here in Mutare. It's better that way because my used car business is here and fewer people know me here so I'm less likely to run into nosey people. My mother worries about me though, especially after the incident when I was last home. I don't answer her calls that much anymore because her worrying and nagging and over the phone prayers really frustrate me. I love that woman, but I don't have time for frustrations, I have got to stay focused.

Oh, about the incident. So, I was meant to get my stash whilst I was home but the distributer kept changing shit around. You know when you are a low-level dealer you can't really be like 'give me my stuff because time is money and I don't like being home,' nah, you just have to go with the flow. Anyway, on the day he said I could come and collect my stash- which was three months worth of weed- I was visiting this chick in Norton and so I told him that I would collect it the next day or that evening when I got back to H-town. I guess he wasn't having it because it turns out he got the stash delivered to my house anyways. How he knew where I lived is still a mystery.

So, this guy rings the intercom and when my

mum answers he asks to see me. The woman tells him that I am not around and things should have stopped there but they don't. She goes out to the gate and asks him what his business is with me. I'm telling you that woman does not know how to mind her own! So, the man says he has a business package for me and asks her to pass on my parcel to me when I get home and he hands her the two sealed packing boxes with my name and number on it. Now like I told you, this woman cannot mind her own so she goes to the kitchen, grabs a knife and opens the boxes. She didn't know what packaged weed looked like but Ryan and Jameson knew and they told her when she asked.

Now, I'm not really scared of my parents, especially since I am too old to get beaten and all they can do is shout. They can shout and scold but their words don't really faze me. They used to though, but there is a psychological freedom from your parents that comes from earning your own money from your very own hustle.

That night when I came home the folks were waiting for me in the lounge. My mother's eyes were red like I think she had been crying. That woman cries too much. The others were nowhere to be seen. They had most likely been sent to their rooms. As signalled I sat down on the sofa opposite my parents and had to wait a tense three minutes before the old man- the self-appointed spokesperson of the family- started speaking.

"Your mother found your marijuana. Do you know that it is illegal?" "What you are doing is a sin!" my mother had interrupted.

"Let me speak. We could tell that ever since you left school your mind has not been right. We can tell from your behaviour. Two boxes of marijuana! It will kill you!"

"Dad, I don't smoke weed."

"Do not try to lie to the two people that raised you in this house, Rodney. Smoke anymore marijuana and we will disown you in this house, do you hear me?"

Only then did I start to panic because he was speaking as though something had happened to my two boxes of weed.

"Your mother and I burnt that marijuana in the compost. It was terrible because the smoke nearly killed us all in this house. The young girl is sick she has been asleep the whole day, all because of you. No, we will not accept it!"

I hardly heard him finish his sentence because I was out the door running towards the compost heap to see what I could salvage. Now, I'm a pretty chilled guy, but that heap of black ashes flashes before my eyes every too often and makes me angry. It wasn't so much that they had burnt my stuff to stop me from smoking it- or so they thought- it's their ignorance that angered me. They did not stop to ask questions, they just jumped to conclusions. And now I was stuck in a rut. I did not have product and I did not have the boss's money to pay him for the product. I was in trouble because of their stupidity and that made me angry.

I don't get angry often but when I do I see red and it becomes very difficult for me to control my actions. That's probably why I went straight to the room I shared with Ryan to pack my belongings and leave instead of confronting my parents. They followed me anyway. "Where do you think you are going at this time of night? Rodney, if you leave you shall not step foot in this house ever again!" The old man's dramatic shouting had woken everybody up including Sara who then clung to my heels begging me not to leave. She had no idea what was going on.

"I don't plan to," I told my dad. I remember looking back at the house from the gate just before I slipped out. It was a humid night and the mist added to the mystery of the whole situation. I felt no sentiment to the house, and oddly enough none towards the people in the house. They failed to understand me. My mother's pleading echoed through the damp walls of the house as I closed the gate behind me. Whether she was pleading with Jesus or the old man I will never know.

Mama, 2008

Every single day I prayed for Rodney, every single day.

"Mune mufananidzo wake here? That will make identification easier." Of course I had a photo of my son, though it was taken three years back just before we had left England. Since being back in Zimbabwe we hadn't had as many opportunities to grab a camera and capture a memorable moment. That is not to say we didn't have memorable moments, of course we did, but they weren't as effortless as in the past and besides, my husband had had to sell the camera and all its lenses together with our third car to make some money for the kids' school fees. They say there are some phones with cameras inbuilt into them. I heard Ryan talking to my husband about it. Maybe we'll get one of those and kill two birds with one stone.

"Can you make a copy of this photograph? I'd very much like to keep it," I had said whilst slipping the photograph out of the picture frame I had taken from the mantel piece in the living room. I remember the day it was taken. We were all at the beach even though it was overcast. We went because it was the last time we would be able to go to the beach in a long time to come. I had packed a picnic basket and it was a perfect afternoon until it started raining. But before then, my husband has taken pictures of us all. This one of Rodney was of him in his grey swimming trunks and a wet white vest. He had just come out of the water which none of us went into because we were afraid of the cold. He was always more daring than the rest of us.

"I'll scan and copy and give you back this one," the police constable had said. I had to hunt him down for that photograph back for several weeks later. I ended up scanning and giving him a copy myself. I told the two constables that he worked as a used car salesman in Mutare. I did not tell them that he was a marijuana smoker because the police are less sympathetic to criminals and it was already uncertain whether they would follow up on my missing person's report in the first place, what with the notoriety of the ZRP to not be very helpful unless spurred on by encouragement fees. I had given them tea and cake in an effort to get them on my side but they still said, "Ah, Mutare? That's way beyond our jurisdiction. But what we can do *ka*, Madam, because you are very worried we can see, is that we will transfer this report and your son's file to Mutare and we will try work together with them." At their request, they left with the rest of the cake in a lunch box.

It is nearly over a year since he ran away after I burnt his marijuana. Sometimes I think that I acted to rashly, maybe I should have prayed and talked to him myself before involving my husband. My husband can be stern. Sometimes I feel guilty but the ladies in my cell group assure me that my actions were good because I was saving my son from sin by removing the temptation from his path.

The first couple of weeks after he left I was as indignant about it as my husband was. Rodney was in the wrong after all and I have learnt from the experience of raising children that they always come crawling back to you because sooner or later they need something. I cannot imagine anyone being completely self-sufficient from selling used cars in this economy so I thought he would be back or that he would contact his father for more money as he usually did every couple of months. I was wrong, it has been a whole year since we've seen or heard from him. He won't answer our calls anymore and he is no longer living at the address he had once given us.

I know he is fine. I know it deep down in my heart because God is mighty and I know He is protecting the son that he gave to me. But sometimes your heart may have faith and be sure of something, but the mind is not so easily convinced. I try to ease my mind by involving Rodney in ways I naturally would if he were still living with us. That way maybe, as the saying goes, his ears will ring and he will know that someone who loves him is talking about him and he will come back home. His photos remain on the mantel piece next to his brothers' and sister's, and his clothes remain untouched in his room. Why shouldn't it be this way? It's not like he isn't coming back. It's not like he is dead.

When Rodney comes back we will take him to a rehabilitation centre- they said they had something like that a Harare Hospital. I've already started saving up for it. I started a chicken business in the back yard and it's doing relatively well and so far I've raised enough money, inflation permitting, for the deposit at the rehabilitation centre. After Rodney is rehabilitated, we will keep him at home and he will not go anywhere without me or my husband. My husband will go to Mutare and see to concluding his car sales business if indeed he is still at it. We will help him here at home. The church will keep him close through prayer and mentorship and we will take care of our son until he is on the right path once again.

But how can he do this to me the mother who carried him for nine harsh months? His birth was the hardest thing I have ever gone through. He refused to shift into the correct position when it came time to deliver and the doctors had to cut my stomach open to get him out before both me and him died. Even after that, my stitches kept ripping open and he himself was a sickly infant. The scar still hurts whenever there are clouds in the sky. Now it hurts whenever I start to worry about him, but a little prayer and an aspirin usually help to numb me of emotions and of pain. How can one child cause a mother so much pain? Is it so hard for a living breathing boy to just pick up the phone and call his mother to let her know that he is alright, especially after leaving under such unsettling circumstances? Maybe he doesn't have the money to call, but then he could always post a letter saying send me money for bus fare home. Besides, we have several relations in Mutare that would take him in were he destitute. We have asked them to keep an eye out for him. Maybe it is the marijuana that has affected his brain, but I pray to God to give him at least thirty minutes of clarity so he can at least go to a police station and ask them to contact us. I know he would never get into dangerous illegal activity because we raised him better than that. So where can he be and what can he be doing? I know he is alive. He is not lying dead in a ditch anywhere because God is mighty and besides, I would feel it because mothers have sixth senses about such matters.

I need to stop this worrying. It is a slap in the face of God because it undermines His ability to hear and answer prayers. Now that the police are involved it is only a matter of time before they bring him home. The police keep asking for money to aid with their search. It's hard but we'll keep providing the money until Rodney is back home, which will be soon. My soul is uneasy from all this over thinking.

Would you like to join me in prayer?

Dad, 2010

My wife's health had been declining rapidly since the boy left in 2007. I mean of course after a while I began to worry too but you know women take things to the extreme. It all began when we were grocery shopping for Christmas at the end of 2008. We were in Spar and my wife went to get a few items whilst I was getting some soft drinks for the Christmas period. It was a delight back then to be able to get such luxuries because the shops had been empty for quite some time what with the decline of the Zim dollar but the introduction of the US dollar saw some of the wealthier shops able to restock their shelves again. Thankfully my sister in America was able to lend me some US dollars to help with the children's fees for January and, with my Christmas bonus and- though reluctantly given up- some money from my wife's chicken business we were able to have a comfortable festive season. Though not nearly as luxurious as the festive seasons we had in the UK this one was more authentic and enriching. Having traditional and organic food, for example, was an improvement from all the bland foods one had to supplement with spices to get some flavour in. So anyway, whilst I was getting some soft drinks I heard some commotion. At first I heard what sounded like a wail, and my brain automatically dismissed it as perhaps a customer's heated argument with a till operator or a complaint that was building up. That kind of stuff was, and still is, quite common. The harsh socio-economic conditions have left the county's atmosphere tense and everyone's nerves are raw. Where once we were gentle and peaceful and even caring towards one another as a nation we are now a very snappish people, suspicious of each other in the battle to selfishly provide for ourselves and our immediate families only, and most people cannot even manage that.

It was just one wail which I heard and I wouldn't have paid much more attention to it had shoppers not started to gravitate towards the direction of the noise. The shoppers did not rush to where the noise came from so that they could help, I can say that because when I reached the source of the noise no one was helping my wife up off the floor. They were just crowded around her staring with curiosity, caution and, to my irritation, amusement.

My wife, according to a conversation I overheard behind me as I gathered her up off the floor and brushed the cornflakes off her, had been strolling down the aisle and when she saw the boxes of previously extinct cornflakes on the shelves, had begun to cry rather dramatically. By the time I got to her she was rocking on the floor clutching an open box of cornflakes to her chest and eating some off the floor. "Rodney loved this cereal back in England. Do you remember *Baba waRyan tichimutengera* since he was a small child? He loved this cereal but since we came back here we haven't been able to find it. Let's buy a few boxes for him and surprise him during Christmas breakfast before we go to morning service." We didn't manage to buy anything that day. To an educated mind it was evident that my wife was having a nervous breakdown. I won't lie, before then I had believed that such dramatic ailments were only for white people-we had seen many nervous breakdowns in the UK and even on television. Even then, I wasn't so sympathetic as I believed that she was overreacting. I was, in my embarrassment at the gawking onlookers, even a little rough with her as I told her to get herself together. As I hauled her into the car I overheard some shoppers who had followed us at a not so respectful distance mutter things such as '*muroyi*' and '*mushonga*.' Poor uneducated fools, what had witches and witchcraft to do with an, albeit embarrassing, nervous breakdown? I have since become more empathetic. I took her home and the children tried to console her and she soon fell asleep from exhaustion. When she woke up the next morning she was never the same. Her prayers have increased, but she needs the help of medicine and not God to combat the high blood pressure and depression that arose after that incident.

Rodney's return did make things better though. It seemed to renew her strength. It was this time last year in 2009 on a rainy Monday morning at breakfast before I left for work and the children left for school. My wife had prepared a breakfast of tea, bread and scrambled eggs and was just packing mine and the kids' lunches when I heard her shriek. My first thought was that she was having a heart attack. They say the risk of having a cardiac event or stroke increases by up to forty percent when you have high blood pressure. However, when she started to shriek the name Rodney over and over again I felt some sort of relief knowing that it was probably just a nervous breakdown and not a stroke. The kids gathered around her in an effort to calm her and as I got up to play my part I saw, through the wet windowpane and veil of pouring rain, a figure walking towards the house, unbothered by the rain. The rain made it hard to see clearly, it could have been anyone, but when the figure approached the kitchen door and I swung it open I saw that my wife was right. It was Rodney.

Two years had thinned and darkened him and he was only a shadow of his former healthy and lively self. A father's role is that of disciplinarian and the thought of those two boxes of marijuana and his causing his mother's illness angered me, but I think, ultimately, what made me begin to clap him repeatedly across the face was its smug and unapologetic expression. He made no effort to defend himself but I could see that his smugness had turned to bitterness by the time my wife had managed to shield him with her own body. I went to my bedroom to call the office and tell them I would be late due to family matters whilst my wife and kids smothered the spoiled boy with loving attention and food.

When it came time to return to the kitchen I found my legs resistant to work and I felt an almost too sudden need to relieve myself. That gave me time to think about my admittedly rough reaction to my son's return. I had gone to church plenty, my wife and sons made sure of that, but how could I treat this unapologetic fool like a prodigal son when the two situations were so very different? The prodigal son was apologetic, mine was not. What had he even returned for? My own father had raised me and my siblings with an iron fist and none of us would have ever thought to run away for two years with no communication. I chose love. My icy reception had been enough. All I wanted from him was the truth of where he had been for two years and why he had been silent. Had he been trying to teach us a lesson? A teary plea for forgiveness on bended knee would further appease my mood. Thereafter we would take care of him and, like my wife insisted, send him to a rehabilitation centre and then we would go from there. Having gathered my thoughts, I walked back into the kitchen to find Rodney's skin and bones devouring all the eggs between four slices of bread at once. My wife was making more eggs and Ryan and Jameson were unsuccessfully trying to casually chat him up between mouthfuls. Sara sat at the furthest side of the table staring at him with wide eyes. I sat down as casually as the tense and awkward situation allowed and ate my own food. A father should never be nervous of their own children but I was. I did not know what to say or when a good time to say it would be. When the time came I sent Sara and Jameson off to school. The college going Ryan was on semester vacation, and besides, he was old enough to learn from this messy situation.

Ryan, 2013

"Where have you been?" Dad really wasn't one to beat about the bush, he had never been. Those are the first words he had said to Rodney the last time we saw him and that was about four years ago now. He asked the question we all wanted to ask but were all too scared to in case it reminded him of his silent absence in our lives and made him want to repeat it. Maybe it did. My mother didn't ask- she was just way too happy. She was humming a church hymn of praise whilst making more breakfast. Jameson and I had been trying to sooth him with idle chit chat like he had been on a three month vacation to the Bahamas. We lied to him even, "You look good man," Jameson had lied and I had agreed and asked him if he'd been working out. He never formed a full sentence in response and I, up till this day, could not interpret the weird pinched expression on his face. It was as if he has experienced things he could not put into words, so he stopped trying and only responded to our insistent mother-bird coos in grunts and groans.

In my opinion we should have been patient with him. If I was head of the house I would have left him well alone for some time and let him bath and sleep first before hammering into him. But I was not the head and could only respect his decision, praying that God would be in control of the situation. I'm going to be head of a house soon. I'm going to ask my college sweetheart to marry me because I have been saving up for the *lobola* and we will hopefully manage to get our own little place. The goal is to move to South Africa and build a more comfortable life there-God willing.

"*Mirai ambodya kani Baba,*" my mother had retorted. God bless a mother's heart. The man may be the head of the house but the woman turns that head in the most suitable direction, and so wait he did for my brother to finish eating before he restarted the interrogation again.

"My son, where have you been?" my father asked again after breakfast. The food must have given my brother strength because now he could form short sentences, albeit not very coherent ones.

"*Apa neapa,* here and there. Business as usual," he had said with his mouth but not with his eyes.

"We have tried to contact you almost every

day, no, everyday in fact, even twice a day. We have been to the address you gave us in Mutare to no avail several times. We have police constables in two cities looking for you-"

"You called the police?" This was the first time since he had stepped foot in the house that my brother had shown any sort of emotion and right now I could see fear in his eyes. His reaction confused us all and seemed to rekindle the original anger my father felt towards him.

"*Hatairegi kufonera mapurisa.* Why wouldn't we call the police? Two years! Two years, Rodney *wakatirwadzisa* you pained us my son," and then she started crying uncontrollably.

"Let me speak, Mama," my father interjected. Not like my mother could have continued anyway in between tears and heavy breathing. Obviously, as their child, my roll was that of a spectator and to fetch tissue and water for my mother.

"It is obvious we had to file a missing person's report. In fact, we filed several so that yours would not become a cold case. Imagine our embarrassment when we tell the constables that you walked into the house by yourself today. Rodney, we searched in mortuaries. Mortuaries for you! The pain you have caused us Rodney!" Dad was not being melodramatic. It was true. The first and second time was the hardest of all. My father and I would go alone because we knew my mother's heart could not take it even though she would plead with us and say a mother's identification would be most accurate. We tried to visit as many mortuaries as possible. There were more in Harare, obviously as there were in Mutare. We would go with a photo of Rodney and talk to the mortuary hand. Often the hand would require a dollar or five before he could be of assistance. It was wasted money because after pretending to analyse the photograph for about two irritating minutes he would say that dead people did not look like the living and that we should go in and look at the unclaimed bodies ourselves.

The greedy mortuary hand spoke truth when he said the dead did not look like the living. Death is a territory I personally cannot get used to. The first cadaver we viewed was of a man my brother's age. Where youthful skin should have been being scaly grey skin that clung onto the diseased cheek bones like wet tissue. I expected to smell rotting flesh but I did not, still the smell of preservative chemicals is not at all pleasant and the sight, smell, and the possibility of coming across my own brother in that state caused me to throw up. "Are you a man?" my father had asked that first time before sending me to wait in the car whilst he finished the undesirable task alone. My father is a man I look up to. He is one of the strongest people I know. Still, this whole situation with my brother hurts him, I can see it in his eyes and Jameson says he can tell that his spirit is wounded. Jameson has the gift of discernment and we thank God for that. My father has since become more aloof. Showing affection no longer comes naturally to him, but he tries. He tries for us because he loves us. I hope I am even half the man he is when I become a father.

We also made monthly visits to Mutare under the pretence of visiting the few relatives we have there when really it's in the hopes that we miraculously run into Rodney. I thought we did the one time. We were near a used car garage and we were in the car waiting for the robot to turn green. A vagabond passed right in front of our car, even bumping it a little, much to my father's annoyance. "That's Rodney!" I had said. "Look at his structure, and Rodney had a shirt like that, I know he does because I gave it to him for Christmas back in England. That's Rodney!" and I was nearly out of the car. The layers upon layers of dirt on Rodney's skin and his dirty dreadlocked hair could not hide his true identity from me, his brother.

I got out the passenger side of the car and ran after Rodney. I had to wait impatiently to cross the road because by then the robot was green and the cars were going. I got too impatient and weaved between the oncoming traffic whilst my father parked the car on the side of the road and came after me. I got to Rodney first. His back was to me and he was bent over a bin probably looking for food. My poor brother! I put my hand on his moist shoulder and said, "Rodney, let's go home" whilst forcefully turning him in case he tried to run away.

Life is made out of memories which we replay in our minds like an old video tape. That instant replays in my head in slow motion for some reason. Rodney turns slowly, my hand still on his shoulder. Before my eyes meet his, the smell of him hits my nostrils. It is an arid and assaulting stench like the smell of fermenting urine if urine could ferment, but I don't care. He is my brother. Sometimes I still catch a whiff of that smell and I look around in a desperate attempt to find its source, only to find that I have walked or driven past a public toilet in town. Rodney continues to turn towards me in slow motion. In my mind's eye, I see my own nervous smile- a calculated attempt to make him feel wanted and safe. Finally, in the memory, he is facing me and at the same time our eyes meet he goes limp and weak-kneed and falls to the ground in an apparent fit, complete with loud gibberish which in some churches would have passed for tongues. My stomach flips, not because my brother is a mad man- I could handle that- but because this is not my brother. His face is not Rodney's, his eyes are too narrow and too much of a light brown. I guess I had wanted him to be Rodney so much that my mind had convinced my eyes. By this time it is my father's hand on my sweaty shoulder leading me away as he repeatedly says, "It is not Rodney, it is not Rodney." His voice gets louder as he tries to drown out the onlookers who have begun to surround the vagabond who continues with his theatrics. The onlookers shout at us to leave the poor well alone as if it was my intention to hurt the mad man. They have no idea of what we are going through.

After that incident the mortuary visits became fewer and further apart. My mother only follows up on Rodney's case files about every five months. Only one unsettling thing happened after that. It was in 2012, towards the end just as the build up to this year's presidential elections started getting heated. I can't speak too candidly about issues around the government and the elections as making false claims can land you in trouble, especially around this time. All I know is that some people who are not in support of a certain party are disappearing. Just before the incident happened a journalist disappeared and is apparently still being searched for. The news said 'the puppet has fled to the West.' But I digress. Around November last year when politicians held rallies and visited otherwise forgotten towns in an effort to win votes I received a text. The text was from a number with only three digits- 874-which was unlike any number in Zimbabwe. Mother insisted on going to the police but they said to go to the various telephone companies. Neither Econet, Telecel nor Netone could trace its origins and so the where and who of it remains a mystery. For me it confirms our worst fears. Jameson says it means nothing and continues to have unshakable faith. For some people deliverance is only gotten in heaven and I've come to accept that. Mum and Jameson have not. Not yet.

> Date:27/11/12
> Sender:874
> Text: R. In danger. Asked me to join their group. Had joined for economic opportunity but they intimidate people in rural areas. They cut people long sleeve or short sleeve. I can no longer. I desire to come home. Once joined cannot escape. I will leave and head home but if caught will be killed. Pray for me. R.

Sara, 2015

Oh my gosh if I had known that it would hurt my mother that badly I would not have asked who Rodney was. People don't really understand me. I'm not asking who Rodney is to us, I know he was our brother; I'm asking who he was, like what he was like and stuff and what happened to him. My boyfriend said that people don't really tell me because Rodney is probably dead. I think he is right because if he was alive then my dad wouldn't have taken all his photos off the wall a couple of years ago and my mum would still mention his name now and again. Only Jameson still talks about him like he is around, and that's only to me and to

Ryan when he chooses to, as he says, "entertain his fantasies." Ryan and Jameson are close in age and they are best friends, leaving me as the odd one out. I fight with my brothers sometimes when they are being bossy or telling me how to live my life. The only thing the two of them fight about is Rodney and whether he *was* or *is* our brother.

I don't remember what he looks like. I vaguely remember one morning before school when some skinny dude

came in and ate all our breakfast. They said that that was Rodney. Anyway, by the time I came back from school that afternoon he was gone and the spare clothes in the spare room where gone too and some things were out of place in the lounge and a glass was broken in the kitchen. When I asked Mum where the skinny guy had gone she slapped me and said, "That *skinny guy* is your beloved brother Rodney." That was all she said. She didn't even bother to answer my question. I did press my ear against my brothers' room that night like I usually did and from their hushed conversation I gathered that this Rodney had gotten upset about something to do with the police and had packed the spare clothes- which apparently where his clothes- into a bag and then strip searched the house for money. My dad had left for work and for a skinny guy Ryan and my mother could not restrain him and it wasn't safe to try when he started thrusting a kitchen knife in their direction. After that the police came to our house every other day for like two weeks and my dad and brothers went to Mutare a couple of times. I even heard talk of the mortuary. My boyfriend says he wouldn't be scared to go into a mortuary. I would be. It's gross.

All that stopped a few years ago and it kind of started again after the mystery message. I wasn't allowed to read it but when Ryan was bathing I snuck into his room and went through his phone. That message was so cryptic it was like something out of a James Bond movie. It's been like three years since then and no one seems to care anymore, well, at least not out loud. Only Jameson occasionally asks me if I want to see a picture of Rodney which he hides in his Bible or if I want to hear a story about him. Most of the stories are of when we still lived in England. That's pretty cool but it pisses me off that I was too young to remember living in England. These days when he asks I say no because the stories are starting to get a little repetitive.

Today was the first time I've seen my mother cry in a long time. In fact, as far as I can remember all the times I have seen her cry have been because of the skinny, I mean because of Rodney. I guess I made it worse by asking. I once asked my dad and he ignored me. I was like, that is so rude! I didn't say it to his face obviously.

If Rodney does come back though, like Jameson says he will, I hope he won't be skinny anymore, cause that kind of scared me.

THE PROMISED LAND

In Johannesburg's Park Station, Shepherd, a lean man with a neat beard, wore a red Arsenal jersey, a worn-out leather jacket and dark denim jeans. He stood behind a woman who was dressed in blue jeggings and a champagne coloured jumper. Her hair was long and straight. Directly in front of them was a little girl who was dressed in a purple princess dress. She stared up at the two of them.

Shepherd gripped the woman's arm from behind and gently placed a blood filled-syringe and needle to her neck. He moved his mouth close to her ear. She did not move.

Shepherd whispered, "Give me all your money or I'll inject you with HIV."

* * *

One week earlier, Shepherd and Kaito, a dark, tall and muscular man who was wearing a tank top and black jeans, sat in Shepherd's dingy, dimly lit office drinking whiskey on ice. On Shepherd's lap was Lolo, a curvy woman dressed in a crop top and tight leather pants. She had on a blonde lace-front wig. Shepherd's dirty-finger-nailed hands caressed her curves. A tipsy Kaito raised his whiskey glass, "You inspire me daily."

"My man, that was nothing," Shepherd replied.

Kaito grinned, "We are going to make a lot of money off that Range Rover."

Shepherd grimaced in response, "We, are not. I'm not selling it. It's about time I reward my-self. I've earned it."

Lolo caressed Shepherd's cheek and pecked him on the forehead, "Yes you have, Baby. And I will have your old car. Like we discussed, because, I have earned that."

Shepherd looked at her lovingly, "Yes you have, baby girl." Lolo kissed Shepherd on the head again and got up. As Lolo turned to leave Shep-herd smacked her bottom. Both Kaito and Shepherd stared at it as she left.

"Bitches getting greedy these days," Kaito commented.

"Watch it. That's my girl," Shepherd snarled in response.

"One of them!" Shepherd and Kaito snickered and fist bumped over the table just as Tatenda, a scrawny young man in tattered clothes, walked in. Kaito turned his head to look at him, "Fuck you want?"

"Boss..." Tatenda stammered. Shepherd sighed and brought his whiskey glass down hard on the desk. Tatenda continued, "Diva was arrested." But still there was no verbal response from Shepherd, so Tatenda continued again, "And then there is an old lady here... to see you."

"Old lady?"

"Yes..." Tatenda confirmed hesitantly.

Kaito stood up and pulled his gun out of its holster, "They're using old ladies now?"

"Who did she say she is? Where is she?" Shepherd inquired suspiciously.

"I, I ..." but before Tatenda could finish stammering an answer Sheila, a short, thin middle-aged woman wearing a faded white T-shirt with a picture of Mugabe on it and a long black skirt and head wrap marched into the office. She and Shepherd stood in silence staring at each other. Kaito raised his gun to her head slowly.

Shepherd forced himself to snap out of it, "Alright, everybody out."

"What?" Kaito began.

Quietly, with his teeth gritted, Shepherd repeated, "Everybody, out." Without waiting to be told again, Tatenda left the room followed by Kaito who took the whiskey bottle with him. Sheila walked around the table and hugged Shepherd whose one arm hovered just above her back. Finally, Shepherd asked, "What are you doing here, Maiguru? How did you find me?"

Sheila sat in Kaito's chair across from Shepherd, "How did I find you? Every Zimba

who enters Musina learns about you, and you know me, I'm smart. There's nothing I can't find out if I want to."

Shepherd sighed, "I guess what I am asking is, why?"

Sheila leaned back in her chair and examined Shepherd's face. "*Makadini Babamunini?*" Sheila asked, "How are you, Brother-in-law?"

"Ndiripo kanamakadiiwo. Matwins Arisei? Nemhuri?" Shepherd replied politely, "How are the twins? How is the family?"

"The twins are good." Sheila confirmed, "They both received awards for exceptional A'level results." Shepherd said nothing so Sheila continued, "Ruvimbo is also good..."

Shepherd stood suddenly and retrieved a whiskey bottle and two clean glasses from a cupboard behind his chair, "Want a drink?"

Sheila laughed and Shepherd poured only one drink for himself before he sat back down. Undeterred, Sheila continued, "I actually saw them on Easter in Chipinge. The family gathered for Mbuya's tenth anniversary of her death. It was nice. Did you hear about that?"

"No."

"Tambirai is just delightful. Honestly, she..."

Shepherd interrupted her, "I'm actually incredibly busy. So, unless you have something urgent to discuss I'm going to have to ask you to..."

Sheila interrupted him, "I need help, Shepa. I'm desperate. I've hit rock bottom many times and I managed to pull myself up, but this is a new kind of low for me."

Shepherd rolled his eyes impatiently, "You know, even those of us in South Africa are struggling too."

"I'm not here to beg for money," Sheila snapped.

"So why are you here?"

"I need a job."

"A job? I'm no employer."

"I want to join your... family," Sheila finally confessed. Shepherd chuckled, smiled and downed the whiskey in his glass before pouring himself some more. Sheila continued, "Shepherd, please. I am serious." Shepherd chuckled again and Sheila went on, "Things are so hard at home. After your brother died my buying and selling sustained my boys and me, but you know the government has banned imports and the boarder is chaos."

"Sheila..." Shepherd tried to interject but Sheila continued.

"I put money aside every time I had a cent to spare because I knew my boys would need to go to college. But the banks stole all our money when the government shifted to U.S. dollars. And now, I have nothing."

"Maiguru, I hear you, but I am also struggling," Shepherd finally managed to say. There was silence for a while before Sheila said quietly, "You are skinny, Shepa. So, I am not under the impression that you are living the good life, believe you me."

Shepherd buttoned up the second from top button on his shirt, downed his whiskey again and poured himself some more, "Go home, old woman."

"Think of your nephews," Sheila pleaded.

"A gang is no place for a woman, let alone one

your age," he snapped.

Sheila leaned over and grabbed Shepherd's glass of whiskey and downed it. She coughed and spluttered as Shepherd leaned back in his chair and watched her. "The devil is a liar." she managed to say between coughs.

"It's a dangerous game." Shepherd finally responded.

"I'm desperate."

"We'll see."

* * *

Shepherd, Kaito, Sheila and a group of about twenty men ranging in age stood and squatted around in a dimly lit storage unit with the gate rolled down. Shepherd was in front of the group pacing up and down and Kaito stood in front also with his arms folded across his chest.

Shepherd addressed the group, "I protect you motherfuckers and how do you repay me? Eight of you were arrested in the past fucking month alone." Shepherd turned and glared at Tino, a short, skinny man wearing a worn-out shirt and shorts. Tino quickly looked down. Shepherd walked up to him and put his face too close to his. "Tino, what the fuck is happening?" Tino shuffled backwards. Shepherd shoved him and he stumbled. "The other seven of you come forward." No one moved. Some of the older men looked around at the younger boys. "Godi, Craig, Xolani, Nhlanhla and Umkhulu. I said, I said, step forward. Didn't I?" Godi was tall and wiry. He took a deep breath, held his head high and began to wade through the crowd to the front. Craig was a short but muscular man. He followed Godi. Xolani was a boy who still had a considerable amount of baby fat. He and Nhlanhla, a strong dark boy, had to be pushed forward by the men around them. Umkhulu was a sixty-nine-year-old man. He had razor cuts on his face and was stooped and thin. He walked quickly to the front. The five of them knelt before Shepherd and Kaito, Umkhulu taking a little longer to kneel. Que, a tall and muscular man who had on a white vest and denim pants stepped through the crowd with a baton and joined Shepherd and Kaito in the front.

Shepherd walked over and stood in front of Umkhulu, "Life is about give and take, isn't that what the old and wise say, Old Man?" Kaito raised his rifle to Umkhulu's head.

Sheila screamed, "Please no!"

"*Engizisebenzele iminyaka eminingana. Lena ukon-iwa kwami kokuqala* ...I've worked for you for several years. This is my first offense..." Umkhulu calmly replied. A murmur rose from the gang. Que pulled Umkhulu up to his feet. "*Sihloniphe abadala yakho*. Respect your elders..." Umkhulu said a little less calmly. Shepherd punched Umkhulu in the stomach twice whilst Que held Umkhulu's arms behind his back.

"Stop it, stop it please!" Sheila begged. Umkhulu went limp. Que let him drop to the ground.

The gang looked on in shock and Sheila covered her mouth with her hands.

"Kaito, finish up." Shepherd instructed. Kaito aimed his gun at the kneeling men.

Que interjected, "Why don't you show the fuckers how it's done, Blood?"

Shepherd pushed Kaito's gun down, "I'm going to show you fuckers how it's done one more time. Park Station, Saturday at seven." He wiped some spittle off the corners of his mouth. He raised the storage unit gate and walked out, "Motherfuckers."

* * *

Shepherd, with the office lights still off, poured himself some whiskey then sat down in his chair. There was a knock on his open door and he looked up to discover Sheila whose eyes were red and swollen. He downed his whiskey. Sheila walked in, took a seat opposite him, turned on his desk lamp and stared at him for a while. “What happened? What happened to you?” Sheila sobbed. There was silence. Sheila continued, “That old man, Umkhulu... I think he’s dead. You kil...”

“I’m not going to apologize to you if that is what you came for,” Shepherd calmly retorted.

Sheila stopped crying and dabbed at her eyes with the collar of her shirt.

“It’s not,” She whispered.

“Then leave.”

Sheila did not leave, instead she said, “Have you ever seen someone struggle to stay alive? Someone you know? My brother, Sheanesu, during the xenophobia ...”

“Sheila.” Shepherd downed his whiskey and poured himself some more, “You know, I made a friend on the bus on the way here, his name was Peter. When we boarder jumped, well, swam through the Limpopo, he got lost in the chaos. I went back for three days after that." Shepherd downed his whiskey, "Crocodile must have got him."

Sheila dabbed at her eyes with her collar again. Shepherd sniffed and got up and poured himself more whiskey with his back to Sheila. "I guess we all know pain…" Sheila eventually said.

"What happened to me, Mai Matwins?" Shepherd suddenly said sharply, "My country happened to me, and *this* country happened to me."

* * *

Five years earlier at Road Port in Harare, Shepherd, healthy but not sculpted, kissed baby Tambirai on the cheek before handing her back to Ruvimbo who was a beautiful and curvy woman with an afro, dressed in jeans and a floral blouse. Ruvimbo, whilst looking at the baby, said, "If you don't come back in time and things here get too hard you know I'm going to have to sell her off for a bag of maize meal, right?

Shepherd smiled, "Well, she's so beautiful that her *lobola* will be enough to feed us for the rest of our lives." They both laughed and then they hugged with the baby between them. Still in each other's arms they stared at each other and both their eyes began to water. "Don't cry, Baby," Shepherd urged his wife.

"I can't help it," Ruvimbo sobbed. Tambirai giggled. This made Shepherd and Ruvimbo both laugh again. "She's so happy you'd never think there's anything wrong with her," Ruvimbo's smile faded and she began to cry again.

"Stop it. Stop it now, you've got to be strong for our little family," Shepherd cooed at his wife. They embraced again. The bus started its engine and people who were saying their goodbyes to their loved ones began to climb on. Shepherd wiped his face with his palm.

"Remember to pray every day, okay? Everything will be alright," he said to his wife. Ruvimbo nodded. The bus began to move slowly. "I love you okay? I'll call you soon as I can."

"I love you more, I love you so much," Ruvimbo replied. Shepherd ran and hopped onto the bus.

Ruvimbo dabbed at her moist eyes. Tambirai chortled again and Ruvimbo laughed down at her then they watched the bus drive away.

Shepherd walked down the aisle of the old bus until he reached his seat. He sat down next to Peter, a small but handsome boy in faded jeans and a red T-shirt. Shepherd waved at his wife out the window until the bus was too far gone. Shepherd wiped his face with his hand. “Isn’t it meant to be the small boys like me crying instead of you, Chief?” Peter said sheepishly.

Shepherd laughed and settled back into his seat. Peter unwrapped a plastic bag holding two ears of boiled maize and offered one to Shepherd.

“It’s okay don’t worry about it,” Shepherd declined.

“I’m not worried. Just that you are a little too skinny. Don’t want to make it obvious to theSouth Africans that we’re struggling,” Peter quipped. Shepherd laughed again and nudged Peter before taking the maize that Peter offered him. They shook hands. “I’m Peter.”

“Peter. I’m Shepherd.”

“Great to meet you, Chief. Just sad it’s not your

beautiful wife sitting here next to me instead of you." Shepherd laughed and nudged Peter in the arm before taking a bite of his maize.

* * *

In Johannesburg, Shepherd inserted coins into the call box phone and dialled, his small luggage bag at his feet. "Hello?" Ruvimbo answered.

"Baby, Hi! Ya, I arrived safely, called you soon as I got the chance," Shepherd's brow furrowed and he wiped his face, "Ya of course, got past easily really, no hassle... I miss you more baby..." Shepherd's eyes narrowed. "I can hear Tambi crying in the

background, why is she crying? She what? Did you take her to the clinic what did the doctor

say? Listen... Listen to me baby, I swear to you I will get this money and our little girl's heart

is going to be just fine, you hear me? Okay..." Shepherd's eyes began to water. "I love you

more baby girl... I love you... I'll call you again soon... I love you too. Give her a kiss for

me... Bye my love." Shepherd slowly replaced the receiver whilst leaning on the call box. He rested his head on the phone and for a while there was silence. He put a hand over his face,

let out a sob then hurriedly dabbed at his moist eyes, picked up his luggage and walked away.

* * *

Shepherd, dressed in a brown suit, sat in a well-furnished office opposite a balding Mr Fitz-henry who was looking at his CV and other documents. “So, you said you don’t have a work permit?” Mr Fitzhenry asked.

“Not yet. Not at the moment,” Shepherd confessed.

“Well, I mean, we would have taken you on as a junior location engineer, your qualifications are really good but...”

“I’ll get the permit,” Shepherd interjected.

“Passport?” Mr Fitzhenry quizzed. Shepherd looked down at his lap.

* * *

Shepherd, dressed in the same brown suit and a hard hat, stood with Brent, a well-built man in a work suit and his hard hat cocked in his arm. He looked at Shepherd's documents. "We have a vacancy but we can't take you," Brent said finally.

Shepherd responded, "I could help with the BEE-"

"You aren't from South Africa and you don't even have the right documentation," Brent said flatly.

"I've been trying to get them and I'm sure soon-"

Brent cut him off, "Sorry man." He handed Shepherd back his documents and Shepherd walked away.

* * *

A much slimmer Que who was in a dark tracksuit and a cap stood against a pillar in a dingy car park. Shepherd walked towards him. "Shepherd?"

Shepherd stopped a few meters in front of Que, "Que?" Que nodded. "Are you sure it'll be fine? It looks legit?"

Que replied, "No ID, no work in this country." He took a South African ID booklet out of his pocket and opened it to the page where Shepherd's name and face was.

He handed it to Shepherd who looked at it for a while before exhaling, "This is great."

"Money." Shepherd handed Que a rolled-up wad of cash and Que counted it before putting it in his pocket and jogging away. Shepherd continued to look at his picture in the booklet.

* * *

Shepherd sat in an office opposite a smartly dressed Mr Wells. Mr Wells looked at the South African ID booklet under Shepherd's name, "Well, Shepherd. We're glad to take you on board. We'll start you up right away as a location manager."

"Thank you. Thank you so much," Shepherd smiled.

"Go see Packer, he'll get you geared up." The two men stood up and shook hands.

* * *

Shepherd was in a work suit. He worked on fibre equipment along with Packer, who was also in a work suit. Mr Wells got out the car which had just driven onto the site followed by Mr Lewis, who was dressed in a dark suit and tie and was holding documents. The two approached Shepherd. With a grave look on his face Mr Wells said, "Shepherd, a word please." Shepherd went over to the two gentlemen and extended his hand in greeting but neither shook his hand. "Shepherd, this is Mr Lewis, the company lawyer. Your papers are fake." Shepherd stared at Mr Lewis. "Our accountants verified this when they were trying to register you onto the company's pay roll. Shepherd?"

"I, I'm a permanent resident," Shepherd stammered.
Mr Lewis interjected, "No, Shepherd you are not. Your passport too is invalid."

Shepherd ignored Mr Lewis and continued addressing Mr Wells, "Mr Wells, I can, I can fix this." Mr Wells ran his hand through his hair. "Please Sir, I am desperate. Let me fix this."

Mr Wells finally spoke, "The best I can do for you Shepherd right now is to let you go."

"No," Mr Lewis retorted, "We are going to call the authorities and get him deported back to his country James, that's what we agreed on."

Mr Wells ignored Mr Lewis and said to Shepherd, "Shepherd, I like you and I feel for you and I'll include you in my prayers but, just leave. Leave now."

"Unbelievable," Mr Lewis said in Mr Wells' direction, "I can't believe this. I'm calling." Mr Lewis turned his back to them and dialled a number on his phone. Shepherd looked at Mr Wells and then hurriedly took off his work suit revealing his tracksuit bottoms and vest underneath. He left his hardhat and work suit beside Packer and walked away.

Days turned into weeks and weeks into months as Shepherd tried in vain to secure a job. One gloomy day, Shepherd walked through several rows of informal settlements dressed in his crumpled brown suit. He paused at one and timidly knocked. Ndau, a stooped, very old woman in shabby clothing hobbled out. "*Sawubona, Gogo.* Good evening, Grandma," Shepherd greeted her.

"Ah, Shepherd. *Noma yimuphi inhlanhla namuhla*? Any luck today?" She softly inquired.

"*Akukho, Gogo.* Not today."

"We keep praying. You should not lose hope. I remember a scripture that says..." She trailed off as she tried to think of the scripture.

Shepherd ceased his opportunity, “Actually Gogo, I was wondering if perhaps *ungase ngenanele ifoni yakho* so I can call *unkosikazi wami*? I was wondering if perhaps you could lend me your phone so I can call my wife?”

“Of course, of course!” the old lady said as enthusiastically as her age allowed, “Boss gave me ten rand airtime to make some calls but you can use it, and I’ll get some more on my way to work tomorrow.”

“Are you sure?”

“*Yebo ndodana.* Of course, son,” Ndau replied without hesitation. Ndau took out a Nokia 3310 from her pocket and a strip of airtime and handed it to Shepherd.

“*Ngiyabonga. Ngibona kakhulu.* I will pay you back as soon as I can, I promise.” Ndau smiled and waved him off. Shepherd entered his own little shack beside hers. His shack had an old mattress and blanket on one side and a pot and meagre groceries on the other side. His small suitcase of unfolded clothes was at the foot of his mattress. He fell onto the bed and entered the airtime into Ndau’s phone before dialling and putting the phone to his ear.

As Ruvimbo tried to change a crying and fidgety Tambirai's nappy her cell phone rung and she reached over to grab it, "Hello? Shepherd?"

"How did you know it was me"?

"The country code. I'm so happy to hear from you... I miss you too..." Ruvimbo used her shoulder to hold the phone to her ear and continued to change Tambirai's nappy. "How's the job hunting? Listen... Listen... just come home then we'll sort something out... I'm helping Mama with her chicken business and we are going to start a quail business soon and that's going to bring in a lot of money..."

Still lying on his mattress Shepherd responded, "No, you listen to me... listen...I'm not going to let you down. I'll keep trying. I'll find something... Okay? Okay? How is she?"

Ruvimbo looked down at Tambirai who smiled up at her suddenly, "Today she is happy. She's happy and strong today but she misses you Daddy, we both do... I know... We keep praying. Okay my love... I love you... Hello? hello?" Ruvimbo looked down at the phone and saw that the call had ended. She looked down at Tambirai and playfully tickled her. "Daddy ran out of airtime, but Daddy loves you so much. Yes, he does!"

Shepherd looked at the screen of Ndau's phone which displayed that the call had ended, "Dammit!"

Shepherd knew that he would not get a job as an engineer, which is what he had studied in university back home. He began to go from gate to gate in the suburbs asking anyone who would give him the time of day for any sort of job. Many times, his pleas were met with aggression, one man even threatening to set his dogs on Shepherd for ringing his intercom. One day however, a gate opened after he rang the intercom, and he walked in to meet Susan who was dressed in a floral dress, at the top of the driveway. She looked him up and down then exhaled smoke from her cigarette before addressing him, "You are looking for a job?"

"Yes Madam," replied an exhausted Shepherd.

"My gardener left so you're hired," She told him. Shepherd tried to hand her his papers but she waved them away, instead she asked, "There have been so many randoms coming around these parts. Where are you from?"

"Zimbabwe, Harare," he said cautiously.

"Oh?" she exclaimed, "Hard working fellows, you Rhodesians are. Our maid was from there." Without waiting for a response from Shepherd she continued as she walked, "You can start immediately. As you can see, we have a big yard so it's twenty -four-seven. Half days Saturday and off Sunday. Living quarters are in the back behind the ivy wall. Keep it clean and no illegal business. Last guy was brewing some sort of traditional beer in there. Not allowed."

Several months into his job, Shepherd, dressed in overalls, collected garden tools from a flower bed and piled them into a wheel barrow which he pushed against the wall of the house. He picked up a small dark plastic bag and began to walk towards the gate. Susan appeared at the kitchen door in a simple white summer dress, "Shepherd, where are you going?"

Shepherd walked back towards her, "I'm going to the car wash, Madam."

"Have you finished your work for the day?"

"Yes Madam," He replied. Then hesitantly, "Madam... I was wondering when you'd be able to pay me for the months I've worked here."

Susan placed a cigarette between her lips delicately and lit it. She blew out smoke and then looked directly at Shepherd. "I don't know if my husband would appreciate the fact that you have another job."

Shepherd sighed, "It doesn't interfere with my work here, Madam. It's just a weekend job." Susan waved her cigarette at him and turned to walk away. "My money, Madam?"

"You'll get your money, Shepherd! Why is everyone obsessed with money?" Shepherd stood and stared into the kitchen for a while before he turned and walked towards the gate. He exited through a small door in the main gate.

The car wash was a small one just outside a large shopping mall. There were three cars being washed by two men in blue overalls. A black BMW with tinted windows drove up and Dumi, a fat, middle aged man wearing a suit, struggled out of the driver's seat. Lolo, dressed in tight shorts and a tank top got out of the passenger seat. "Full valet clean, and polish the tyres boys,"

Dumi said in the direction of the workmen. To Lolo he said, “Let’s get that dress you wanted, Baby.”

“Go on Babes, I’ve got to make a quick call and cancel my plans for tonight,” she replied as Dumi pulled her towards him and gave her bottom a squeeze with both his hands before planting a wet kiss on her lips. She giggled.

“I love it when you cancel your plans for me,” he whispered loudly. Lolo giggled and hit him playfully on his chest before he waddled off. She took out her cell phone, and leaned against the car.

“Shepherd, Big Man, full valet clean,” the first man shouted as he approached Lolo. He opened his mouth to speak to her but Lolo held up her manicured index finger to his lips.

“You couldn’t afford me,” she said seductively.

The second man snorted, “We’ve had better than you for free.” The two men laughed and high-fived each other. Lolo scoffed and turned her back towards them just as Shepherd came out of the small shed with cleaning detergents and walked towards Dumi’s car. He began work at the opposite end of the car to where Lolo was standing.

"Hey, Shepa!" Lolo chirped in his direction.

"Madam."

Undeterred by his curt response she continued, "How was your week? How's work?"

"Fine."

"*Uriwekumba.* You're from home," she informed him.

"How do you know?"

"Your accent. Plus, a Zimbo knows a Zimbo... And your bad Zulu gives it away. I remember when I first came to Jo'burg." Shepherd walked away to get a cloth from the next car. He walked back to Dumi's car. Lolo was now talking into her phone, "Coming, Sweetie." To Shepherd she said, "I have to go. Nice to see you again." Shepherd wiped the car and avoided looking at Lolo. After a pause, Lolo strutted away towards the shopping mall. The two men looked after her and whistled while Shepherd continued to wipe the car.

A week later, Shepherd was cleaning a small red car whilst Dumi's car drove up. Dumi struggled out and walked towards the shopping mall. Lolo leaned against the car dressed in a red jump suit. "Come on! Tell me, *kumusha ndekupi*? Tell me, rural home at least?" She begged Shepherd.

"Kwekwe," Shepherd gave in with a sigh.

Lolo laughed, "I knew it." Shepherd smiled and continued cleaning. Lolo opened the boot of the car and retrieved a brown paper bag. "Nearly forgot. *Nyimo.*"

"What? Really?" Shepherd looked surprised.

"Take them. You said you missed home food. My cousin sister brought them for me yesterday." She insisted.

"Give them to your sugar daddy," Shepherd said flatly.

Lolo tilted her head and stared down at Shepherd who was polishing a tyre. She shoved the package at Shepherd. "Take them Shepherd. I'm serious."

Finally, Shepherd took the parcel, "If you insist." Lolo smiled and began to strut away toward the mall. Shepherd stashed the parcel in the bucket with his cleaning utensils and called after her, "Thanks, Chido."

Lolo turned and pointed a finger in his direction, "Hey, only my mother can call me that."

As she walked away the first man came out of the small shed, "Dude, you can't afford her." Shepherd clenched his jaw and went back to polishing the tyre.

* * *

Shepherd, dressed in old trousers and a worn-out T-shirt stood stooped and barefoot in the kitchen in front of the coffee table where Susan, dressed in black trousers and a white blouse, was seated drinking a cup of coffee. “Look Shepherd, the economy is bad for us all. My husband will pay you soon as he can.”

“Madam, is it alright if I speak directly to Boss?” Shepherd hazarded.

“I am your boss, Shepherd.”

“But it’s nearly two months now, Madam. I cannot work for free, I need the money for my daughter. She needs heart surgery desperately.”

Susan sipped her coffee, “If I recollect, I did pay you last month.”

“That was less than half of what we agreed on, hardly enough to live by.”

Susan slurped her coffee again and flicks her hand in Shepherd’s direction, “Look, I feel for you, I really do but life’s tough for all of us. Get back to work Shepherd.”

Shepherd stood up straight, “Not without my pay Madam.”

Susan slammed her coffee cup on the table and spoke through gritted teeth, "Well then Shepherd, you are welcome to leave."

Shepherd spoke as purposefully as she had, "Not without my pay, Madam."

"I'm going to have to let you go then, Shepherd."

"You heard what I said."

Susan stood up, "Excuse me?"

"I am not leaving, especially not without my money."

"Shepherd? May I see your passport and work permit please?" Shepherd clenched his jaw but did not move. Susan examined her manicure, "Because, you know. It would be highly illegal for you to be here without the relevant documentation, highly illegal. You could go to jail."

"Madam, please, I just need my money then I'll be on my way," Shepherd's voice trembled only slightly.

"In fact," Susan continued, "let me phone the police and just verify the facts. Should I call the police, Shepherd?"

"That won't be necessary, Madam," Shepherd was defeated.

Susan sat back down and slurped her coffee, "Goodbye then, Shepherd." Shepherd made as if to say something but then stopped himself. He turned and walked out the door.

* * *

Shepherd was talking to Andile who was a chubby grey-haired man who was sitting at a small desk doing some calculations with his reading glasses on at the car wash. "There won't be much use for you during the week Shepa, but I can give you an extra day- Friday," Andile said.

"I could do admin, maybe, during the week," Shepherd responded.

Andile took off his reading glasses, "Well, that's my job, isn't it?"

"Okay," Shepherd turned to leave and Andile replaced his reading glasses.

"See you Friday."

"Ya."

"Wait," Andile called after him, "why do you have luggage with you?" Shepherd continued walking away without responding.

Day turned to night and Shepherd walked slowly down the street past the windows of a few stores. He finally settled with his luggage in the doorway of one of the stores. He opened his luggage and retrieved a thin blanket which he wrapped around himself. With his head against his luggage his eyes closed. It began to drizzle. "Fuck."

Days later at the car wash, Shepherd cleaned the windows of Dumi's car whilst Lolo leaned against the bonnet. Beside the black BMW was a Toyota which the second man was cleaning. He finished cleaning the Toyota and moved on to the little green car beside it. A group of three boys, David, Graham and Paul walked up to the car wash. One went into the shed and came back out with the car keys. He unlocked the Toyota and then tapped at the pockets of his jeans. "David, do you have my phone?" Graham asked.

"No, why would I have your phone?" David responded.

"Can't find it."

"Check your pockets," Paul advised. Whilst Graham checked his pockets Paul and David checked theirs. "Maybe you left it at the mall?"

"No I never, I never used it, it still needs a sim card. Is it in the car?" Paul and Graham checked inside the car whilst David checked the boot. The phone was not found and Graham slammed the car door shut. "Shit."

David said, "Dad's gonna kill you. Should I try calling it?"

"It has no sim card, dumb ass."

Andile walked out of the shed, "Problem, gentlemen?"

The boys looked at each other mischievously and then Graham's eyes widened and he took a few steps towards Andile. "Yes. One of your people stole my phone."

"I don't think so. No one here steals," Andile replied calmly.

"I left it on my seat and now it's gone. I'm calling the police," Graham responded.

"Wait. Who cleaned the Toyota?" Andile asked. The second man was crouching behind the green car. He looked at the first man who looked back at him then stepped forward towards Andile.

"It was Shepherd."

Shepherd and Lolo were chuckling by themselves by the BMW but when Shepherd heard his name he quickly spun around, "Ya?"

"Come here," Andile ordered.

"See you," Lolo said as she turned to walk towards the mall as Shepherd approached the shed entrance.

David sidled up to Graham. "Gray, did you remember to get the phone back from Sarah when she asked to see it in Mug and Bean?" David quietly inquired. The three boys looked at each other before getting into the car.

"Wait, where are you going?" Andile asked.

"I don't know." Graham hurriedly responded

whilst starting the car.

David stuck his head out the window, "To the police!"

"Dude, shut up," Graham said to David. To Paul he said, "Call Sarah will you." Then they drove off.

"Jesus" Andile said as he turned to walk into the shed as a bewildered Shepherd followed. "You stole a phone."

"What?" Shepherd asked.

"Those boys said you sole a phone from their car."

"What do you mean? I didn't even clean that car," Shepherd said.

"Don't lie to me Shepherd! They are going to inform the police as we speak," Andile could not stay calm any longer.

"You can search me!" Shepherd also began to panic.

"They said you stole a phone. If not you then who? The other two have been with me for years," Andile paced up and down then finally stopped in front of Shepherd. "Get out."

"What? No."

Calmly Andile said, "If I don't fire you they'll bring the police here and that'll cause trouble for my business." Shepherd stared at Andile with his mouth open. "Please Shepherd."

"But I did not steal anything." Shepherd stood his ground.

"Is there a problem?" asked the first man, walking into the shed.

"Shepherd is fired, he is leaving," Andile announced.

The first man made to grab Shepherd's arm but Shepherd shrugged himself free.

"If you want to fire me then fine, but I'm sure as hell not leaving here without my money."

"Just leave easy, Shepa," urged the first man. Shepherd overturned Andile's small desk. Andile backed away and the first man grabbed Shepherd's arm and began to pull him away. Andile grabbed a couple of one hundred rand notes out his pocket and threw them in Shepherd's direction.

Shepherd picked them up and stormed out of the shed, "I will be back for the rest." As Shepherd left the shed Lolo backed away from the entrance which she had been standing at and tried to grab Shepherd's arm but he shrugged her off and stormed off.

"Shepherd!" Lolo called after him. Shepherd did not stop and everyone stood there and watched him leave. Lolo began to walk after him but Dumi appeared.

"Hey Baby. Where you going?" he asked whilst crushing her body against his own.

Looking over his shoulder at Shepherd she replied, "Nowhere, Darling," before they both got into his car.

"Everything alright?" Dumi persisted.

"Yes." They drove away and passed Shepherd on the road.

Shepherd dug into his pocket and retrieved a few coins which he inserted into the call box before he dialled. He listened to the dialling tone for several minutes before dialling again.

Meanwhile, a Doctor listened to Tambirai's heartbeat with a stethoscope. Tambirai wailed as Ruvimbo held her still for the doctor. Ruvimbo's phone rang until it stopped. It started to ring again and this time she fished it out of her pocket. "Doctor, it's a South African number, I'm so sorry but I have to take this." Ruvimbo hurried to the far end of the room and turned her back to the doctor and answered her phone, "Hello? Baby?"

"Why did it take so long to answer the phone? You know it's not easy for me to call," snapped Shepherd.

"I'm at the doctor's with Tambi... I don't know... Couple of nights ago she just started shaking... I thought she was cold but it carried on and I had to rush her to Pari..." she responded. Tambirai wailed louder and Ruvimbo turned to look at her. "Shepherd, I really have to go..."

Shepherd gripped the side of the call box hard, "I hear her crying... How bad is it? Wait, can I speak to the doctor is he there... Ya okay, I understand... Wait... Hello?" Whilst he was still on the phone Lolo ran towards him. She reached him just as he slammed down the receiver. "Dammit!"

"Shepherd?"

"What are you doing..." Shepherd began irritably.

"Take this. It's my number and address." Lolo shoved a piece of paper into Shepherd's hand and ran back the way she came before Shepherd could respond. He watched her go before crumpling the piece of paper and stuffing it into his pocket.

Shepherd was back in his sleeping nook with his luggage and his thin blanket serving as a bed. It was a windy night and Shepherd struggled to pin the blanket down. The street was noisy with shouting and car engines revving and drivers hooting. Shepherd sat up and rested his head in his hands for a while before he got to his feet, folded his blanket, grabbed his luggage and began to walk down the street. At the street corner, he came upon a call box. He retrieved some coins and the crumpled piece of paper from his pocket and dialled Lolo's number. The phone rang for a while and just as he was about to put the receiver down Lolo answered.

"Hello," she answered, panting. Shepherd heard grunting on the other end of the line.

"Did I catch you at a bad time? I'm so sorry," he gushed.

Lolo's room was bare save for a double bed and a night stand with a lamp on it. The lights were off. She sat up in bed naked and Dumi, also naked, lay with his head in her lap panting as she spoke into her cell phone, "Don't be silly, don't apologize. Where are you? Okay, I'm coming to get you now. Don't leave that spot. Bye." She put her phone down and stroked Dumi's head.

He looked up at her, "Who was that?"

"My brother... He's just come from the rural areas. I'm gonna go fetch him." Lolo got out of bed and began to get dressed.

On the other end of the line Shepherd put down the receiver and eyed the phone wide-eyed.

After a while he sat down beside the call box with his blanket around his shoulders.

Shepherd was asleep with his head against the call box. The headlights of a car illuminated him and the sudden light intensity awakened him. A taxi stopped just in front of him and Lolo jumped out of the passenger seat and hurried towards him. He got to his feet.

"Shepa."

"I wasn't going to call you, really," he began.

"But you did." The two stared at each other for a bit before Lolo turned and walked back towards the taxi. "*Pano pakaipa.* Hop in. This area is dangerous." Lolo got into the passenger seat and Shepherd got into the back seat. The taxi drove off.

"We're going to your...house?" Shepherd hazarded after a while.

Lolo chuckled, "I guess you could call it that."

Shepherd continued timidly, "I... I'll obviously pay you back every cent you've spent on me."

"Don't worry about that."

"I'm not a charity case," he declared.

Lolo looked back at Shepherd and placed a hand in his, "You're my brother, Shepa. Birds of the same country need to stick together." Shepherd looked out the window as Lolo turned to face the road ahead. The taxi stopped in front of a brothel that looked like a block of flats. "We're here." Lolo handed the driver some money and Shepherd and she got out of the taxi. Lolo walked ahead but Shepherd stopped just before the entrance of the brothel. Faint sex sounds could be heard.

"Chido, I don't think I ..." but before he could finish Lolo walked back towards Shepherd and pulled him by the arm. They walked down a corridor with doors on either side. Shepherd looked straight ahead as he walked. They reached Lolo's room and she unlocked the door and the two entered. Lolo turned on the lights. Her bed was unmade. Shepherd stood rigid in a corner whilst Lolo pulled a thick blanket out of her cupboard. She dropped it on the floor beside her bed.

"I don't have a problem sharing my bed but I know you do. So, the floor is all yours," she said kindly. Shepherd smiled slightly and placed his luggage on the ground.

* * *

Lolo lay on the bed, face down and shivering. Shepherd, after another day of unsuccessful job hunting, entered the room and switched on the light. He saw Lolo on the bed shivering and dressed in a small silk night dress. "Lolo, are you still working? Should I come back later?" He inquired. Lolo did not respond so he continued, "If you are expecting a customer I can come back."

Only then did Lolo let out an audible sob. Shepherd removed his brown suit jacket and knelt beside the bed and turned her over gently. Lolo had a bruise on her cheek and on her chest. She covered her face and continued to sob. "Who did this to you? Tell me who did this to you. Was it that Dumi?"

"No, no. It wasn't him," Lolo managed through sobs, "It was a customer... I asked him to use a condom... And he said he had paid for the no condom package."

"Jesus," gasped Shepherd as he held her in his arms.

"There is no 'no condom package,'" Lolo sobbed quietly.

"We're going to the police."

Lolo stopped crying and laughed bitterly, "Shepherd, be serious."

"He can't get away with this. I won't let him."

"Shepa, he's gone."

Shepherd looked down at Lolo and wiped the tears off her face, "Tell me what you need."

* * *

Lolo, still in her silk night dress, was now under the blanket. Shepherd, still in his

suit, lay beside her on top of the blanket holding an ice pack gently against her eye. The two giggled.

"No, but Shona parents were smart. They'd whip us where the marks could be covered by clothes," Shepherd quipped.

Lolo laughed hard until she began to cry again, "I can't work with my face like this. Make up won't cover this."

"Then don't work." Lolo turned her face to look into Shepherd's eyes, "What?"

"This room is two hundred rand a day. I need to work at least once a day to make rent. Especially since Dumi is out of town at the moment."

"Don't worry about that. I've got you," Shepherd soothed.

"Shepa you-"

"I said I'll cover us. Don't worry."

Lolo and Shepherd stared at each other for a while. Then Lolo said, "I was beaten so much as a child."

"Ya, I can tell you were naughty. No well-behaved child grows up to do this kind of work." Lolo punched him playfully on the arm and they both laughed. As their laughter died down they stared at each other again with their heads close together on the same pillow. Shepherd moved his head closer slowly and then Lolo pecked him on the lips. He began to kiss her as he rolled on top of her. Lolo kissed him back and put her arms around his neck just as he pulled back, wiped his mouth and got off the bed.

"Shepa?" Lolo furrowed her brow.

"Sorry, I-"

"Shepherd, it's okay," Lolo tried to calm him.

"I, I have to go..."

Confused, Lolo sat up in bed just as Shepherd

grabbed his jacket off the floor and walked out the door. “I’m sorry,” she called after him.

Shepherd inserted coins into the phone machine and dialled his wife’s number. He listened until the dialling tone stopped then tried again. He tried one more time until he slammed the receiver down and hit the side of his fist into the call box, “Dammit!”

* * *

Park station was full of people with luggage arriving or leaving on buses or buying tickets at the various bus company stalls and families seeing their loved ones off or welcoming them back. Shepherd went from person to person, at times with his hands cupped in front of him begging for money. Most people responded to him by gathering their belongings closer to themselves and walking away from him. Some people dismissed him with a flick or their hand or a shake of their head. One elderly lady gave him two five rand coins and Shepherd clapped his hands in gratitude before he moved on to the next person. Mr Ndebele stood out in the crowded Park Station because he was dressed in a grey three-piece suit and carried a brief case as his only luggage. He was talking into an iPad when Shepherd noticed him and approached him with his hands cupped in front of him. "Chief, if you could help me with some money, please Boss," Shepherd begged. Mr Ndebele flicked his hand in Shepherd's direction and turned his back to him. Shepherd persisted, "My daughter desperately needs a heart operation Boss, please, anything would help."

Mr Ndebele spoke loudly into his iPad, "*Mira, mira Taku, pane benzi ririkundinetsa.* There's an idiot bothering me."

Shepherd grinned when he recognised his native language, "*Saka muri wekumba? Neniwo!* Will you help your little brother out please?"

Mr Ndebele turned around and faced Shepherd, "You low life poor excuse of a man. Your so-called daughter should be ashamed that her no-balls-having father is begging and thieving instead of earning an honest living. *Pfutseke.*" Shepherd's eyes widened and he stood still as Mr Ndebele began to walk away from him. He walked after him after a while, grabbed his arm from the back and with his other hand pressed his index finger into the small of Mr Ndebele's back. Mr Ndebele froze.

"You don't know my story. Motherfucker," Shepherd snarled into the man's ear.

"I don't care to, I work in Mugabe's office so unhand me before I fuck up the rest of your life even more than it already is," the big man said defiantly.

Shepherd pressed into his back harder, "Give me your money before I shoot you." Both men were breathing heavily.

Mr Ndebele did not give in easily, "I will fucking ruin-" But before he could finish his threat Shepherd grabbed the brief case out of Mr Ndebele's hand and ran away with it. "Thief! Thief! Police, where are the police?" Mr Ndebele shouted after him but people just stood and stared at him in his panic as he pointed in the direction in which Shepherd had disappeared.

Shepherd, brief case in hand, exited the building and ran at top speed into an alley a few blocks away. Shepherd crouched behind two bins panting with the brief case clutched against his chest. He looked down at the patch of dampness between his legs. Shepherd placed the brief case on the floor and opened it with trembling hands. Inside he found a newspaper, documents and thick wads of two hundred rand notes. "My god," Shepherd licked his finger and began to count the money before giving up and stashing it all into his pockets.

Shepherd looked at a display of various smart phones in a phone shop. A Clerk watched Shepherd from the next display. Shepherd picked up one of the phones and the clerk quickly trotted towards him. “Can I help you?” asked the clerk nervously.

“I’d like to buy this phone.”

“Okay, we can get you that one. Let me get you one in a box,” he said. He came back with a packaged phone and walked Shepherd to the counter where a till operator stood behind the counter.

“Great choice,” the till operator chirped, “that one is MTN and with some paperwork you pay R299.99 a month for the next...”

“I can’t pay at once?” asked Shepherd.

“Absolutely!”

Shepherd took out a wad of cash from his pocket and counted out the money.

* * *

Shepherd sat on a park bench and dialled his wife's number on his new phone. He listened to the dialling tone.

"Hello?" Ruvimbo answered.

"Hey, Baby... I'm good, good, how are you and my little angel?"

Ruvimbo was in the kitchen stirring a pot at the stove and holding the phone against her ear, "The past week has been a good week for us, no, no incidents she's been healthy and happy...

Oh, I did see a missed call, Baby but you know I had no way of calling back... We were sleeping it was quite late... But was everything alright?"

Shepherd, still on the bench, rubbed both his eyes with his thumb and index finger before responding, "Ya... everything was alright, of course. I guess I was just missing you...

Anyway, listen. I've got some money for Tambi... Don't get excited... listen, it's not all of it but maybe if we arranged with the hospital-"

"Oh, thank God! They'll definitely allow us an arrangement, Dr Ncube knows us... Oh thank God... Shepa now you can come home."

Shepherd had his head resting on one hand whilst speaking on the phone, he snapped at her irritably, "Are you listening to me? I said it's not all of it I have to stay here and make more...

I miss you too but if I come home with no more money then what... Listen, I'll go to Musina tomorrow and I'll give the money to Mai MaTwins to bring to you... Ruvimbo, your chicken business will not sustain us at all." Shepherd sighed as he sat back on the bench. He gently continued, "Sweetie, doesn't matter how I got the money, my goal is Tambi's life first then after that to sustain us... I'll work here a bit more then when I've made enough I'll buy a kapenta rig and open a business in Kariba, TK told me that it's quite lucrative. Stop crying Baby."

Ruvimbo sat on the floor. She wiped her eyes then she smiled slightly, "Maybe...

maybe after Tambi is fine we can relocate to South and start a new life. I know, was just thinking out loud. I love you too. I will."

Shepherd stood up, "I've got to go now but I'll call you soon... Save this number it's my number... Don't get excited. Baby I've got to go... Yes, God is good... You pray also... Love you too. Bye." Shepherd sat back down and stared at his phone screen.

He thought back to a time just before he married Ruvimbo. In his mind he was back in his small room in Harare. On the sofa was a box of silver wedding invitations to his and Ruvimbo's wedding. Shepherd lay in bed asleep. The door opened slowly and Ruvimbo walked in and climbed into his bed. She shook Shepherd awake, "Hey."

"What are you doing here? You are meant to be with your family," he had asked, startled.

"You are my family silly. You paid *lobola* today so I'm your wife now. No returns!" she rolled on top of Shepherd and he put his arms around her and chuckled.

"Well, I don't know if your uncles would agree. I didn't finish paying."

"No one ever does, no one is supposed to," she said as she began to unbutton her shirt.

Shepherd's eyes widened, "What are you doing?"

Ruvimbo paused, "Trying to make love to my husband but he seems reluctant."

"I, I thought you wanted to wait till our wedding night. I guess tonight is our wedding night." Shepherd rolled Ruvimbo over and was now on top of her, "It's our wedding night."

* * *

The bar was dimly lit and quite packed. Shepherd sat on a stool and examined a drinks menu before he signalled to the Barman who was bold and had a tattoo sleeve, "Hey man, can I have a, ahh, whiskey please?"

"Right up." The barman poured a whiskey for Shepherd and Shepherd downed it and coughed.

He signalled to the barman again, "Could I have two more please?" The barman brought Shepherd his drinks. Shepherd looked down into his glass, smiled and shook his head.

Lolo was lying on her bed in the dark. There was a hard knock on the door before it swung open and Shepherd stumbled in holding a bottle of wine. Lolo sat up and turned on her desk lamp, "Shepa!"

Shepherd knelt on the bed holding up the wine bottle, "Let's celebrate. I did good today."

Lolo giggled, "Looks like you've already started." Lolo grabbed the bottle from Shepherd as he collapsed face down onto the bed. She stroked his head. He turned and looks up at her. "Where did you get money?"

"It fell from the heavens!"

Lolo giggled again, "Be serious."

"I stole it. From a man. In Park Station." Lolo's eyes widened. Shepherd turned and faced the other direction. "You're not allowed to judge me." Lolo lay back down on the bed and continued stroking Shepherd's head. She also stroked his shoulders and his lower back. She slipped a hand into his shirt and Shepherd turned towards her suddenly. "It just, it's just a little something till I find a proper job, a lot of money which will cover till I find a job hopefully, not gonna happen again."

Lolo kissed him on the lips, "I'm not judging." Shepherd's eyes closed. Lolo turned off the lamp and lay down, "I'm proud of you." Shepherd opened his eyes and began to kiss Lolo passionately whilst undressing her.

It was morning and Shepherd and Lolo lay asleep and naked on the bed. Lolo's arm was across Shepherd's chest. Shepherd's eyes opened, he looked over at Lolo still asleep beside him, "Fuck." Shepherd slowly removed Lolo's arm and slipped out of bed. He put on some clothes, grabbed the wad of cash that was on the bedside table and slipped out of the room quietly.

Shepherd did continue to try to make an honest living, but life as a foreigner was hard, even with the fake documentation. The money ran out, and in desperate need to make a quick buck to sustain himself, he took to purse snatching. The snatching soon turned into intimidation and he purchased a small pen knife to help him. Business was most lucrative when he operated from Park Station, where it all began. The relatively quick cash proved too much of a temptation for him, and so did Lolo.

* * *

Shepherd's room was similar to Lolo's room except the bed had no linen on it and there was nothing on the dressing table. Shepherd walked in holding his luggage and blankets followed by Lolo holding a small duffel bag. They put the bags down and stood staring at the bed. Lolo linked her arm with Shepherd's. "It'll have to do for now," Shepherd commented.

Lolo rested her head against Shepherd's shoulder. He turned towards her and she put her arms around his neck, "Wanna break the room in?"

"I... I better just settle in tonight."

Lolo pulled away from Shepherd and opened the bedroom door, "Fine." She left the room and Shepherd closed the door behind her. He sat on the bed and used his phone to dial his wife's number. "Ruvi, hello."

Ruvimbo was sitting in the waiting room chair next to her Mother. She had the phone pressed to her ear. She talked softly, "Hey Baby... No nothing is wrong, we're in the hospital... It was scheduled for today, had you forgotten? It went well, praise God... I'm waiting to see her and hopefully I can nurse her... Shepa... It's been a while why haven't you called? Yes, I've been getting the money... You do? That's great... We'll be able to pay off her final operation with that." Ruvimbo's mother patted her hand. "Mama is so happy; do you want to talk to her? Okay... So, does this mean you can come home? Right, capital, Okay. I love you. Shepa? I said I love you."

Shepherd sat on the bed with the phone pressed against his ear, "I love you too. So much. More than you'll ever know. No matter what happens. Give her a kiss for me. Bye my baby girl." Shepherd stared at his phone before he fell back onto his bed. He stared up at the ceiling.

* * *

The light was turned off in Shepherd's room. The room was littered with Shepherd's clothes, including a black leather jacket, a brown leather jacket and a waistcoat. There was a poster of an AK-47 on the wall and one of the movie 'Tsotsi'. Shepherd, who now had very short dreadlocks, and Candy, a short and slim prostitute, were in bed together. Shepherd's cell phone rang and he put his hand over Candy's mouth and reached over and snarled into his phone, "Do you have my cut or not? Because if you don't..."

There was a pause before Ruvimbo answered cautiously, "What are you talking about?" Frazzled, Shepherd responded, "Oh shit, I mean...

Ruvi, my love... Sorry... was just someone from, err, work... I know, I know I haven't called but it's really been tough lately. Aren't you getting the money? So then? I know, but I need capital remember? I will I promise. Hello? Hello?" Shepherd wiped his face with his hand and stared at the phone for a while before he replaced the phone on the side table and continued to have sex with Candy. He stopped abruptly, "Get out of here."

"What?"

"Get out," Shepherd repeated.

Candy hurriedly got dressed and left the room. Shepherd lay on the bed on his back and covered his eyes with the palms of his hands. When he removed them, his eyes were teary and he sniffed. His cell phone rang again and he answered it softly, "Hello?"

"Hey bruv," a man's voice said, "I've got your cut. Come through."

"Ok," Shepherd hung up the phone. He sat up in bed. He looked through the contact list in his phone and when he got to Ruvimbo's name he stopped for a moment before pressing block and deleting the number. Shepherd put on a pair of jeans, shoes and a shirt before he placed a small revolver in his back pocket and leaving the room.

* * *

Shepherd sat behind his desk. Sheila sat in the chair opposite him and stared at him, "That's...

There's a God Shepherd and he has a plan to... You've just got to..."

Shepherd sat up and downed the glass of whiskey on his desk before slamming the glass down hard, "Oh save it, Maiguru." Shepherd stood up and put on his leather jacket.

"Wait, Shepherd..."

Shepherd walked out of his office and then called back, "Welcome to the Promised Land, Maiguru. Milk and honey."

Sheila got up and walked around the desk, she looked out of the window at the industrial factories below.

* * *

Shepherd, with blood shot eyes, drove into the parking lot of Park Station. Kaito sat in the passenger seat and Sheila and Que sat in the back. Sheila looked at Que's revolver which was on his belt and sighed. He turned and looked at her and she looked up at him, shook her head and turned to look out the window as she continued to shake her head. Shepherd parked his car and a group of his gang members came from all directions and surround the car as he, Kaito, Que and Sheila got out. His car did not have number plates. He stood against the bonnet of the car and his gang members, including Tino, Craig, Nhlanhla, Themba, Godi, Xolani and Umkhulu, who was being propped up between two men, gathered around him.

Shepherd addressed his people, "I'm going to show you this once, and once only. Once we get in there you will not crowd around me like you are doing now but you will disperse yet still be able to see me."

Themba raised his hand eagerly, "Blood, will you use a shank or a pistol?"

"Neither," Shepherd looked at his gang as they quietly murmured, "Today I will be using the fear of AIDS." The gang members shifted in their places and the murmuring got louder. "Shut the fuck up and watch closely." As Shepherd walked forward the crowd made way for him, Kaito and Que to walk through. They entered the building. As usual, the building was crowded. A group of passengers, having just gotten off a bus entered through a side door and dispersed. A woman, dressed in blue jeggings and a stylish jumper with long and straight hair stood with her back to Shepherd and his gang members. Shepherd pointed to her, "That one."

"Why?" Themba inquired.

"She is well dressed and has a fashionable hand bag, obviously, she is carrying a lot of cash with her."

"*Kukhona ingane naye.* There's a child with her," Umkhulu said feebly.

Shepherd turned and looked at Umkhulu, "Glad to hear you still have your wits about you, old man. Now watch and learn motherfuckers." Shepherd began to walk towards the woman. The gang stood and stared.

"The fear of AIDS," Craig said to no one in particular. Some of the younger gang members snickered.

"What did Blood say? Disperse mother-fuckers," Kaito barked. The gang members quickly dispersed in different directions but they each kept their eyes on Shepherd.

As Shepherd walked towards the woman a little girl reached up to hold the woman's hand, in the little girl's other hand was a bag of KFC. As Shepherd got closer to the woman he took out a needle and syringe from his back pocket. He rolled up his jacket sleeve, stuck the needle into his arm and drew his own blood. He pulled the needle out. By now he was directly behind the woman. Shepherd gripped the woman's arm from behind and placed the blood-filled needle to her throat and his mouth close to her ear. The woman did not move. The little girl stared up at Shepherd. "Give me all your money or I'll inject you with HIV," Shepherd whispered.

The woman turned around slowly and stared at Shepherd with wide eyes. Shepherd took a step back, the hand holding the needle dropped to his side and he stared back wide eyed into Ruvimbo's eyes which were now moist with tears. Tambirai looked from her father to her mother and back to her father.

As Shepherd and Ruvimbo stared at each other Park Station's crowd grew louder and busier like an angry swarm of bees. Just outside, passengers disembarked from a Greyhound bus which had just arrived. People went about their business.

Outside, crowds of people went about their business too.

All around Johannesburg, in fact, people went about their business.

DNA

Our parents sent us to private schools where we became part of a very small sprinkle of colour. They puffed out their chests and boasted to their friends when we won awards for writing and speaking the Queen's English better than any white child could. We were taught the history of wars we had no roots in, neglecting our own liberation struggles, and we mastered the geography of oceans and glaciers our landlocked, sun-baked, Savanna selves would never see.

But now our parents jeer at us in our adulthoods asking, "How do you not know the word to this?" and, "Why must you speak your mother tongue with that accent?" Every Christmas when we make the long drive back to their old homes far from where we were nurtured, they warn us, "Do not embarrass us in front of Grandmother and Grandfather," and they scold their daughters, "What kind of a man will marry a girl who cannot cook our tradition's food to perfection?"

So, who are we? Who can we be, we who are trained in split personality? Our heritage rejects us as imposters, tourists in our own land, and that which we mastered we mastered in the hopes of acceptance and opportunities. The very same acceptances and opportunities being denied and taken from us with accusations of not being the originators. We are we who belong to a niche yet to be discovered. A niche that is there and that some of us know that we will one day take ownership of, but a niche we are yet to be allowed.

Through us the children, our parents showed he who came to steal and replace that we savages of Conrad were not so. It could not be so if we showed him that we could best him at his own colour game. But in so doing both they and him sacrificed their children.

We are now mutants. By association we have become our own breed of brown kids. We guard our cultural identities fiercely, but every now and again a small piece of it flakes off of our peeling skin as we journey into the Global Village hoping, subconsciously, that we can always follow the trail of brown skin back to where we came from, even when are parents are no longer there as points of reference.

CHAOS AND CONFUSION

Two forces acted against each other subconsciously and although both forces were attached by blood, the sinews that pulled them towards each other were strong but had with time lost their tension. Though both forces moved towards each other over various hurdles and around many bends they were stopped a distance apart, leaving between them a gaping no man's land that neither could or would explore, until it was too late.

The no man's land belonged to nobody, no country, no entity, and it was general knowledge that to trespass onto nobody's no man's land was to make oneself vulnerable to an enemy that was invisible but whose bullets one felt piercing through flesh, muscle and bone leaving a path of charred flesh. It would likely not just be one bullet, it would be several bullets. If one paused the pain receptors and numbed all other senses one would see flash, flash, flash from all directions, like a politician sees as he is photographed in compromising positions. Each individual flash would start off as a small burnt orange spark that would turn golden and then yellow as it changed from a spark to a temporary explosion. If one- still with numbed senses- could also then activate the slow-motion settings of the eyes, one might see little golden ships sailing across the sky. In reality these would be the bullets and if one waited long enough, one would see them making contact with one's own body in this no man's land. For sure it would be a confusing sight for if one followed the path of one particular bullet one would see it making gentle contact with one's skin, but one's skin being so abhorred by this unwanted physicality, would split or explode open- seemingly without provocation- tearing, around the bullet, into tiny little pieces of skin like the fraying of the ends of a satin scarf. The ripping would send little droplets of purple blood in all directions as the bullet now determined on its path, would continue through layers upon layers of muscle, flesh and fat, tearing a hole to give the foreign body way into a space they had sworn to protect. The flesh would react in much the same melodramatic way as the skin. The muscle, on the other hand, would try and stand its ground, almost, but not quite, causing the bullet to go back the way it came before giving way suddenly by sucking itself back from the violence and ripping a slit in itself by mistake. The fat, the insulation layer, would not put up much of a fight as its purpose is not one as prestigious as the muscle's purpose. No, the bullet would already have its nose some way into the fat before the fat realised the need to bubble back and give way. But bone, bone would be the most interesting of all. Bone would not give way at all. Bone would take no insult, pass no judgement and be abhorred by nothing, like a dead thing. It is this stubbornness that assures that bone is that last substance of anybody's remains that remain. It is with bone that the bullet would get most incessant. Bullet would push his way forward in his path and if lucky, cause the bone to shatter into a million little splinters which themselves would turn rogue and stab one's own flesh. Bone having shattered, the bullet would finally come to its destination. The bullet would perhaps stop in awe of the Mighty Muscle, the all-powerful muscle that was so well designed it could beat outside the human body given the right amount of oxygen and nutrients. What an oxymoron it was that such a mighty organ would not withstand even the gentlest of touches from the hot metal bullet. The bullet would not pause for too long in admiration as it would know of its one sole purpose. Like an athlete into a pool of deep water, the bullet would dive deep into the heart, but unlike water that changed shape to facilitate displacement, the heart would maintain its true form, tearing instead like a tapestry stabbed by a sharp two-edged object- each string snapping and rolling away to its edges. This too is how the capillaries and veins would meet their end, they would snap. The heart compromised, blood would ooze out of every possible opening. The heart, the mighty warrior that it is, would continue to try and beat, but only for a few seconds until it faded- no energy even for fibrillations. The omniscient presence of one's body- the brain, seeing his partner lost, would watch and mourn, knowing that without the heart he cannot survive and he too would eventually suffocate.

The senses and real time reactivated, one would see this as a potentially fatal situation and choose not to venture into this nobody's no man's land for fear of a pain so great it would cause loss of life. Neither force would venture into no man's land, even with the white flag of surrender, until the invisible enemy was gone and one was sure of one's own safety. Only then would it be safe to timidly peek over the top of one's wet, slimy, death and rodent infested trench and throw one weary and injured leg over the top and clutch at the dirt to pull one's skeletal body out of a premature grave. One would lay very still for many minutes to be sure that the invisible enemy was indeed gone. Then one would slowly stand to their shaky feet like a bean plant germinating, and clutch at their hard hat- if they were lucky to still have one on- and blink in the sunlight as they looked around. A few minutes more and one would feel alright and confident enough to venture out further and explore the scarred and ashen land that now belonged to them.

* * *

The dog died. The dog died, but not before it killed the cat, intentionally or unintentionally. It was the little blue cat that it killed. It killed the little blue cat- the Star. Chaos had seen the dog, which was a short and stocky creature, a black mutt of a creature that responded to the word ‘Charcoal’, Chaos had seen it with her own eyes- that Charcoal carrying the little blue Star by any loose skin on her delicate body. Chaos had not seen the Star in protest those few days ago, but Chaos was still concerned. Her concern was a little too late that night though because she discovered the Star’s mangled and lifeless body in the garage on the floor beside the Box Sunny and Chaos had deduced that the dog had killed the cat.

It was at that moment that the chaos began. It began deep within as the adrenaline rushed through pulsing veins. Her brain brought back the message that in the choice between fight and flight, she should choose fight. She had it in her, that fight, because it had been building up in small tiny things, ready to break out at any moment and she had been waiting for the chance and the opportunity to fight, to release all the tension and regain the calmness of an empty vessel void of all inward pressure. It was a combination of regaining calm and wanting to feel physical pain. She wanted to feel physical pain because physical pain was easier to bear than the type of pain that is on the inside that no one can see. That is why she subconsciously welcomed to opportunity to fight- even if that fight was against a dog- a smaller creature, a vulnerable creature which was not able to reason like her. She did not care because in her mind at that exact time her actions were justified, and not even an enquiring matriarch could satiate her wrath.

She stared at the dead cat because the injustice of it all fuelled her hate fire. She saw it as an injustice because the poor little blue Star was small and defenceless and yet some higher power had still allowed this terrible thing to happen to a creature that did not deserve such treatment. She decided to take matters into her own hands because beg as she had no one else had dealt with the issue before it had thus escalated. Perhaps no one saw the issue the same way she did and so perhaps no one was able to help her with the issue in the way she was not even aware that she needed help in. However, it was all too late for that, no one could commune with her now. She was at a level in which she could not be reasoned with and no form of questioning or pleading could penetrate the whirlwind within and satiate her thirst for pain, even if it was no longer her own. It was as a man turning into a werewolf-painful and unstoppable- a process that needed to happen. She thought she knew just what to do and at first, she did it in silence.

Chaos marched into the garage to the tangled pile of cold, metal garden tools. At the very back, among the broken ones, was a cold, heavy, rusty chain. She reached into the tangled pile of cold metal and latched her fingers around the chain of determination and destruction, dragging it out of the pile in which it had long been of no use. The tools clung to the chain, perhaps sensing Chaos' dark intentions with it, but she was strong with rage and dark, incoherent thoughts and so she yanked and pulled and dragged, shaking the brave tools off the chain until finally, the chain was free and cold in her hands. The noise and confusion brought attention to the situation and worried faces emerged from the house. They stood in the doorway and their silhouettes were still and staring against the dirty, yellow light that shone through from the kitchen. Cold, black, staring silhouettes. Until...

Chaos caught the dog named Charcoal and roughly secured the chain around its neck. Charcoal had come to be among them carelessly. The inbred was simply dropped on the premises by a careless relative who had too many dogs and too many children and whose flea and mange ridden canines kept breeding and breeding, trapped in the unkempt yard of a crumbling home. The relative gathered the sickly puppies and dropped one off in the yards of unsuspecting relatives, getting rid of his own problems by adding them to other people. He had informed Chaos that he had brought her a present, a little black ball of fleas and disease and he had been taken aback by the way Chaos had stared at him wordlessly instead of falling to her knees and clapping her cupped hands in gratitude as was the custom. Perhaps Chaos knew, perhaps she knew that no good would come from an unsolicited gift.

Chaos caught the mongrel named Charcoal and chained him. Unsurprisingly the little beast was not used to being yoked, especially not buy a cold and heavy chain which smelt like death and destruction. Charcoal yelped. He yelped and his brain told him that between fight and flight he should flee and so that is what the little black creature tried to do. He attempted to run for his life because he knew that no good thing was about to happen. He was no match for the angry Chaos who held onto the one end of the rusty chain which had him secured tightly and roughly around his thick black neck. Digging his powerful hind legs into the ground with his nails to secure him he pushed his front legs back to pull away from the chain, but the chain neither slipped over his head nor out of the dangerous one's hands. He panicked because the more he pulled, the tighter the chain got around his neck, choking him. His panicked yelps mixed in with coughing and retching sounds, but still mostly desperate and ear-splitting yelps that turned from aggressive to wretched.

Up until then Chaos was not completely sure what she would do with the dog, but she had an idea so she began to pull on the chain, her hands jerking every now and again as the dog kept tugging at it from his end. She pulled the strangled dog and it began to panic even more as its brain became starved of air. As it was pulled along it left a trail of liquid from between its legs as its bladder, in fear, released, continuously.

The mother of Chaos begged and pleaded for her to be rational but Chaos was past the point of no return and so she continued to fight with the dog for dominance, making slow progress towards the gate. The terrified little creature had a strong will to live. With the sound of pleading in the background and a beast in pain in the foreground, Chaos had managed to drag the still struggling dog to a patch of shrubbery which the helpless little boy tried to run into for safety. Sadly, the vegetation was not dense enough to protect him and also, he was still secured by a tight, cold chain around his constricted neck.

It was around this time that Chaos and Confusion joined forces. Chaos and Confusion never joined forced and Chaos was happy that her and Confusion could bond over the destruction of something evil. In all the hysteria and confusion, Confusion quickly grasped the gravity of the situation and knew exactly what to do to climax the event. It thus happened that Confusion walked himself into the dark night, the darkness behind the garage where a lot of trees and foliage were. All the while Chaos was still gripping the chain with the tormented beast at the end of it. After some time, the begging and pleading still in the background and the lamenting beast's cries in the foreground, Confusion emerged from the darkness dragging behind him a thick bough of a stick. The grown man dragged it because it was thick and long and heavy and was not easy for him to carry.

It was only at this point that Chaos, out of herself, began to understand that an otherwise subtle situation had taken a turn for the worst because just like Chaos had been, Confusion was now unstoppable. The dog's yelps of pain and terror began to penetrate Chaos' heart as she realized that there was nothing she could do to reverse or stop what was about to happen. Everything was traumatic and unstoppable. Chaos tried to reason with Confusion but chaos had long since entered Confusion's mind and no logic could come of it. He was now a soldier like back in the day, fighting for survival at any cost, and this was gorilla warfare.

Confusion now hovered above girl and dog and the strength of forty years back when he was a warrior had re-entered his aged body as he was now miraculously able to lift the log well above his head. Chaos, now with her wits about her, let the chain fall from her trembling hands. Droplets of blood seeped out from where the rusty metal had cut her. Her own screams mixed in with those of the little, stocky black dog's and she was helpless to the situation that she herself had escalated to a level that it need never have gotten to. Her desperate screams mixed in with those of the dog's, and helpless she willed the urinating little creature to run for its life, but for some reason which she could not fathom the dog was now still and crouching and urinating and yelping. It no longer struggled, it just crouched in one place, its face upturned towards the night sky as confusion had entered its own mind because a dog cannot reason, even though Chaos had believed it could when it killed the little blue cat. Perhaps, and we will never know, but perhaps the dog had given up. Its desperate yelps became softer and softer until they turned into very soft inward whimpers of self-pity and anguish and then there was silence. It was the silence that goes before a man standing before his own gallows with a hood over his eyes, not so much seeing as feeling death's caress and embrace. There was silence all round as even Chaos' screams had been silenced by the still picture that she had painted for herself of a small black crouching dog looking up into the night sky with a heavy metal chain still secured around its neck, and above it an old but magically strong man, confused, and holding half a tree above his own head and above the dog's head as it sat in a puddle of its own urine.

And then it happened. The log swung down, cutting through the cool night air, down, down, down. Down past Confusion's head, down,

down, down. But then it stopped. It stopped just above the silent dog's head because the dog had moved in an attempt to dodge the down-coming log. Confusion growled and moved the log slightly to the right, over the defeated dog's now drooping head and less than half a meter above. And then he brought the log down the rest of the way.

The sound the log made when it made contact was not unnatural. It was what would be expected of a dry log making contact with a hard surface, yet it was still very sickening to those who knew what that surface was. Upon contact, time seemed to stop for several seconds and sound seemed to be muted even though everyone's mouths were agape with gasps and screams of shock. When time started back up again it was in slow motion. The log rolling off the top of Charcoal's head and landing beside where he was still standing, frigid. And then, as a delayed response, Charcoal's pupils dilating, his legs straightening out to their full extent beneath his heavy body as if due to a fast setting rigour mortis, his jaw going slack as a final but inaudible scream escaped from his throat, and then finally him falling over– legs still outstretched- onto his side. The dull thud of his lifeless body hitting the moist ground would be the first sound one would have registered before the screams of rage and sadness escaped from Chaos' already open mouth, cutting her throat as the screams raced to escape into the darkness of the night.

You killed him! You killed him! You killed him!

Chaos stumbled backwards as Confusion stood there staring at what he had done in confusion. Chaos stumbled forward again and forgetting all respect and protocol pushed Confusion out of the way and knelt so that she could loosen and remove the old, rusty chain from the dead dog's neck. The chaos around Confusion confused his mind and made it foggy and he felt the need to defend himself against the verbal blows that were coming in his direction but which he did not understand. He was suddenly outside, circled by people who were upset with him and he did not know why. And why was there a dead dog laying before him? What had happened to the dog? He spun around and growled at Chaos who seemed now to be struggling for breath.

But as life goes, after the climax, things begin to simmer down in a downward spiral towards the conclusion. Chaos continued to scream and Confusion continued to growl and Confusion turned further into chaos and Chaos into confusion. In her confusion, Chaos ran to the gate, called a friend on the phone and hysterically begged her to come and take her away because the pressure, no longer from within, was now from without, a sort of high intensity atmospheric pressure crushing her and she could not take it anymore. The mother flittered to and fro like a humming-bird between too blossoms but more morbidly so. She tried to drag Confusion into the house and tried to stop Chaos from leaving the gate.

If you leave, he'll never allow you back home. If you leave, he'll never allow you back home. If you leave, if you leave, if you leave...

But nothing could ease the very air crushing Chaos for no one knew the madness that flowed through her veins and into her head. She was all confusion and she had to get away and stop the worsening, crushing pain.

But then, just then, after everyone had, in their own individual hells gone their separate ways and then come back to reconvene outside- besides Confusion because someone had convinced him to go back inside- and just as the gardener was being woken up to dispose of the dead dog and whilst everyone was screaming and pointing fingers and crying and threatening and begging... the dead dog came back to life.

Jesus

He first wheezed, and some thought logically that it was the sound of gas leaving a dead body, but then he shivered then very suddenly sat up, looked around, then got up and walked away very slowly and with his eyes downcast. There was silence.

Chaos' friend came to pick her up but the mother convinced her not to leave because otherwise Confusion would never allow her back in the house. She, instead, cried in her companion's supportive arms and tried to make calm out of the chaos and confusion.

After that Chaos rummaged in old cupboards looking for sleeping pills or any sedatives that she could swallow that would shepherd her calmly into the oblivion of a long, easy and deep, dark sleep and maybe, just maybe if God were willing, into a new day with a fresh start and none of the chaos of yesterday. But how can you leave behind what you are?

As for Charcoal, the miraculous and magical cat murderer, he was, the next day, euthanized.

* * *

Confusion still insisted on driving, and quite frankly, you would have to have physically restrained him to stop him from getting into his car. Even if you knew that it would be safer for him not to do something, to actually stop him from doing that thing would have been to kill him faster than the disease that was slowly eating away at his brain, memory by memory. They say, however, that driving is something you can do without memory, that most of it is muscle memory and not brain memory and that one can do it on autopilot, so Chaos was not too concerned. So, Confusion would drive and go about his business, and sometimes he would drive just for the fun of it.

Confusion would get into his old car which was much like himself- mature in age but surprisingly strong. He'd step on up onto the silver step just underneath the doors and swing his leg up into the driver's side and sit on down, slam his door shut- but not too hard because that would be bad for the car- and turn the key in the ignition and head on out.

I'm just passing by church.

But the pastor said he never did pass by the church that Wednesday afternoon. Instead Confusion, sunglasses on, drove down Samora Machel, passed into the once vibrant Newlands neighbourhood by driving off Samora, past Pennywise Liquor Store and Bon Marche and then from Newlands onto Enterprise, taking the third exit at the roundabout and then eventually taking a left turn into Borrowdale road.

Confusion was free. He was free of any confusion temporarily. His Lady Smith Black Mambazo cassette played loudly on his radio and mixed in with the purring of his engine so he was soothed, smooth and without a care in the world. His fingers curled around the worn brown cover of the steering wheel and his mind filled with good thoughts. He did not think about the battles he had fought and the wars that he had won, he did not think about having to sell his beloved Peugeot to make ends meet or having several thousand Zim dollars turned suddenly into less than a hundred US dollars, he did not think of his daughter's kidney disease or his depression or high blood pressure or ... No, no negative thoughts went through his mind, in fact, nothing went through his mind because he did not question anything, he did not wonder where he was or who he was with or why or when or how. In that moment, all he did was listen to his favourite music with the cool late afternoon breeze blowing in his face in his favourite car. He just drove. He was just in existence and that was perfectly fine. That was fine for him and for as long as possible he would make sure that everything remained that way.

Everything was perfect. Everything seemed to work in his favour. The car seemed to glide over the unexpectedly well-maintained gravel road and then, magically, he noticed cars parking to the side of the road to let him drive past. He did not question it because everything was perfect and for once life was treating him with the respect he deserved, the respect he had not gotten in a long time, the respect none of his friends and family showed him anymore. He drove past the stationary cars and smiled at the wide-eyed drivers crouching at their steering wheels looking at him in bewilderment. They must have thought him amazing and he did not know why but he relished the moment, slowing down ever so slightly to let it all sink in, to let the moment last for longer.

Confusion seemed to float through this perfect moment like a seasoned swimmer just enjoying the waters of the deep end. Letting the water take over his body and take him where it would, seeing only a comforting blue haze far from the surface and hearing only the happy gentle tales of each whispering droplet. Confusion thought and in amazement realized that he was not holding his breath, he realized that he was a seasoned swimmer breathing underwater.

And then the water began to take his body up,

towards the surface, each little droplet passing him from their tiny hands into those of the droplet above. He looked up and as the water pushed him upward the comforting dark blue haze that he had been seeing became lighter and lighter and very soon he could see a bright orange sun which grew bigger as he continued to move closer and closer to the surface. The tales of the droplets became fainter and fainter and from a place in the very dark recessed of his mind came a sound he thought he was familiar with but which he could not quite put his finger on. The water formed a barrier between the sound and his ears and so he began to push upwards in an effort to break the surface and hear the sound clearly, for things he could not identify frustrated him. His progress to the surface seemed never-ending and the once comforting water began to seem like a jail that would not let him escape back to what he thought was reality, to what he thought clarity was, and so he began to thrash around with his limbs, pushing the water downwards to surge his heavy body upwards.

And then finally, he broke through the water top and opened his lungs to take in air but to his greatest surprise he found that he could not breathe. He could not breathe but he could hear the shrill sound of sirens in front, behind and beside him causing chaos in his mind. He looked around and stared down one of the barrels of an

AK47 held by one of many soldiers in a camouflage coloured truck driving beside him on the road. Now there was a man in black clothing banging on his door whilst driving a motorbike. The crouched drivers at their steering wheels no longer looked amazed by him but they looked frightened for him. He wanted to go back down to the depths of his water and lose himself in oblivion once again but try as he might he could not. The chaos and confusion frustrated him and all individual noised merged into one loud noise which cracked like lightning in his ears. His sturdy hands began to tremble on the steering wheel as he saw a police motorcycle stop in front of him with the man in black pointing a rifle at him but, luckily, though he was confused, his muscles remembered how to stop his car.

Time seemed to stand still and as if in slow motion he watched as he was surrounded by policemen on their motorcycles and several army men that had jumped off their still moving truck. The truck drove on past his car and then three black Range Rovers with tinted windows sped past him followed by an ambulance, a limousine, three more window-tinted range rovers, another ambulance, another army truck full of armed soldiers and three more police motorcycles. After the last motorcycle passed his car, nearly two minutes went by before the crouched drivers at their steering wheels timidly turned their cars into the road and drove off.

Confusion looked around and wondered where he was and why there were seven men surrounding him with their firearms pointed in his direction.

DON'T YOU KNOW TO STOP FOR THE PRESIDENT'S MOTORCADE?

Confusion mumbled and sputtered, asked the soldier who he was and how there were suddenly so many cars in Salisbury and then he was dragged out of his car, falling to the ground and then he plunged back into the deep blue waters of his oblivion where he sank deeper and deeper into a darkness that seemed to stick to him like liquid tar.

When he broke surface again, he was in a holding cell hunched over a wooden bench with his hand under his thigh. A skinny man in a faded grey ZRP uniform who, Confusion thought, looked like a praying mantis, was crouched in front of him looking into his face.

Where are you from, Grandpa?

Confusion looked around wearily and all was a blur. He was no longer panicking but still the steel bars and stained walls whispered to him, desperately telling him that he did not belong there and that he should escape. He tried to stand but his legs felt leaden and refused to work. The small room itched at the furthermost recessed of his failing mind and he knew he had been in a place like this before. He knew that he had spent many years in a place similar to this place but he did not remember why. He could not remember that it was because he fought for freedom that he had been locked in a cell for many, many years and Constable Marudzi would not believe him even if he had been able to tell him. Constable Marudzi had Confusion's wallet in his hands. He opened it and took out Confusion's ID.

Ah, Mr Confusion, I think I know you, you are Confusion... Confusion, Confusion from Chipinge? That is where my mother is from. So, you are my grandfather for sure! Can you not speak?

Confusion reigned in Confusion's mind and because several questions were competing to be asked at once, what came out of his mouth was a babbling sound and a little bit of drool. The constable gave up, placed Confusion's wallet in his slack hand and walked out, locking the door behind him. Confusion turned his neck to watch him leave, every cell in his body screaming at his inner man to run after the constable and once more he tried to stand and his legs failed him. He looked down at his open wallet and wondered who this Confusion was, and then he wondered at the growing patch of dampness between his legs.

Confusion was once again in his deep blue waters when a voice called him to the surface.

Dad, Dad, let's go home.

Confusion broke the surface of the water and to his delight found that he could breathe oxygen, for standing there in front of him at the water's edge was his beautiful wife of nearly thirty years looking down at him with her hand outstretched. Confusion wondered why her eyes were red but he ignored it and instead shook her outstretched hand enthusiastically and asked her when she had arrived. His sight began to tunnel-vision and he saw only her as hand in hand Confusion and his wife walked out of the holding cell and in that moment, his mind was free because he knew that finally, he was safe.

* * *

To a mind that has no choice but to grieve for someone who is still living each small event and discomfort is like an increase in temperature to the water in a small contained pot on the stove.

The temperature increases, or stays the same, but it never decreases. It can take minutes, days or months for the water to reach boiling point, but it always inevitably does and then the water boils and boils and then suddenly the little black pot on the stove can no longer contain the boiling water and the water dances aggressively against the lid of the pot, steaming and pressuring it until the little lid topples off and falls to the floor with a loud clash followed by the aggressively dancing water which spills itself down the sides of the pot and onto the hot plate where it is evaporated into steam with a harsh hissing sound. Left to its own devices, which it often is, the water will boil itself into nothingness and the pot will be left empty – numb.

When Chaos heard that Confusion was lost for the second time in a week, first, they were informed, when he was taken away after driving into the president's motorcade, and then by simply getting out of the car which his wife had told him to stay in and wandering off, Chaos reached her limit, she reached her boiling point and the dancing waters could no longer be contained. She sat on her bed, fuming and steaming and her subconscious wondered how best to transfer pain, for pain is a thing that often goes from one host to the other if not harnessed. And then she heard it, she heard the yelps of pain of an injured animal before she saw, out of her bedroom window, a gruff brown dog with its ribs all but piercing its skin and with fur so matted that it looked like an old, long forgotten stuffed animal come to life, mounted upon her own little brown lady of a dog.

That fucking mongrel again...

Chaos' inner woman smiled a deep evil smile as her dilated pupils locked on her next target. She folded the seams of the old denim shorts she was wearing so that they went from knee length to midway up her thighs and then she retrieved her fibre glass hockey stick which she had last used three long years ago from behind her washing basket and ran outside. The mongrel saw her coming, dismounted, turned and ran towards the fence. It pushed up with its malnourished hind legs and in one swift and practised leap landed on top of the wall, looked back briefly with its tongue lolling out and an unapologetic expression on its face before jumping down and disappearing on the other side of the wall. Chaos was determined though, and so at full speed she ran out of the gate of her own yard and followed the mongrel which, with a limp, still ran faster than she could. She chased that dog with her hockey stick mid-air, ready to swing a fatal blow had she gotten close enough and she did not care for the bewildered looks she got from neighbours and vendors that saw the young girl in makeshift shorts, wielding a hockey stick and chasing after an injured dog. The dog could run but could not hide. Until it once again showed an uncanny athleticism and jumped over the bars of a manual gate. Chaos saw red and once again there was no reasoning with her, she was out for blood and the transferal of pain and so she stood in front of that gate and ran her fibre glass hockey stick over the metal bars all the while making nonsensical but threatening sounds in the direction that she thought the dog had disappeared in the stranger's yard.

Eventually, from the direction the dog had disappeared in appeared a dishevelled and frightened woman whom Chaos addressed roughly and accusingly. The frightened woman cowered under Chaos' bullying and tried to convince her that it was not their dog but an annoying stray which also jumped into their yard for unsolicited visits. The frightened woman turned down Chaos' offer to do a yard search for the notorious dog and so Chaos, having hit a brick wall, turned and walked back the way she had come.

Chaos was still a raging pot of boiling water in her mind even if, physically, she was all but drained of energy. She had not managed to kill or even hurt the offending mongrel and so had all but kept her pain to herself. She knew of no one she could start a fight with. That is until she came to a guard house at the corner of her road. She stood, a girl in subconscious confusion but unexplainable pain, staring at the little wooden brown guard house which so annoyed and offended her in that moment that she lifted her fibre glass hockey stick high above her head and brought it down hard against the side of the unoccupied guard house. To her surprise, her stick bounced off the wood back in her direction and she only just managed to keep a hold of it. She looked at the tall wooden structure with wide eyes filled with first surprise, then betrayal, and then determination as she found a weak wooden panel in the structure's side, hooked the curved end of her stick into the wooden panel below the loose one and then with all her strength backed up with all her weight and pulled. The wooden panel gave way and popped off and she fell backwards onto the dusty gravel road, scratching her thighs and the palm of her hand which had flung back in an attempt to break her fall.

Ouch

She liked the pain and she liked the adrenaline that coursed through her blood at the thrill of having found a worthy opponent to fight her. She stood up with one foot forward and swung and pulled and jerked and kicked and spat at the guard house. She stopping only temporarily as an elderly neighbour addressed her.

Don't do that, that guard house doesn't belong to you. Why are you destroying it?

The elderly neighbour stumbled backwards against the hot gaze of Chaos who was now sweating, grunting and frothing at the mouth like a rabid predator. She turned and power walked away, looking over her shoulder every so often to make sure the rabid predator was not following her home or swinging its one lone, hooked claw in her direction.

Chaos reigned and ruled her own world for several minutes more, only stopping when she was thoroughly spent and in more physical pain than emotional pain. That was how she preferred it. She looked at her craftsmanship and was amused to see the guard house still standing tall with only a few wooden panels unhinged and one or two cracked. She turned and walked on home, too exhausted to feel.

Chaos would forever be chaos, but for now the water had evaporated itself leaving only a small black metal exoskeleton with no inner substance.

* * *

Confusion is several years gone but Chaos remains chaos though the water boils over less often now. She will forever be an empty exterior with only darkness within. She is a lone soldier exploring a no man's land which over the years has turned into a waste land. Every day she walks cautiously in a direction she knows not of. She is cautious not to step on a landmine which she herself buried long, long ago in a bid to destroy her enemy but which now threatens to destroy her. She is a lost soldier, wandering, wandering, and everyday falling into a deeper state of confusion wondering where her enemy is, what her enemy looked like and if the soldier who died really was the enemy or if, maybe, they were allies all along fighting against a bigger enemy. The enemy is gone but the battle is lost and with it so is Chaos who wades through a no man's land which has become her land. She runs on the trenches of the enemy in agony because she has discovered that the peace she so long longed for is far, far more painful than the sounds of warfare and the pain of bullets and shrapnel cutting and piercing one's flesh and bones. She fought for peace, and waited and watched for peace, but not the peace of a death that was not hers.

Now confusion has set into her own mind as she grasps at memories that are quickly fading and runs towards an injured soldier who disappears like a mist before her very eyes leaving her fists dampened but empty. She is a beast in pain, a beast that howls into the night only to be answered by her own echoes. She is a miserable and a wretched chaos. She is the worst kind of chaos. She is a chaos alone.

But maybe one day colourful wild flowers will begin to grow again in no man's land.

TRENCHES

The Reverend knelt in front of where Marshala sat on her mourning mat. She was rocking gently- or being rocked by the three women whose duty it was to stay by her side during her time of mourning lest she harm herself with grief.

It was not common, suicide, in the Shona culture at a funeral. No one slit their wrists in grief, and although some mourners skipped some meals, it was unlikely to lead to starvation. The meal skippers were likely those who had had a bad experience with eating food at such a large gathering and had maybe contracted food poisoning or a slightly upset stomach. No, Shona people did not commit suicide out of grief at funerals, but that did not stop them from proposing to do other things. It was not uncommon for a bereaved wife or sister to threaten to jump into the grave as the casket holding her beloved husband or brother was being lowered. The bereaved would preferably be foaming at the corners of her ashen lips with her hands hanging limply atop her covered head and her feet stumbling towards the mouth of the grave which she was trying to convince the gathered mourners, but mostly herself, that she would jump into. In such cases, it would be the job of the women assigned to her, usually cousins, aunts or close friends, to hold her back at a safe distance from the grave mouth whilst giving her enough room for her to continue to dramatize her intentions.

Not Marshala though. Reverend Chitiyo was at first taken aback by her composure and calmness when he first walked into the gathering that afternoon. Even when the other women saw him and started keening and writhing on the floor to express their grief, Marshala just continued to sit on her mat, even smiling a little when he first knelt in front of her to grasp her small hand in his. In fact, he was so unsettled at her reserve that he felt the need to make excuses for her. He supposed that she was so composed, even getting up now and again to give instructions on how meals should be prepared for the gathered mourners and where to find an extra blanket for relatives who had come from afar, because she had been preparing for her loss for a long time. Marshala's mother had battled diabetes for as long as the Reverend had known her- which was going on fifteen years. In the past three or four years she had had to have a hip replacement operation after a bad fall and she had seemed to just go downhill health-wise from there, contracting pneumonia which never seemed to completely clear up and her arthritis worsening, until finally passing away peacefully in her sleep the previous night in her early nineties.

Her passing affected Reverend Chitiyo greatly. Mai Marshala had been good to him and supported him every step of his journey in his walk to becoming first the youth pastor and then the reverend of their church. She would invite him for lunch every Sunday afternoon after church service and also to join her family for Easter, Christmas and any other holiday when he was a struggling university student because she knew that he had no family nearby. Even when he got married, Mai Marshala and Marshala herself did so much to help organise his humble wedding, going to the extent of catering at his reception at no cost to him and allowing his young bride, Cynthia and her bridesmaids to use her home to dress before the ceremony. Mai Marshala and Marshala had become his family and so he felt like he had lost a mother. Cynthia had sat beside him on the bed and held him when he had received the phone call with the news of Mai Marshala's passing. He had cried and Cynthia had allowed him to, and then he had gotten on the first bus to Harare, excusing himself to the Superintendent overseeing the church conference in Mutare, to gather with the mourners in Arcadia. Cynthia was to follow him after the afternoon ladies' meeting in which she was one of the speakers.

After a while Reverend Chitiyo had checked himself and prayed for forgiveness for judging Marshala's composure. He knew that people grieved in different ways and no matter how long and how much you prepared for loss, it was never easy. Sometimes the deepest grief was the one that paralysed your heart whilst allowing you to continue functioning like an empty shell of a human.

Marshala and the Reverend looked into each other's eyes for a while whilst she was being rocked gently. She smiled slightly and looked at him pityingly as if he was the one who had lost a mother and was now alone. He quietly praised God for her strength and then she broke free of the women beside her and hugged him long and tight.

"I'll see you tomorrow morning, Marshala," he promised her as she melted back into the arms of her support system.

"Thank you, Reverend," she said, her voice

breaking a little. Reverend Chitiyo shook the hands of the women beside her before getting up and walking out of the living room, making sure not to accidentally step on any of the many women sitting and mourning on the floor. He walked right out into the midst of the gathering of mourning men who were seated on chairs and low stools around a fire just in front of the house. They were discussing politics and were in the middle of a heated argument about whether or not it was possible to acquire a mine without any political affiliations. However, when they saw the Reverend the argument fell into a hushed silence and they looked down at their laps or into the orange flames of the fire as if deep in thought and contemplation of their loss.

"I'd say you'd need strong political connections to buy a mine," the Reverend said. He preferred to be relatable to all and did not like people to forget that he too was just a normal person much like them. His efforts were met by chuckles and nods and well wishes as he walked on towards the open gate at the end of the yard to where his car was parked outside. Marshala's brother, Miguel, who lived in the UK but was home for his mother's funeral, jogged up to the Reverend with a castle lager in hand. He put his arm around the Reverend's shoulder.

"Thank you, Pastor, for everything you've done

for my Ma," he slurred.

The Reverend remembered that people handled grief in different ways. He did not know Miguel, only having seen him in photographs. In fact, this was the first time seeing him in the flesh.

"It was the other way around. She basically took me in as her own son," the Reverend assured him.

"Nah, nah. I heard how you'd come pray for her and shit. I appreciate that stuff, from the heart you know," Miguel insisted, tapping his chest with his beer bottle.

"Okay..." the Reverend managed. He felt his phone vibrate in his pocket and took it out and saw that Cynthia was calling him. He let it ring as Miguel continued.

"And that sermon, that sermon Pastor, it spoke to me here." He tapped his chest with his beer bottle again before continuing, "About not knowing the time and all, that Jesus will call you home and all. Powerful."

"Thank you, Miguel. Thank you. I have to get home to my wife now but I'll see you tomorrow morning," the Reverend said as he opened his wife's message that had just come in.

"You travel safe, Reverend," Miguel slurred as he walked backward back the way he had come, pointing at the pastor with his beer bottle all the while. Reverend Chitiyo turned back towards the gate and walked on, responding to his wife's message all the while. Before walking out of the gate, he turned back towards the house and said a silent prayer. He prayed that God's spirit would remain and comfort the gathered mourners and for a peace that surpasses all understanding. Then he turned back and walked out the gate, smiling because suddenly he could smell Mai Marshala's favourite perfume which he had bought her for Mother's Day a couple of weeks before she had passed away.

"Nyasha *gara pasi mhani*, sit down. There is another police road block ahead," Mai Simba said turning back in the passenger seat and swatting at whichever of her three young children she could reach in the back seat. The children shielded themselves from the attack and Simba managed to pull his younger sister down into a sitting position. Only then did Mai Simba retrieve her fleshy arm and settle back into her seat comfortably. She looked out the window at the suburban houses in Mt Pleasant. She had been trying to convince her husband to buy them a bigger house and she loved Mt Pleasant. Now she grimaced at the gapping trenches that ran alongside most of the durawalls. "Zvii izvi? What are these atrocities in front of these nice houses now?" she complained to anyone who would listen.

"Our teacher says they are digging all over Harare to put in fibre glass for phone internet or something," piped up Simba, who was at the age when children thought they knew everything.

"Simba *nyarara mhani,* keep quiet," his mother said with a half-hearted swipe of her supple arm in his general direction.

"I think it's good. It's improving our country. With these telecom improvements, there'll be Wi-Fi everywhere and with the power of the internet only then will Africa rise to the levels of the West!" This was Baba waSimba. He had the opposite temperament to his wife. This meant that he listened more than he spoke, he liked to avoid complaining and he tried to see the good in every single situation. He believed in the power of positive thinking and believed that Africa was only a few words of affirmation away from being as great as America and Britain.

He was driving his family to his sister's son's graduation party. He could not wait till his own children graduated and he was already so very proud of all their small accomplishments.

"Still," Mai Simba said eyeing the trenches dubiously, "they are so ugly all over Harare." Sometimes her husband's positivity annoyed her as she felt that he purposefully disagreed with her. She worried that Simba was becoming too much like his father- purposefully disagreeing with her too. Her phone pinged once in her purse which she clutched in her generous lap. It pinged once, and then it began to ping almost continuously. She opened her purse and, elbow deep, tried to fish it out of her bag. "*Ko* who is this bothering me on a Saturday like this? People are obsessed with this whatsup, whatsup!" she tutted.

"It's 'WhatsApp,' Mum!" Simba corrected and chuckled. The look that his mother turned and shot him shut him up quick and he covered his mouth with his hand as a form of surrender. Mai Simba turned back and unzipped the cover of her phone to check who it was that was looking for her as Baba waSimba looked at his son via the rear-view mirror and winked. Simba grinned and winked back, with both his eyes. Mai Simba swiped the screen of her new iPhone to unlock it and she pressed the green WhatsApp icon where she discovered that the messages pouring in were all from the *Ruwadzano* church woman's group. It was Cynthia Chitiyo who had first messaged in the group informing everyone that Mai Marshala had passed away peacefully in her sleep the previous night. After that it was everyone offering their condolences to Marshala, who was silent in the group, and asking about the funeral proceedings.

"*Amaiwe zvangu*!" exclaimed Mai Simba after she had finished reading all the WhatsApp messages and typed in her own condolences. Although he was generally a calm and composed man and although he was well used to his wife's sudden exclamations this one was so loud and forceful that Baba waSimba swerved the car a little. Mai Simba was never one to need encouragement to express herself and so she continued on before he could ask her what was wrong. "Mai waMarshala, she is dead!"

"Who is Mai waMarshala?" asked Simba, practising his newly acquired private school accent.

Mai Simba turned back to scowl at him, "*Iwe usatiitire benzi panapa.* Don't be an idiot. *Hauzive* Mai weMarshala *vane bvudzijena*? The woman with white hair who sits in the front middle bench two people from the right in church," Mai Simba turned back and stared at her phone as the messages continued to stream in.

"Oh her! I know her, she gave Nyasha a sweet last Sunday," Simba said, proud to know who his mother was on about.

At that Mai Simba whipped around and swatted at the unsuspecting Nyasha who had all the while been dosing off in her seat with her head against her baby sister Memo's car seat. "Nyasha, what did I tell you about eating everything from everyone?" Nyasha's wide eyes stared back at her mother in bewilderment.

Baba waSimba interjected before the situation escalated, "Mai waMarshala was a valuable member of the church. She will be missed."

"She's the one who sewed those shimmering golden curtains for the church, remember?" Mai Simba said in the direction of her husband. Her husband nodded and for a while there was a solemn silence in the car save for the pinging of the messages that were still coming into Mai Simba's phone.

"You know you can mute group chats, right?" Simba was first to break the silence.

Mai Simba readied her powerful neck to swing back and shoot her son a look that would have let him know that he had overstepped but Baba waSimba put his hand on his wife's shoulder and asked, "So, where are the mourners gathered so we can go and pay our respects for that lovely woman who is now resting in God's arms?"

"*Hameno*, I'm not sure yet. Marshala is offline. Let me ask again." By this time, Baba waSimba had reached his sister's house in Chisipite and turned his car into her gate. He rang the intercom and the gate opened without anyone having enquired who was at the gate. He drove on in as Mai Simba used the little mirror on the underside of her sun visor to add another layer of foundation to her oily face. "*Ndichafona manheru* after the party. I'll call Sara in fact, she is Marshala's cousin that one so I'm sure she'll know where the mourners are gathered." Baba waSimba parked the car and killed the engine. Simba ran out towards the direction of the party followed by Nyasha who was rubbing the sleep from her eyes. Baba waSimba unbuckled Memo from her car seat whilst Mai Simba finished applying her second layer of makeup.

It was late in the night and Baba waSimba and his family had arrived home forty minutes earlier. He had just put Simba and Nyasha to bed and

Mai Simba was sitting on the edge of their bed breastfeeding Memo before putting her down for the night in the cot next to their bed. Baba waSimba emerged from the bathroom with his pyjama longs on. He climbed into bed, laid down and yawned. In Mai Simba's arms Memo's sucking became softer as the baby began to fall asleep.

"Did you phone to find out about the funeral proceedings? It would be good to go and pay our respects first thing tomorrow," he enquired whilst rubbing his wife's back with his hand from where he lay.

"*Amaiwe zvangu*! I had almost forgotten. Let me call Sara now," Mai Simba replied. She put the sleeping baby into her cot and covered her with a warm blanket before returning her breast into her shirt and fishing for her phone in her bag again. She retrieved it, unzipped its cover and scrolled down her contact list until she found Sara's name and pressed the green call button next to it. She put the phone to her ear and sat back on the edge of the bed.

"Sara! *Nematambudziko*. I'm so sorry about Mama Mai Marshala," Mai Simba shouted into her iPhone.

On the other end of the line Sara was packing

a small bag with her phone secured to her ear by her shoulder. She packed a *zambia* into her little bag and wrapped a thin woollen blanket around where her waistline used to be. She listened patiently as Mai Simba, perhaps her hundredth caller since her aunt had passed away, said all the necessary words of comfort. Finally, Mai Simba tapered out and just as she had predicted and like all callers had done before her, she asked how Mai Marshala had died. On auto pilot, Sara responded. She informed Mai Simba, like she had the past one hundred callers, that her aunt had died peacefully in her sleep and that she believes that the diabetes, arthritis and old age had caught up with her and that no she did not think that an autopsy was necessary and yes indeed that would be an added expense and that no Marshala was not online as she was probably organising her mother's wake and funeral and yes her aunt had been a part of the church's burial society and yes indeed what a good thing that was. After she finished giving Mai Simba the detailed directions of where the mourners were beginning to gather she sat on the old brown arm chair in the corner of her room and allowed herself, finally, to cry.

Sara loved her aunt, who she and all her siblings and cousins referred to as Aunty MooMoo. They're extended family had never really been exceptionally close but whenever they did gather, be it in celebration of a birth or academic or social success, it had always been Aunty MooMoo who had initiated it and it was always Aunty MooMoo and Marshala who had done all the cooking, and boy could the mother and daughter duo cooked up a storm every single time. Sara sobbed quietly because she would miss the love and kindness and warm and sweet-smelling embrace of Aunty MooMoo, but she cried most of all for Marshala. Without Aunty MooMoo Marshala was now very much alone, especially since she, her closest cousin and friend, was moving to Johannesburg to marry an Afrikaans man she had first met online on a dating app a year ago. Without Sara, the timid and soft spoken Marshala would be very much alone in that quaint house in Arcadia. Marshala had never moved out, she had stayed first to help her mother take care of her alcoholic father who had stumbled back into their lives when Marshala was in her mid-thirties. He had died nearly twenty years back from liver failure. After that Marshala stayed for her mother, to make sure she was never lonely and then as her health began to decline, Marshala, who trained as a nurse, stayed to take care of her mother. Marshala was now in her fifties and Aunty MooMoo once confided in Sara, one time when Sara came to visit her after her hip replacement operation, that she was worried that it was her fault that Marshala had never married. Marshala had overheard the conversation and laughed it off telling her mother and closest friend and cousin that it was just as well she wasn't married because all men were trouble. Sara racked her memory and tried to remember if Marshala had ever told her about or shown interest in any boys when they were young. Like the average girl she had gotten many catcalls and been asked out many times in her teenage years all the way into her early thirties but she never reciprocated any of the advances.

"Not everyone is meant to be a half of a whole," Sara remembers Marshala telling her after Sara's high school crush had stood her up at the school dance, "God created me and you already whole." But her words had failed to comfort Sara who never seemed to be lucky in love. Until now, in her mid-forties her niece had convinced her to try online dating and that's where she had been found by Hans, her Afrikaner, who she was moving to South Africa to marry in a couple of weeks. Sara couldn't believe her happily ever after, but just thinking about it made her all the sadder for Marshala, who, without Aunty MooMoo, was now completely alone.

Sara went into the bathroom and washed her face. The cold water against her warm face gave her the resolve she needed to be strong for Marshala and support her all the way through everything. Perhaps Hans would be willing for Marshala to come and stay with them sometime after the wedding. Either way she would take one day at a time beginning with that evening. She picked up her little bag off the bed, switched off the geyser and made sure the gas was shut tight before leaving the house, locking up and driving off in her little blue Datsun in the direction of sweet, soft spoken Marshala.

Sara met Marshala at the funeral home where they were keeping Aunty MooMoo. The two hugged for a long time before Sara pulled back to look into Marshala's face. She wiped the one solitary tear from Marshala's cheek and hugged her again. "I am so sorry, my love," she said.

"I'm sorry too. You've lost your Aunty MooMoo," she'd comforted Sara back. They pulled away again and headed home where already a handful of relatives from Skies were setting up camp. In the car Marshala said, "She was so happy you know, about your wedding. She had nearly finished weaving your matrimonial blanket."

Sara gasped, "she still had her loom?"

"Oh yes!" Marshala looked over at Sara in the driver's seat, "It's a shame I never had the time to sit down and really learn. I would have finished the blanket for you."

"I want it! However far she'd gotten, whatever piece of it there is. I want it. I'll frame it and keep it forever." They drove on in silence, bracing themselves for what was ahead of them.

As soon as it was day break the following day and more mourners had gathered, Marshala was up and about, shaking hands with everyone and comforting everyone, including the distant relatives, friends and congregation members who insisted on outdoing each other in writhing on the floor and expressing their grief. She made breakfast for everyone- bread and margarine with milky tea. When one great aunt insisted that she couldn't eat any sort of spread on her bread nor plain bread, Marshala cooked her an egg. She answered everyone's questions and made sure that all were as comfortable as was possible at a wake. Sara insisted she sit down and created space for her in the living room where she was accessible to people who wanted to shake her hand and pay their respects but she got up every hour to clean the bathrooms and make sure everyone was comfortable.

All Marshala truly wanted to do was to curl up in her mother's bed whilst her sheets still smelt like her and sleep the pain away, but the culture would not allow her her solitude. She was uncomfortable with the many people that were constantly around her and she was anxious to make everyone comfortable and be as hospitable as her mother had taught her to be. Only when plates of food appeared at lunch time as if by magic and she went outside to discover a small group of her younger female relatives cooking Sadza and relish and goat meat over a fire, did she begin to see some of the benefits of having a large extended family, even if she did not know half of them. She was unable to sit and do nothing so she went to where the men were eating and thanked her Uncle James for the meat. He owned a small farm in Chiredzi so she knew it was him who had provided the food. She made a few phone calls and ensured that her mother's burial would be the following day after which, on everyone's insistence, she went to sit back down against a wall in her living room on her mourning mat where Sara and other women put their arms around her and rocked her gently. Marshala wasn't angry with God for taking her mother. Her mother, she knew, had lived a good and full life. Despite any hardships, her mother had remained gracious and generous and Marshala only hoped that she was even half the woman that her mother had been.

Marshala opened her eyes and only then did she realize that she had nodded off. She looked around embarrassed and then saw, kneeling in front of her in a fine fitted dark blue suit, Takudzwa Chitiyo, the Reverend and the man whom she considered to be her adopted little brother. With tears in his own eyes he took her hand in both of his and expressed his condolences. She did not know what to say as she saw in his eyes that his loss was as bad as her own, and so she smiled to comfort him and let him know that it would all be all right. She was relieved that he was there as she knew that the Reverend would shepherd not only herself but all the mourners through the grieving process.

"I'm sorry I couldn't get here sooner," Reverend apologised. "Cynthia sends her condolences. She had to preach at the ladies meeting in Mutare this afternoon but she's on her way now to Harare and she'll come as soon as she can." The Reverend smiled at Marshala weakly and Marshala smiled back. "I hear Miguel is coming? Your uncle has gone to wait for him at the airport..."

"I am so glad you are here Reverend," Marshala finally managed.

The Reverend stood up and turned to pay his respects to each one of the gathered mourners. As he did so he saw Mai Simba get out of her car and walk toward the gathering. She was a proud and mighty woman, what with her husband making many generous donations to the upkeep of the church. On Sundays, she sat in the front pew with her meek and good-natured husband beside her and she said the loudest amens and held her chubby manicured hand up the highest during praise and worship. The Reverend, who was watching her advance, was somewhat surprised when she first seemed to trip and then began to stumble along toward where he was standing in the centre of the living room. By the time she had gotten to him she was crawling and she had long since began her ear-splitting keening. He bent at the knees to support her as she continuously rose then fell and rose then fell and keened and wailed and listed, between piercing sobs, all the nice things that Mai Mashala had ever done for her and the church, including the time, last Sunday, that Mai Marshala had given her small daughter, Nyasha, a sweet. By this time Baba waSimba who prior had been shaking hands with the male mourners outside, had heard his wife's mournful wails and was now helping the Reverend keep his wife standing until someone created a space on the floor against a wall for her to sit. Thus secured, she continued to whimper and sob, smudging the top layer of her foundation whilst the women beside her rubbed her body. It was only when she was brought a plate of food that she arrested her sounds of despair and dug in.

"*Yuwi*," Sara whispered into Marshala's ear whilst rubbing her back. Marshala smiled and squeezed Sara's hand under the blanket that someone had thrown over them.

Although Reverend Chitiyo had presided over many funerals he always made an effort to personalize each funeral sermon he gave according to the word that God impressed upon his heart. He sat in his dark blue Toyota corolla just outside the yard and prayed to God to open his heart. Very quietly he heard a whisper upon his heart.

...you are a mist that appears for a little while and then is gone...

The Reverend opened the Bible on his lap to the book of James chapter four, verse fourteen and began to prepare his sermon.

"Life is so unpredictable, you know? It is so unpredictable and there is nothing you can do to change the unpredictability of your life besides to live life to the fullest whilst you still can. Do you hear what I am saying? You can do everything right and follow the rules and never stray from the law. You can study till your head aches and get one hundred percent on every single exam. You can have the perfect CV and the most pristine suits. And you still won't get the job that you want or the spouse that you thought was perfect for you or that promotion or your family's acceptance and praise. My brothers and sisters, there is nothing that you can do to guarantee anything in life. Nothing. It's like there is nothing you can do to guarantee the grace and love of God in your life. It's not about how many bulls you sacrifice or how often you remember to pray or how many days you can go without sinning, it is about God choosing to love you and God choosing to be gracious and merciful to you because let me tell you a secret, none of us deserve God's grace, but He chooses to give it us anyway. You can eat healthy every single day of your life and still get sick whilst someone who drinks and smokes every single day and eats the lard off a side of pork for breakfast, lunch and super never even gets the flu in his whole entire life.

"Life is unpredictable my friends and so you've got to learn to stop constantly trying to be in control. Let go and let God. Put your trust and faith and hope in God and trust that everything will work for His glory and in your favour because He knows the plans that He has for each one of us, that is Jeremiah twenty-nine, eleven. All you can do in this life, whilst you are letting go and letting God, is to make the most of your life. I think that everyone who knew Mai Marshala, or Aunty MooMoo as some of us affectionately call her, will have seen a great example of someone who lives life to the fullest. She was a soldier of God, she fought the good fight. What does living life to the fullest mean? It means yes, do what you are supposed to, sow when the weather demands, but, my friends, do not forget to reap and enjoy the fruits of your labour. It means find joy in the tiny everyday things. It means forgive yourself and laugh and give yourself room for trial and error. It also means that whilst you are alive also make someone else's life a little bit easier and more pleasant. I do not think that there is anyone in this room whose life has not been made even a little bit more pleasant by Aunty MooMoo. I know she made my life more pleasant. Without her love and support I would not have been able to graduate, without her wisdom and encouragement I would not have had the guts to approach the girl I liked in church, and without her cooking, which we all loved, my wedding would not have happened. She made us promise not to tell anyone but she hand-made my wife's wedding dress because we could not afford to buy or even rent one.

"I grew up in an orphanage. Many of you do not know this, but I did, I am an orphan. Life was tough, food was scarce and it was scary and lonely most days. The day I met Mai Marshala, I knew in my heart that God had finally sent me a mother. She may be physically gone but her love will remain forever. Because of her I will live every single day to the fullest. I will laugh readily and love without hesitation. I will be at peace with the things that I cannot change and trust God. I will be bold and courageous like the Lord commanded and never be afraid to do anything with God's blessing.

"You see, brothers and sisters, you must never waste a day. James four verse fourteen says this, 'Why, you do not even know what will happen tomorrow. What is your life? You are a mist that appears for a little while and then vanishes.' A mist- here today, gone tomorrow. That being so, does it not then make sense to live each day as if it is your last? It may be. If you have kind words to speak to somebody, speak them now. Tell that person that you have not spoken to for ages that you love them. Apologies to that person you wronged many months ago. Forgive that person because life is way too short and too precious to hold grudges.

"Before you invest too much time in something ask yourself if that what you are doing will get you closer to God, if not then do not stress over it. Can you take it with you when you die? Probably not! So, seek ye first the kingdom of God and all else will follow. Amen?"

The mourners were attentively looking and listening to him now, including the men who had moved their chairs and stools into the veranda so that they too could see and hear the Reverend's preaching. In unison, everyone answered his Amen.

"You are but a mist my family. No one knows the day or the time that God will call for you, that He will call your name and call you home to Him. And oh, what a joyous day that will be for you, Hallelujah! Especially is you've fought the good fight here on earth because you do not get a second chance on this planet. This is the only life you have so enjoy it, live it, love it and be confident so that the day that you are called home you are content and happy knowing too that you have left the world better than how it was when you entered it."

Just like in his sermons during Sunday service, people were encouraging him to 'say it louder' and to 'tell them pastor.' People swayed as though his words held some sort of inaudible melody and he watched the effects of the Spirit amongst them. He thanked God silently for using him as His vessel.

"Let us bow our heads in prayer. Almighty God, we come before you today and thank you for the time that we had with your sweet servant Aunty MooMoo, Mai Marshala, Dorothy deKindle. Lord we know that you have called her home, Jesus, but we who remain mourn at our own losses as this earth has lost an angel dear God. I pray for your spirit to come upon us and comfort us, especially Marshala and Mai Marshala's closest family and friends. Dear God we pray for a peace that surpasses all understanding as we know that Aunty MooMoo is now enjoying a painless and joyful eternal life in your kingdom Jehovah. I pray for your guidance and supervision during this mourning period and with the funeral preparations Lord. Watch over all our comings and goings and protect us all with the blood of Jesus. In Jesus' name, we pray. Amen."

There was a resounding Amen from everyone in response. Reverend Chitiyo looked around and saw that he had indeed managed to get through to the mourners and again, he thanked God. He excused himself, knowing that he had to hurry home to his wife and kids, but he promised to be back the following morning with his wife. He began to go around the room shaking everyone's hands, thanking them when they thanked him for his heart felt sermon, and willing them to carry on being strong.

Only death reminds the living of how precious life truly is and how one should live it to the absolute fullest. It is another's death that reminds people that life should not be taken too seriously, nor for granted. Everyone always makes a new resolution- that they have made at every other funeral but forgotten- to live each day more purposefully and to find peace and joy despite the hardships that each new day brings.

* * *

"Mommy, where's daddy?" Cynthia's three-year-old daughter Naomi asked as she climbed into her bed from the side her husband usually lay on. Cynthia opened her eyes and discovered, to her surprise, that it was already morning.

"I'm not sure, Sweetie." She had fallen asleep on top of the covers without changing into her pyjamas or even taking off her bedroom slippers which she used to walk around the house. She turned and faced her daughter and stroked her hair until she fell back to sleep. She then got up and walked to the kitchen where she saw the pie dishes and plates she had laid out for her husband's dinner untouched. Cynthia was confused, she was sure that her husband had said that he would not spend the night at the wake but that he would come home and then they would then go to the funeral together in the mourning. Cynthia rubbed the sleep from her eyes and yawned. She was terribly confused. She walked back to her bedroom and retrieved her phone from under her pillow where it had fallen out of her hand when she fell asleep whilst texting her husband. She opened her WhatsApp to her and her husband's chat and saw the ellipses that indicated that her husband was typing a message. She stared at the screen for a long time, waiting, but then looked at the time and decided to prepare her children for school whilst Takudzwa finished typing and sending his message. She had a strong feeling that he wouldn't be home in time to do the school run that day. She ran a warm bath in the children's bathroom and painstakingly managed to rouse both Naomi and Ester for their morning baths.

"Why do we have to go to school in winter?" whined Ester as her mother scrubbed away at the green marker that she had let her little sister draw all up and down her right arm the previous day.

"It's too cold for crèche!" wailed Naomi with her eyes closed.

"What does daddy always say? Education is key!" admonished their mother. "And," Cynthia continued happily, "in two weeks it'll be holidays and then where are we going?"

"Kariba!" the girls said in unison. Cynthia was more excited than the girls were for their first family holiday. At first she had worried that they'd better save the bonus check she had gotten from work for the girls' school fees for the second semester, but then she had thought that life was short and needed to be enjoyed and so her and her husband had planned to vacation in Kariba on a houseboat offered for their leisure by one of the wealthier congregants as a belated Christmas gift. With the congregant's generosity, they'd still have some extra cash left over from their holiday so everything was perfect and Cynthia was excited.

With the children bathed and changed Cynthia gave them cereal for breakfast and packet them jam sandwiches for their break time at school. She poured herself a bowl of cereal too and sat at the table with the kids. She picked up her phone to read her husband's message and found that he was still typing a message. She thought that, perhaps, he had forgotten to log out of WhatsApp, but still, the last message had been hers and it was one in which she had asked him if he was on his way home. She checked the time and saw that the girls were behind time for school so she got them and their school bags into a taxi as quick as she could and they all drove off. She was determined to get the girls to school on time and prove her husband wrong about how she was always late for everything.

With the girls safely in class she took a kombi home. She walked the few meters from the bus stop to her gate and entered her yard and house. She saw that her husband's car was not in the yard and she began to feel uneasy. She understood that her husband's line of work was unpredictable and that perhaps he had decided to stay on at the funeral and comfort the bereaved but one thing she always boasted about in their relationship was the great communication between the two of them. It was not the first time he had failed to come home because of church obligations but it was the first time he had failed to call or text her and tell her where he was.

Cynthia sat on her bed and dialled her husband's number. He did not answer. She made herself a cup of tea to ease her rising anxiety and sat back on the bed thinking about what to do. Finally, she decided to call someone who was likely to be at the house where the mourners were gathered. She called Mai Simba because Mai Simba had posted on the *Ruwadzano* group chat that she was at the wake and kept updating everyone as to how everything was going. Her last app before the one saying good morning to everyone on the group at five AM was one where she was reporting on how powerful Reverend Chitiyo's sermon had been and a summary of what he had preached about. She dialled Mai Simba's number.

It was a while before the phone was answered

and when it was it was a male voice on the other end of the line.

"Hello?" Cynthia said, "Oh is that Baba waSimba? It's Cynthia, Cynthia Chitiyo."

"Oh, Mai *Mufundisi*, how are you? Sorry Mai Simba's phone was on the charger. She's in the house let me go find her for you," Baba waSimba offered.

"No, no don't worry about it. I was just phoning to ask if the Reverend was still there this morning?" she asked.

"*Aiwa*, no. The Reverend left last night after he preached. I saw him walk out even. *Asi* you can't find him?" he asked.

"No..." responded Cynthia dejectedly.

"Let me go see if his car is still outside. I parked right next to his Corolla just outside," said Baba waSimba helpfully as he walked toward the open gate. Baba waSimba saw a small crowd of men gathered just beside the gate. He walked past them with his phone still to his ear and saw, parked next to his Mazda 323, the Reverend's unmistakable dark blue Toyota corolla. He spoke into the phone. "Yes, his car is still here Mai *Mufundisi*. Maybe, maybe then he changed his mind and decided to sleep here. I'll check around and call you back."

"Thank you, Baba waSimba. Bye," said Cynthia. She hung up the phone and exhaled. The tea was now cold in its cup next to her on her bedside table. She had felt a pain in her chest as all sorts of thoughts raced through her head. She took a deep breath and rationed with herself that Mai Marshala had, after all, been like a mother to her and her husband, and so it was not surprising that he could have changed his mind and decided to spend the night at the wake. It was also a possibility that his phone had run out of battery and that he could not find a charger to charge it and communicate his whereabouts to her. Cynthia took a sip of cold tea and dialled her husband's number again, just in case.

Earlier that morning Miguel and Uncle Blue, a man he had only just met and who claimed to be his late father's second cousin, had walked back to the house from a nearby bar. Miguel hated funerals and family gatherings with every bone in his body but his Nigerian girlfriend had convinced him to go and even helped him fund his air ticket because, after all, it was his mother's funeral and he hadn't seen her or his sister Marshala for twenty years. It was an airtight argument but it did not change the fact that he did not want to be there among all those people who wanted to pat him on the back and have deep conversations with him about what he was doing in life. That is why he opted to visit the nearby bar because alcohol always helped him cope with things he'd rather not have to. At the bar he had bonded with Uncle Blue over too many beers and told him his life story and why he was back in the country and wondered aloud if he would be allowed back in the UK because he did not know if he had all the right papers to re-enter. Uncle Blue had asked about his family lineage and discovered that he was his uncle and decided that he needed to go back to the house with Miguel to pay his respects to his sister-in-law's family. Miguel agreed and so the two staggered back to the house.

"Perhaps, perhaps we shouldn't have drunk so much at a funeral," Uncle Blue considered out loud.

"Jack, the pastor said we must live life to the fullest!" Miguel said turning back to address Uncle Blue. "Come on, you'll be left behind."

They reached the house and Miguel lurched forward and grabbed the side of the open gate to steady himself.

"You see, I told you we should sober up a bit more before we go in... wha!" Uncle Blue tripped just before the side of the gate and managed to stop himself from falling forward only by grabbing onto Miguel. He looked back and saw what had tripped him. "I almost fell into one of these stupid trenches, bru…" he trailed off, looking into the trench he nearly fell into.

Miguel straightened up and followed his uncle's gaze. "Shit."

Baba waSimba always tried to keep to himself and mind his own business but as he turned away from the Reverend's Toyota Corolla and began to walk back into the yard his curiosity got the better of him. He heard, from the small crowd of men, a phone ringing and he wondered why no one was answering it. He heard someone say, "Nah bru, don't touch anything. We have to wait for the police to get here otherwise they'll say it's tampering or something. Don't touch anything."

"Well, where are the police?" someone else interjected.

"We called them like five hours ago they said they were getting petrol and then they would come," the first voice responded.

"We got robbed last year November and we had to drive and go pick up the police," another voice chimed in. Baba waSimba pushed through the crowd, wondering what everyone was looking down at.

His heart sank. "*Amaiwe zvangu*!" he exclaimed.

Marshala had finally broken down. She had lost all composure when, against everybody's advice, she had pushed through the now large crowd at the gate to see what everyone was staring at. She had joined all the women as they writhed and keened on the floor in the yard. Sara put her *zambia* over the ditch and tried to lead her cousin away from the commotion into the house.

Baba waSimba sat down under an avocado tree away from all the noise. He used his wife's phone to dial Cynthia's number. She answered.

"Did you find him? Is he there?" she enquired calmly.

"No, no... we didn't ... find him," Baba waSimba responded.

"Oh," Cynthia exhaled long and loud.

"Umm... we, I, I'm not sure if the car I saw this morning is your husband's car. I think, I think maybe you had better come and see... if it is his car..." Baba waSimba suggested shakily.

There was silence on the other end of the line.

"Hello? Mai *Mufundisi*?" he said into the phone.

After some silence, she responded, "Alright. I'm on my way." Her voice was hoarse.

The kombi dropped Cynthia off and she ran the rest of the way to Mai Marshala's house. Just outside the gate she saw her husband's little blue car like she knew she would. She knew that Baba waSimba and every other member of their church knew her husband's car from a mile away because, after all, they had all helped to buy it- Baba waSimba and his wife having contributed the most towards it. Nonetheless she went around to the front of the car to check the number plate even though she knew she did not need to. She stared at the number plate for a long time, ignoring the crowd that was by the gate.

"Jesus please, Jesus please, Jesus please, Jesus please, Jesus please," was the prayer she kept repeating under her breath. Suddenly, she felt arms around her and looked up to see a pink faced Marshala looking at her imploringly with quivering lips. Marshala pulled her towards herself in a hug but Cynthia shoved her backwards where she fell to the ground and stayed, looking up at Cynthia. "Leave me!" Cynthia said as more women tried to stand in her way. She pushed through every woman that tried to stop her from going towards the gathering of men. "Leave me!" she shouted again so loudly that subconsciously the crowd of people gathered around the ditch made way for her.

Cynthia looked down at the ditch and saw an orange cloth covering it.

"Jesus please, Jesus please." She blinked hard to expel the angry hot tears from her eyes and then knelt on one knee and in one movement pulled away the orange cloth.

"... Jesus please, no, no, no..."

And before anybody could stop her, Cynthia jumped into her husband's shallow, makeshift grave, and clung to him.

HOW DADDY HAPPENED

You work hard in school. You work hard in school because you know that that is the only possible way to break through the walls of the substandard life you have now. You've seen the possibilities. You've walked through Mt Pleasant on the way to fetch your little cousin from St John's High and seen the possibilities. You've seen the ladies in the crisp white blouses and turquoise skirts from Arundel School being driven home in shiny BMWs and Land Rovers by their drivers. You know they get driven by drivers because your dad used to be a driver and he used to pick up his boss's children from school at three o'clock- or five o'clock if they had sports. Now he's unemployed but he sometimes gets to drive your mother's church-friend's boss's commuter omnibus. That is probably the only reason your dad grudgingly goes to church every Sunday now- to keep up appearances for his part-time boss- and not, as your mother will have anyone who will listen believe, because 'God answers prayers'. You've seen how it is possible for a black girl to level with a white girl because you've seen their picturesque smiles as if in a magazine as they drive home in the same car. You have tried in vain to emulate these smiles of equality with Sophie and Johnny-your mother's boss's children- on the occasions that you have gone to their house to help your mother with her housework when they throw their big parties. You have seen the confidence with which an impatient girl has chastised her tardy mother for being late and how the guilty mother has apologised profusely. It reminds you of the one time you sulked and refused to greet your mother the time when she was five hours late to pick you up from crèche and how instead of an apology or explanation you received a smack across the face for being insolent. You have even seen – though this you do not approve of - a happy father kissing his smiling daughter right on the mouth in greeting.

It's too late to be an Arundel lady now. Just before you wrote your grade seven exams you coyly suggested to your parents that Arundel would be a good school to send you to but they only laughed. Your parents hardly ever carried a spirit of unison but that night when you made them laugh by suggesting you wanted to go to Arundel School they laughed in unison like a happily married couple. After the words left your lips your mother stopped breastfeeding your little brother for a second and your father's hand stopped midway to putting a ball of sadza into his mouth and they looked at each other and they both started laughing. They even high-fived and when their laughter began to subside one of them would say 'Arundel Girls' High' and they would look at each other, high-five and then begin to laugh all over again. This annoyed you so you finished your sadza and relish faster than usual and got up to leave but before you could escape your father said, "Where are you going? *Handiti* you said we must send you to Arundel Girls' High?" Once again your parents high-fived, looked at each other and began to laugh hysterically again. After about five more minutes the eight o'clock news started on ZBC and your father became instantly serious and transfixed with the news. Knowing that the news was important to your father your mother tried to suppress her giggles. Your father shouted at her to grow up and keep quiet. After you did the dishes you sat at the dining room table and did your homework. You finished just as the news finished. Your mother looked over to you and said, "Arundel Girls' High is only for smart girls."

"I am smart!" You had retorted. Both your parents looked over at you in shock. Whether it was because you dared answer back to your mother or that you thought you were smart you'll never know. You prepared yourself for a smack across the face for either one of these transgressions but instead your parents looked at each other and laughed, this time falling into each other's arms, and then they told you to go to sleep. That night you tried to stay up as long as possible without being noticed so that you could study hard and prove your parents wrong. You stayed up way past the time your parents got up and went to bed. It must have been an hour after that that you decided to go to sleep, not because you were tired, but because there was something disturbing about the way your mother's muffled giggles turned into unsuppressed moans in their bedroom across from yours. At least he wasn't beating her again.

At the end of the year you had left no room for them to doubt your intelligence what with your five units: One for maths, one for general paper, one for Shona and two for English. You were very proud when you came home and showed them your results and the fact that your father scolded you for disturbing his three man gossip session in the back yard did not dampen your mood like a scolding usually did. When they acted nonchalant you asked them why they weren't proud of you. Your father told you that you weren't the first person to pass an exam and besides, you would never get a good job with two units for English. Your mother, on the other hand, was all songs and praises, but praises to God and not you. Still, she made an effort, and that night she mixed in the chicken gizzards she had bought from Mai Nyasha next door with your sadza and relish in celebration.

You broached the subject of attending a private school again casually after dinner but before the eight o'clock news. This time your father asked what the point of furthering your education was and when you told him that it was so that you could get a good job and become successful, he told you how your mother had a good job yet had no formal education. Your mother then verbalised her thanks to God for having given her a good man who was a good provider (even though she was the breadwinner in the family) and your father pretended not to have heard and when she touched his arm and repeated her thanks to God he hid his approval by telling her gruffly to stop being crazy. The conversation stressed you out but that night your mother crept into the room you shared with your little sister in grade three and your baby brother who wet the bed whenever his nappies were in the wash and she whispered how you should stop dreaming as you would not go to a private school, let alone 'Arundel Girls' High' but that she would make sure that you would go to school.

Your good results ensured that you could get into any school you wanted to but of course it was not up to you. Your father chose the co-ed school in the neighbouring neighbourhood for you because he said that it would cut down on transport costs. When you suggested that you wanted to be a boarder in a school in Rusape that your friends were going to he reminded you that money did not grow on trees regardless of what the kids of today thought. In the end, you were just thankful that you were going to go to school.

School is your escape from reality, even though it is now comparatively harder than primary school. Still, you have persevered and have for the last three years placed in the top five. Your parents take it for granted but your doing so well makes everything you go through and overcome well worth it. You are really good at mathematics which surprises your elderly male relatives and when asked what you want to be when you grow up you say either a maths professor or a doctor. You either get shocked or amused looks in response to this. Nevertheless, numbers make sense to you more than people do. You can organise numbers and make them obey you. But you cannot seem to organise people, not even your own self. Even though you play sports and drink a lot of water you haven't been able to control your body. In form one you woke up with the worst pain in your lower abdomen that you have ever experienced. Worse than the time you ate the yellow chicken that your mother had insisted was fine even though the chicken had died of unknown causes before spending an additional twenty plus hours on top of a bus in the scorching heat on the way from Beit Bridge to Mbare. So, when you woke up with a pain worse than the yellow chicken pain and then looked down to see blood coming out of you, you bypassed the rule of not going into your parents' bedroom- especially when your mother was not there- to wake up your father as he was the only adult because your mother had gone on a three day church retreat. When you entered the room you temporarily forgot your pain because you saw two bodies instead of one in your parents' bed. You were relieved because your mother was home but when you walked closer to rouse her you saw that it was not your mother but your mother's younger cousin who was in upper six and who you were instructed to call Mainini. You wondered why she slept in your parents' bed instead of with you and your sister like all female relatives usually did, but then you surmised that it was probably a space issue. You had no time to wonder why her clothes were scattered on the floor or why she was naked because just then you remembered your pain and so you went to the other side of the bed to where your father was snoring. You timidly roused your father and his shock at seeing you in his bedroom in the middle of the night soon turned to rage and even after, between painful sobs, you tried to explain the cause of your rudeness, he told you to stop being stupid and to get out of his line of vision and wait for your mother to get back before he belted the demons out of you. His shouting woke Mainini up and she brought a sheet up to cover her naked breasts. The next morning she was gone.

You painstakingly located the source of bleeding and nearly died of shock when you discovered that there was a hole other than the one you urinate from. You filled your bathing bucket with cold water and took it to the bathroom to wash away the blood and rinse your underwear and stained pyjama bottoms. After that you went back to your bedroom, knelt beside the bed without waking your sleeping sister and prayed to God to first of all stop the pain and also not to let you die. You also prayed that this was not the doing of one of the spirits your mother was so fond of casting out when she prayed and finally, that you were not pregnant, even though you were taught by your *tete* that girls could only get pregnant once they had graduated into womanhood by getting married to a man with a car. You made it through the night. You made it through the night and you woke up relieved to feel that the pain had lessened. However, you nearly fainted from shock a second time when you saw that there was again blood between your legs and also on the sheets. You repeated the last night's cleansing rituals and kept up a constant stream of pleading directed to God and, out of desperation, also your dead great grandparents. When your father shouted at you asking where his food was you decided to make do and so you stuffed half a roll of toilet paper and your face towel between your legs because as you were bathing you noticed that a small trickle of blood kept coming. You prepared your father's breakfast and as you served him he shouted at you to walk normally.

By the time you had walked to school the blood has seeped through the tissue and there were three red spots on your brown skirt so you decided to turn back and head home. Some girls a few forms above you pointed and giggled and one of the boys known best for his theatrics pretended to vomit. Your father was surprised to see you and asked what you had done to be sent back from school so early. You showed him your skirt and when he pulled a face you burst into tears. He asked you why you were crying and before you could answer he told you to stop disgusting him and make his lunch. You didn't go to school for the next two days but instead stayed indoors tending to your father and sister and washing and rewashing your bloody face towel. Your little sister asked if you were sick but you lied and said no because you did not want to worry her.

On the third day your mother came home as jovial as ever. She asked you why you looked like you had seen a ghost and to make dinner because could you not see that she was tired from her long journey. She was dismissive and that hurt your feelings so you decided to show her what was wrong. You went to your bedroom and removed the wad of toilet paper from between your legs. There was nothing. There was no blood and when you examined yourself you discovered that the blood had stopped as suddenly as it had started. This made you both sad and happy. You were happy that you would not die yet you were sad because now your mother would never know the extent of your suffering. Even if you told her what had been happening the past three days would she believe such a bizarre story? At dinner when she asked how everything had been whilst she was away you told her casually that you had nearly died from blood that was coming out from a new hole down there. Your father said "*pfutseke*," and your mother told you not to say inappropriate things at the table whilst your sister gasped and clutched your arm- the only one who was concerned about your well-being. Your mother scolded your sister and told her to stop being a crazy person, all the while whipping out her breast to feed your baby brother who had started crying as if on cue after your dramatic statement. Her bare breast reminded you of Mainini and so in an effort to lighten the mood you mentioned to her that Mainini had come for a visit. Your father looked at you sternly and your little sister looked confused as she had not seen Mainini so you said she had not slept in your room. Your father interrupted you and told your mother that you had been sick and hallucinating for the past three days and said that Mainini had come only for five minutes to ask for money to help with her college applications and that he had generously given her five dollars. Your mother praised God for her husband's generosity towards her side of the family and said that some husbands only want to bless their own side of the family, but not him.

The next day your mother threw three padded cotton towels onto the bed beside you and told you to put one between your legs when you bled again. Why did she say when and again? She also, without looking at you, told you that it is important for women to be hygienic and that you should bath as often as possible now. She finished off by telling you not to do ungodly things. You later learned in biology class that menstruation was one of the natural yet burdensome parts of being a woman. You wondered why it seemed like a big secret or something to be ashamed of if it was natural and when you asked your mother this she told you to stop being stupid and to make yourself useful and sweep the house.

Several months after you started your period you caught your uncle staring at you in a weird way when he came for one of his after church visits. It made you uncomfortable and so you went to change into one of the few dresses of yours that still fit modestly and that were not affected by all the fat you had gained around your thighs and on your chest. Your mother hated the fat, as did you. After your uncle made a comment about how big you were getting your mother made sure to remind you every day that you were fat, even pinching your fatty bits for emphasis. You tried to starve yourself so that you could get your former boyish build back because your fat caused uncomfortable attention, even from people you did not know. In form two teachers sometimes mistook you for a senior girl because of your uneven fat deposits. Sadly, no amount of starving yourself alleviated the situation and when you refused to eat the rice and beef stew at Tete's house she scolded you to stop being ridiculous as growing hips and breasts, as she put it, was a natural part of womanhood. The thought of you getting closer to womanhood excited you yet the stares and occasional catcalls still made you uncomfortable. Your mother continued to scold you for becoming a woman and many of the children in your form at school did to. Besides your two friends Chipo and Hope, no one else wanted anything to do with you.

That is, until you noticed at break time, one of the senior boys smiling at you. You smiled back to be polite and just before you looked away you noticed him whispering something to his friend which made him look at you and smile too. From then onward the senior boys began to say hello to you on occasion. One of the boys in form four even offered to carry your bag to class for you but you politely declined. One of the boys in lower six took an interest in you and the more he waited for you after school and talked about everything as he walked you to the road just before the road which you lived on, the more you took an interest in him. One day on a particularly hot day in summer he bought two freezits, a blue one and a red one, and he offered you the blue one- a rarity both in deed and colour.

All the attention stopped as unexpectedly as it had started. Your father saw you walking home with the boy in lower six and he saw you happily sucking on his freezit. That night he and your mother took turns beating you with a hosepipe till your crying and pleading turned into gagging as your spit and tears blocked your throat. You promised to never let him or anyone else walk you home or buy you freezits again and when your father told your mother that you were probably pregnant you silently wondered how that could be since you were not married to a man with a car. You went to school the next day with welts on your legs and a swollen face. After school you ran home, not wanting to have to explain to your lower six boy why he could no longer be your friend. You did not understand the pain you felt in your chest two weeks later when, by chance, you saw your lower six boy walking a light skinned form four girl home. You did not understand the pain in your chest but you took one of your mother's aspirins for it and that seemed to help.

As if by your parents' doing the swelling on

your face was replaced by little bumps which you learnt from some of the whispering girls is called acne and, like one of them pointed out, in your case, a severe case. Your face hurt as some of the pimples oozed and popped and left little black scars. The senior boys stopped smiling at you and your lower six boy with the light skinned form four girl pretended not to have heard you when you said hello two times when you passed each other on the fields at break time. Apart from Chipo and Hope- who also had a few bumps on her face- everyone seemed repelled by you.

You are now in form four and a lot has happened in the past two years. Most importantly you are doing well in school and you feel no fear for your O'level Zimsec exams in a few months. Most of the rest of your form seem to have graduated into womanhood and a few of them even have a severe case of acne. Yours is no longer that severe however and the black marks have just become a part of your identity. Apart from the monthly visits, the acne scars and your rounded hips and bouncing chest, your stretch marks are the only other sign of puberty. However, apart from physical signs there are no social signs of puberty. The boys prefer the other girls over you. They prefer the lighter skinned girls or the ones who smile perfect smiles and wear silky weaves. Even Sekai who is the darkest human being many people have ever seen has a boyfriend in lower six. Maybe this is because she walks around with her luminous green or pink bra straps easily visible against her charcoal shoulders. None of the girls are interested in your friendship either except for Chipo. Hope and her family moved to South Africa at the end of form two. You aren't rich or pretty enough for the other girls, and even though Chipo is still your friend and you often study together on weekends, she has been skipping out on more and more study dates in favour of other people's parties which you obviously are not invited to. You cannot blame anyone though, it's not like you make an effort to befriend anyone. You prefer the company of numbers and even when it is the other person who makes the effort to befriend you, you usually decline. Last term, Godi the ugliest senior boy, the one with the chapped lips, dry greyish skin and no muscles, asked you if you wanted to spend break time in the bathroom with him. Being asked to spend break time in the bathroom by a senior boy is, according to the whispering girls, a prestigious thing. You aren't sure what spending twenty minutes in the bathroom with a boy achieves because when you asked the whispering girls they laughed and told you not to worry as it would never happen to you but what you do know is that after those twenty minutes your friendship circle doubles and you are invited to a lot more places by a lot more people. Nevertheless, when Godi the ugliest senior boy asked you to spend break time with him in the bathroom you blushed and politely declined, ignoring the growing part of you that felt alone and rejected. Surprisingly, after you declined his offer ugly Godi tried to chat you up every day. He had a way of standing too close to you which was irritating because he spits when he talks and he does not smell decent. One day when he had spat on you one too many times you yelled at him to leave you alone. He took a hold of your wrist and more than his tight grip, his sandpaper skin hurt you. He came closer still and whispered into your ear how no one rejects G-man and gets away with it, which is a curious thing to say because it is a widely known fact that everybody rejects Godi. After he said this he planted a moist kiss on your ear before running off and that night you went home and rubbed your ear with a towel dipped in Dettol and hot water until your skin started peeling off. The next day and for several weeks after that people pointed and laughed at you more than usual and you were confused as to why, until one of the whispering girls- the coloured one with the long slender fingers who smelt like lavender- came up to you, tapped your protruding stomach whilst you were eating a peanut butter sandwich and said, "Eating for two *nhai, Amai Godi*." It infuriated you that ugly Godi would start such vile rumours, but even more so, that other girls did not know that much like the entire female population, you would rather join a nunnery than ever end up with Godi.

Not long after you turn down ugly Godi and

the rumours subside due to Amari's- one of the whispering girls- actually being pregnant, an older man with a car rolls down his windows and calls you beautiful on your way home from school- something a boy your own age has never uttered in your direction- so you are bound to feel some kind of special, right? Then he offers to buy you ice cream- a luxury you last had before 2008 when your father still had a steady job. That's the stuff that fairy tales are made of. He comes back tomorrow and the day after that, your shoes no longer know the Zimbabwean dust because he picks you up in his air conditioned car and makes you feel loved, like you are worth more than the dog your mother says you are every time a man looks at you the way your uncle did three years ago after church. Your mother also said no man would want you because of your particularly bad acne and even after it got better she makes an effort to remind you of the black scars that have become part of your identity.

Did I mention that this older man, whom you now affectionately call Daddy, gives you pocket money? You share it with Chipo because after all she was there when you were nobody- before the new clothes and perfumes and fresh chips and pizza. Daddy is an answer to a prayer you didn't know you prayed.

You did not think you would fall in love so easily, especially not with an older man. You clapped your hands in disgust together with the other women in your neighbourhood whilst gossiping about Linette who only lived in a good house because she was willing to do things for and to older men. You also look down on the senior boys who prey on form ones and twos. But with you and Daddy it's different, this is real. You know it is real because he chose you. He drove past all the light skinned, perfectly smiling girls and stopped his car next to you even though you were obviously a loner as you were walking by yourself. He did not ask to spend twenty minutes with you in the bathroom without even knowing your name. Instead, he named you Beautiful. You agreed to get into his car because you had had enough of being alone and also you wanted to show everyone that you could do much better than ugly Godi. You got into his car the next day because he drove you home safely the previous day without hurting you or asking for anything.

So after a month of being treated like a princess when he put his hand up your thigh whilst you ate the burger he bought you in his air conditioned car you didn't think much of it. There was nothing wrong with him touching you after everything he'd done for you. However, when he takes your school shirt and bra off completely before dropping you home from a school debate event at seven in the night your mind jumps to the scriptures they hammered into your head at church. But who can think with warm and wet lips going down their neck? You push him away before it goes too far yet he holds on for a while longer and calls you beautiful. After you insist that he let you go he sits back in his seat and straightens his tie whilst you get dressed and lectures you on how you should know that he would never hurt you and how, quite frankly, he is hurt that you do not trust him after everything he has done for you. Alone in your room that night you cannot concentrate on homework because of how those few minutes made you feel. Daddy made you feel things you had never before felt. Your body tingled and you wondered why you needed the toilet as soon as he let you out the car. Above all, however, you feel some sort of guilt. You resolve that it will never happen again. That this one time was your way of thanking him for the new cell phone he got you.

He comes to your gate on a Saturday whilst your parents are at a funeral. He has never really paid attention to you on a weekend so you are feeling all sorts of princess.

"Hop in beautiful," he says, "I'm taking you to lunch." What? He'd never taken you anywhere besides between home and school before. He takes you to Meikles- not Chicken Inn like the boys your age would have done if they even paid attention to you. You eat a gourmet chicken and avocado burger and curly fries. He eats lasagne whilst making you laugh. "Do you want a taste of my vodka cocktail?" You blush and tell him you don't drink beers. "Ah come on, how can a beautiful woman like you not drink? It's time you embrace the woman you are. Can we have a vodka cocktail for the lady?" he yells at the waitress. The waitress returns with the drink. Behind her forced grin you can see the judgement flowing from her eyes. You think that she herself probably drinks so why is she judging? Not knowing that her main concern is of the ambiguity of you and Daddy's relationship. He is old enough to be your father. "Do you want dessert, Sweetheart?" Dessert? You've never had dessert before which wasn't an apple or banana or, during the rainy season, a bull mango. You have malva pudding and another vodka cocktail because with the strawberry flavour you can hardly taste the alcohol. Plus, it makes you happy and relaxed and that makes Daddy happy and he is paying for the meal which makes you happy. He takes out his iPhone and takes an unsuspecting photograph of you which makes you giggle and when he shows you how your eyes were half closed in the photo you insist that he deletes that one and that he take a better one. He promises you that he will take plenty of photos of you later on which excites you because you will ask him to Bluetooth them to your new phone so that you can show Chipo and the other handful of girls who have decided to be your friend since Daddy came into your life.

Whilst you finish off your dessert a suited man comes up to the table. He looks similar to Daddy complete with a balding head and pot belly. He smells like a typical Zimbabwean business man- like quantity and not quality. “Pastor Mugwati, how are you?” This is weird, you’ve never seen Daddy look nervous before. “Oh the wife? Yes, the wife and Baby Maka are fine! They went to visit Mainini in Jo’burg.” Thoughts are racing through your head. What is he talking about? “Pastor Mugwati, meet my niece. Yes, she’s visiting.” The pastor takes your limp hand in his firm and sweaty grasp in a calculated handshake before leaving. Daddy wipes his brow with a handkerchief once you two are alone again.

“Why are you asking questions?” he says when you begin to ask questions. In the air conditioned car you tell him that you don’t want to see him anymore what with his wife and child. “My wife and I are in the midst of a divorce.” He turns your sullen head to face him. “My wife is not as sexy as you are. No one is.” What did he just call you? You once heard one of the whispering girls, the ones who could afford the long weaves from China, you once heard one of them in the bathroom say for a man to call you sexy means that he thinks of you as a real woman, as desirable. And who doesn’t want to be desired? “I’ll make it up to you, Baby. How about I take you to a hotel tonight? You said your parents are only coming back tomorrow evening? We can go to a hotel and watch DSTV. Have you ever watched DSTV?" DSTV is something you've only heard of but never watched. The thought of it excites you so much that you release your inhibitions. You agree to be picked up at seven p.m.

The hotel is actually one of those lodges you pass by between town and home but you don't mind because you've never been inside anyway. After some pizza he removes his shirt and lies down on the squeaky bed, "It's hot, come lie down." You giggle and comply. When will the DSTV begin? You both lie still for a long time, he smells like his air-conditioned car, a smell you later learn is Axe Body Spray. You lie very still, too afraid to question the authenticity of the possibility of DSTV. Since lunch you have been day dreaming about watching Gossip Girl and Top Gear and The Simpsons- all the programmes that people with DSTV at home constantly talk about and discuss at break time.

Your heart nearly jumps out your chest and you let out a startled exclamation when he suddenly rolls on top of you. He puts his hand over your mouth, "Don't be scared, Sweetheart, I love you. Haven't I shown you that I love you all this time? You are the most exquisite woman I've ever laid eyes on." In all your life you never dreamed that a man like this would love you and say these words to you. Temporarily, you forget DSTV.

"I want you forever. I love you, I've shown you that. So how will you show me?" With that he begins to methodically and expertly undress you. He begins by unbuttoning your blouse. It is the sky blue one that he bought you a few weeks ago. You are slightly embarrassed when your shirt comes off because you are not wearing your one good bra as you did not anticipate this. The one you have on is old and is a rather off-white colour- no longer ivory. The strap ripped off a year ago so you sewed it back on with red thread- not your best craftsmanship. You are relieved when he doesn't seem to mind. He fumbles with the clip at the back for a few seconds before it snaps open. You remember the night you promised yourself that this would never happen again, but he had taken you to lunch and now you were in a fancy lodge, where would you have gotten such opportunities were it not for him? You try to relax and allow him the pleasure of kissing your chest but you panic. You panic, and he can tell from your anxious breathing because he tells you to relax, perhaps a little too roughly. He begins to unbutton your black bootleg jeans. You want to leave but if you tell him you are scared won't it seem like you are ungrateful? And yet you are grateful, very grateful. But you don't think your mother or Tete would like what you think is about to happen, and in any case, it may be too late now because he is also naked and saying anything may anger him and you don't want that because he may stop loving you. You are confused because is this what it means to graduate into womanhood? Is this the man with the car who will make you a real woman? Before Daddy, no one had ever told you they love you. So, Daddy must love you as it is not a statement freely said. Daddy said he'd take care of you forever and so far, he has, more than anyone ever has. He is on top of you and he is heavy but you can handle it because you are a real woman. That's what he called you- a real woman- and you nervously think you feel like one for the first time ever.

Condoms. You remember the condom adverts on ZBC. "Condoms are for people who don't love each other. Come on, Sweetheart, I love you. Don't you love me?" By now you can feel a painful thump where blood started coming out of four years ago when you sought help from your father whom you found sharing a bed with Mainini.

If you back out now you aren't a real woman. If you don't let it happen you'll lose the only thing that has ever made you feel alive. Your mother always scolds you to close your legs when you forget to sit like a lady on hot days. Daddy never scolds you. He says he loves you. So, you open your legs and let Daddy happen.

GOD OF MAN

"U*ne* wrist band *here*?" Banele shook his head at the usher who was crouched beside him to indicate that he did not understand. "Do you have a wristband? The healing power wrist band," the usher repeated. Although his English was much better than his Shona, Banele stared at the usher blankly such that the usher sighed and continued. "A healing power wrist band. You need one for the process. I assume you are here for your healing, yes?" The usher's eyes flittered over the bulging growth protruding out from under Banele's right armpit. Banele saw the brief look of disgust and hoped he had cleaned himself enough for the growth not to smell, at least for the morning. He covered it up with the knitted blanket his mother had made him for that purpose before he left from Bulawayo to Harare. Banele looked around at the throngs of people surrounding him, their hands upraised in praise and worship. He noticed that each and every person he saw had a healing power wrist band fastened securely to their wrist. Some people even had two wrist band on their wrist or one on each wrist. The plump, beige woman with the manicured finger nails near the stage in the front appeared to have three wrist bands on her right hand, and the left hand which was holding up her leatherbound Bible, had five.

As Banele turned back towards the usher who was pocketing some money he had received from someone two rows back and breaking off a wrist band and handing it over, a sharp pain ran through his body from his right armpit all the way down his spine to his left leg. He winced in pain. The usher turned to leave. "How much is healing power band?" he asked through gritted teeth as the pain began to subside.

"Six US dollars or twenty-four bond note," the usher replied. He tore off a wrist band and held it out towards Banele. Banele reached his left hand across his torso, trying to ignore the pain. He looked at the thick red wrist band. It was beautiful and he could feel its powers as his hand got nearer to it. The words 'Healing Power' written on its circumference were in the prettiest font he had ever seen and to his amazement he saw that there was a string attaching a small cardboard print out of the prophet and his prophetess to the wristband where you clip it. Suddenly, the power he felt exuding from the wrist band was withdrawn as the usher pulled it away from his reaching left arm. “Six dollars please, for your healing power wristband.”

Banele opened his mouth to speak but seemed not to be able to find the words to tell the usher that he did not have that kind of money. His mother had sold their only rooster and most of their hens to get him the ten dollars he needed for the bus ride to Harare and the five dollars she had given him as pocket money had all been taken when, at a police road block, the bus conductor had demanded that they all pay two dollars each for the road block fees or be left behind. There had been seven road blocks on the journey and Banele had only survived being thrown out when the other passengers had threatened to beat the conductor up for trying to leave a sick man behind. He was staying with his mother’s cousin and his family in Chitungwiza but he knew that they did not have any extra money to lone him. Just him being there was a strain on their resources and he remembered seeing his uncle taking a lone two-dollar bill from under his mattress and giving it to his wife to go and find meat to celebrate his nephew’s coming. All seven of their children had been excited at supper time that night besides the fact that they only got a piece of meat the size of a kidney bean each. "I don't have the money," Banele finally confessed.

"Well, you need it for your healing," the usher said in his monotone voice, waving the bunch of wrist bands in Banele's general direction.

"Please. What if I just take it for now. I will return it afterwards. I'm telling you truth," Banele pleaded with the usher.

"Maybe you can talk to an elder," the usher said waving the bundle of wrist bands in the general direction of the front row of men in pristine Italian suits near the stage. Someone whistled and the usher turned back to see a man signalling for him to come. He turned and hurried away.

"Please..." Banele called after him taking out the five-cent bond coin he had in his pocket which was for his transport back to Chitungwiza. It was too late; the usher had disappeared into the throngs of people together with his bunch of wrist bands and their healing powers.

* * *

Divine Chamunoda was an IT administrator by profession. He had, however, not been able to secure a full-time job since he graduated nearly five years ago, so whilst he was still looking he worked in an internet café doubling up as the cashier and the tech assistant. He was born and raised in rural Nyanga where his mother still lived but after form four he had decided to take a chicken bus to Harare and force his father to take care of him and pay for his academic endeavours. He arrived in Harare to find that his father had a whole other family and that his step-mother was not too fond of him. Be that as it may this never deterred Divine from his goal to get a higher education. He had always been a hard-working but rather average student and his mother had always told him that education was his only way out of a life of poverty and so he would stop at nothing to obtain a degree, which he did after only having to repeat two out of his four college years.

On his off days Divine still came into town, partly to get away from his nagging step mother but also to hustle. He would stop at nothing to get his big break and so he would walk from building to building dropping off his CV which he sealed in a crisp brown A4 envelope. On one particular day he was seated on a bench in Harare Gardens during lunch eating a pork pie and drinking a cascade when a street preacher took the opportunity to evangelize to those resting in the park during their lunch break, sitting on the park benches and frolicking on the grass with their significant others. He was so emphatic with his deliverance of the gospel that within ten minutes a sizable crowd had gathered around him. He preached about how he was an ex-convict and how in jail he had found the Lord, or rather, the Lord had found him, and now that he was released he went around the city and other jails delivering the gospel to all who cared to listen. Forty minutes later he finished his sermon with a prayer and at the end of it all the crowd dispersed, leaving him standing in a pool of bond coins and even a couple of scrunched up dollar bills which he quickly gathered up in his fedora before hurrying off to the next park or street corner to deliver the same sermon. Divine, more of a follower of the African Traditional Religion, had not been one of those that had crowded around him. He had remained on his bench a way off eating his pork pie, but he did notice, from where he was, the glint in each coin as it reflected the hot sun off of its polished surface. Two men sat opposite him discussing how it was possible to turn one's life around after having been in jail. "I tell you though," joked one of the men whilst opening his lunch box which contained his lunch of sadza and *mazondo*, "the quickest way to make money in this day and age is to start a church." Divine took the last sip of his cascade, threw the pork pie wrapper on the grass and left the park bench with a new-found resolve.

* * *

Thandiwe was a sceptic but she was glad that she had been put in charge of the story because then, she believed, she'd be able to get to the bottom of it. The editor-in-chief had announced in their weekly meeting the previous week that Mrs Chikwewa had finally agreed, at a fee, to allow them, and exclusively them, to interview her about Makomborero- her miracle baby. All five journalists had volunteered to go but in the end the editor in chief, remembering the warm evening he and Thandiwe had shared the previous Friday, had picked her because, he said to the other journalists, Thandiwe was a woman so would better understand maternal matters.

Thandiwe stepped out of the company vehicle which left her just outside of the Chikwewa home and brushed off invisible dust particles from her grey pantsuit. She was giddy with excitement about the upcoming interview and she had done her homework thoroughly. She liked to think herself above all the other journalists in Zimbabwe because she knew none of them put in as much research as she did, after all, she had watched every bit of footage that had the slightest thing to do with Mrs Chikwewa and Apostle Patrick – the apostle who untied her womb through prayer. Thandiwe was ambitious and in her five-year plan she indicated that she wanted to be the government's top investigative journalist by the time she was thirty-five, no matter what it took.

Thandiwe had done her homework, and as such she knew that there was footage of the Wednesday church service that Mrs Chikwewa received her healing, but, surprisingly, there was no footage of Apostle Patrick administering healing upon her. Thandiwe had had to pay money from her own pocket, amongst other things, to acquire footage from that day that wasn't broadcasted. From an almost aerial wide shot taken from the very back of the church and which showed the entire front of the church including the side doors that led to prayer rooms she saw, or thought she saw a woman that resembled Mrs Chikwewa and Apostle Patrick enter into a prayer room, unaccompanied by any guards, ushers or cameramen. They entered the room just after the midday lunch break and only came out just before the end of the service. Apostle Patrick looked powerful as he strode out of the room confidently, but Mrs Chikwewa looked small and meek and slightly bewildered. A man's hand just off screen to the left of the frame was then visible pulling Mrs Chikwewa along until she too was off screen whilst the powerful Apostle Patrick climbed up on stage and took his seat among the other apostles behind the man of God who was giving his closing encouragements and suggesting the third impromptu offering collection of the day.

The company vehicle hooted once again and startled Thandiwe out of her day dream. It drove off when a small smiling man pushed the gate open. Thandiwe identified him as Mr Chikwewa, father of the miracle baby and possibly the owner of the off-frame hand. He was a short, smiling man with greying hair on each side of his head but not the front or the middle. He good naturedly ushered her into the small house and offered her a seat on the maroon velvet sofas before going to call his wife. A beaming Mrs Chikwewa walked into the living room nursing the miracle baby Mako herself. Before taking her seat, the proud mother held the baby in front of Thandiwe for her to see and then sat down and returned the fussing baby to her breast.

"Let me make some tea," the little Mr Chikwewa said. He got up and hurriedly shuffled towards the kitchen.

As soon as he was out of ear shot Mrs Chikwewa enquired, "Have you got my token of gratitude?"

"Ah," Thandiwe said, fishing out of her brief case the small brown envelope with Mrs Chikwewa's thirty-eight US dollars and the sound recorder she had purchased online to use to record the interview because, she thought, pen and paper was so old fashioned.

"Thanks, Dhali. You know," the miracle mother said as she stuffed the envelope into her bra against the breast that was not being suckled on, "I'm more than happy to do this interview. It is like a testimony, although I already gave my testimony at church last Sunday, but this one will reach even the drunkards who spend their Sundays in the bars as even drunkards read newspapers." Thandiwe had watched her testimony footage also just the previous night. She examined Mrs Chikwewa closely as she turned to watch her hobbling husband bring in a tray with tea and Lemon Cream Biscuits. The woman that sat before her was very different from the woman she had seen on screen. On screen Mrs Chikwewa was small and timid with a constant look of bewilderment. She always had a head wrap on and she held her head to the side when she talked. However, the woman in front of her was confident and in control with her head held high and a dark brown Rihanna weave which she tapped at occasionally.

Thandiwe thanked Mr Chikwewa for the tea and poured herself and the Miracle Mother, under her close instructions of course, a cup. Mr Chikwewa, after some time, excused himself saying gently, "This is woman talk I see, I'll leave you to it."

Thandiwe pressed the record button on her recorder and set it on the table next to the Lemon Cremes, "Let us begin. First of all, congratulations."

"Thank you," Mrs Chikwewa beamed. "She was born on the fifth of November at four kilograms by C-section at Harare Hospital after the apostle prayed for me, under instruction of Papa of course."

"Papa being ..."

"The Man of God of course. He is our father," Mrs Chikwewa clarified, rocking her baby gently. Thandiwe looked down at the gurgling baby and smiled at it the best she could. She found infants to be rather inconvenient.

"Can you tell me about the actual time you received your healing? What was it like?"

"Well... you know," Mrs Chikwewa began dubiously before regaining her confidence. "Well, it was normal. I was prayed for after purchasing all the necessary symbols of faith and I was taken to the front during the time of miracles and healing and Apostle Patrick laid hands on me and…"

"Oh, so you weren't prayed for in one of the prayer rooms?" Thandiwe interjected, eyeing a lemon creme unsurely.

"Well, I mean…" there was a pause here. Mrs Chikwewa put Mako on her shoulder and tapped at her back until the baby burped. "Oh yes, I remember now. You see it was nearly ten months ago now. Yes, the Holy Spirit told Apostle that he was to pray for me and so he divinely singled me out of the crowed and I was blessed that I was to get a private prayer session."

Thandiwe could feel tension rising in the room. She had taken an online course in interviewing and so she knew not to push Mrs Chikwewa too hard too fast. It was important for her to always feel comfortable. Still, Thandiwe was sceptical of this particular miracle and of all miracles in fact. "So, what was it that you suffered from that the apostle administered healing to?"

"It was my womb. It was blocked you see, probably by a jealous relative. I'd been barren since I got married eighteen years ago even though we tried for a baby every day. I am lucky to have a God-fearing man for a husband who did not leave me to find a fertile woman," she responded with a smile. She continued, "The man of God simply prayed for me and then said go and meet with your husband and then a week later I was pregnant. Isn't God great?"

"Yes, He is," Thandiwe said. She herself had last set foot in a church ten years ago and she did not believe what she had just agreed to. Still, she thought, it was important to keep Mrs Chikwewa happy. "So, can you describe what happened when the church leader..."

"Apostle."

"Yes, when Apostle prayed for you," she said. She picked up a lemon crème biscuit, took a bite out of it and leaned forward in her seat, waiting for what she had been waiting for all week long.

"He simply laid hands on my womb and prayed for me. I felt something move within me-the Holy Spirit healing me through Patri, err, Apostle Patrick, and then I went home and met with my husband," Mrs Chikwewa finished. She was now wiping at her baby's face with a blanket and Thandiwe thought she seemed to have lost some of her confidence.

"Oh, the Apostle prayed for you. For two hours?" Thandiwe hazarded. She had gotten enough to write her article for the paper but now she just wanted information for her own morbid curiosity.

"No, no, it was a brief..."

"The video recording showed that you were in the prayer room with the Apostle for three hours nearly," Thandiwe interjected ruthlessly. "What were you two doing in there with no guards or ushers or cameramen?"

Mrs Chikwewa rocked her baby even though the baby was now fast asleep. She tapped at her Rihanna weave and then dug her index finger in between the cornrows under the weave and scratched hard. "We, ah... he was praying for me. You know healing doesn't always come fast like how we expect it to..."

"But luckily this time it did come, right?" Thandiwe was basically snarling now.

Mrs Chikwewa looked confused, "Ha, what? Yes of course, that is how my miracle baby Makomborero is here with us today."

Thandiwe threw the last bite of her biscuit in her mouth and clicked her voice recorder off.

"That's all I need Mrs Chikwewa, thank you," she smiled as she stood up and brushed crumbs off her lap.

"Huh, are you sure?" Mrs Chikwewa looked up at her imploringly. Somehow, she had

transformed before Thandiwe's very eyes into the meek and timid lady at church with her head to the side and a bewildered look on her face.

Mr Chikwewa shuffled in very suddenly and seemingly from nowhere. "Leaving already? Let me walk you out."

"Goodbye miracle baby," Thandiwe smiled down sweetly at the sleeping bundle before turning on her heels and walking out the way she had walked in.

* * *

Divine Chamunoda, since that day on the park bench, had joined a church. He had joined one of those new churches that spring up every other month in the Harare CBD, one of those churches that has its Sunday services in a dark musty room on the second floor of a nondescript pre-colonial building, usually above a supermarket. It was a church that the older generation termed as church *yemweya mweya* – one of those churches where people jumped and gyrated and writhed on the floor making troubling sounds during praise and worship and one of those churches that a demon was mandatorily cast out of a congregant whom, until then, had not even been aware that he or she was possessed. Divine had volunteered his demons nearly every other Sunday and this pleased the church's leader who people called Prophet and his wife the Prophetess. They took him aside after a year of his attendance and said that the Lord had shown them that he showed great promise and that he was surely called to ministry if he would just answer Jesus who was knocking on the door of his heart. That very day they made him the church's treasurer and collection collector. This meant also that he was permitted to give a very short sermon before the offering baskets went around and at this, like all other things, he excelled. He moved people so much with his messages of God giving them back ten times the amount that they dropped in the offering basket before the week was over that people felt compelled, by the spirit of course, to empty their purses and wallets into the basket as it passed. For those who did not have cash, Divine acquired a transaction money machine for them, and those with no kind of money whatsoever Divine placed an old TV box near the back of the church against the wall so that people could drop items of their clothing in. The prophet and prophetess promoted him to apostle level and there he stayed for many months, preaching every other month and earning an income. The Prophet and his wife loved him and he loved them. He did all he could for the church and immersed himself deeply in its word.

* * *

The small shivering man was brought to the front during the third forty-minute-long prayer session. Two different ushers had come and scratched Elder Shiri on the shoulder and whispered in his ear that there was a boy who was desperate to see him. The third and fourth time that someone had scratched him on the shoulder it had been the boy himself. His odour had preceded him. Elder Shiri was at first offended by the tenacity of them all. The ushers knew that no impromptu healings were to be brought without two weeks' notice and all the necessary preparations, and the guards had been trained not to let just anybody up past the two thirds demarcation in the stadium. How the small shivering man had managed to hobble all the way to the front undetected he did not know. Elder Shiri was at first offended but then he began to think that perhaps this was a sign from

God. At first he wondered, but then he became very much convinced that today was the day that God would uplift him to higher places and higher powers. That is why he agreed to have the boy brought to him for prayer during the third prayer session.

Elder Shiri, though well respected and revered in the church, was not in the Man of God's inner circle. The Man of God, or MOG as his friends affectionately referred to him, had not yet ordained him to Apostle level and this meant, according to the church's constitution which he knew off by heart, that he was not to pray for healing for anyone unless instructed to or in the presence of one of the apostles or the MOG, the Prophet himself. Nevertheless, he believed that if he brought healing upon the small boy then the MOG would see that he was indeed capable of harnessing the power of the Holy Spirit and that he deserved a promotion.

Elder Shiri told the ushers to bring the boy to him in one of the prayer rooms behind the church together with two out of the two dozen cameramen who recorded the day long church service every Sunday and Wednesday. He wanted to make sure that there was proof for the MOG and the rest of the nation to see, including their sister churches in Johannesburg and Gaborone. His deepest desire was to one day become a

Man of God too and this would be the early days footage that film companies would use in his biopics.

An usher came and told Elder Shiri that the prayer room was ready and that the boy and the camera crew were also ready for him. He walked slowly to the room and prayed for God's spirit to come upon him so that he would be able to perform the miracle. When he entered the room one of the guards – at least one guard always accompanied the notable persons of the church – was spraying lavender air freshener around the room and even on the small shivering boy. It was not enough to mask the stench of rotting flesh that was coming from the bulging growth protruding from the boy's armpit.

Elder Shiri clapped and sang for at least fifteen minutes whilst pacing up and down the room. This was how he got into the spirit and he knew that he really needed to be in the spirit if he was to heal the boy and watch the growth either shrink and disappear or fall off before his very eyes but more importantly, the camera lenses. He preferred that it fall off because that way it could be held up to the cameras and the boy could give his testimony before the church whilst holding it up as this would make for good dramatic effect. He had been singing and clapping for the past fifteen minutes and had encouraged the boy, the two cameramen, the one guard and the usher to join him. Everyone was swaying on their feet slightly by the time fifteen minutes had passed and the boy especially was shivering violently. Elder Shiri knew that this was the effects of the spirit and sensing that the room was saturated enough with the presence of the Holy Spirit for a healing to take place, he began to speak in tongues.

His speaking in tongues went on for ten minutes. It was accompanied by the intermittent moans of the boy who was now hunched over and clutching his right arm with his left hand. He was ready. Elder Shiri jogged around the room, feeling the power of the spirit strengthen in his chest and followed by one of the cameramen he raced around the room three times and then he sprinted to the centre of the room to where the boy was doubled over and struck him on his right shoulder just above the growth and with a booming voice he commanded, "Demon of growths, come out and take your house with you!"

Nothing happened.

Nothing happened except that the boy fell to the ground crying in pain and clutching his shoulder where Elder Shiri had struck him. Nothing had happened so Elder Shiri was confused because the image that God had put in his mind's eye was of him striking the boy's right shoulder and the growth falling off from his right armpit and landing, with a thud, just a few centimetres before his Salvatore Ferragamo shoes. He even saw a splatter or two of puss from the growth land on his suit leg but he did not mind because he would have accomplished God's work. None of this happened and after staring at the boy in pain for a few seconds Elder Shiri snapped back to his senses and remembered that nothing is ever easy. He knew that healing was not easy to administer, he had seen the MOG struggle himself a couple of times, especially with the impromptu healings, and so he told the usher to call in another usher and hold the boy up on his feet. With a round the room run start, Elder Shiri spoke in tongues and demanded the demon to leave the boy over and over and over again whilst striking him repeatedly on both shoulders and even once or twice on the head because it was never certain where on one's body a healer was to lay hands successfully. With each strike and command from the elder the boy cried out in pain as shots of electric anguish ran all over his body from the point of impact. Sweat mixed with sweat, from the boy in pain and the elder who was really over exerting himself in his task. He stopped striking the boy for a while and whilst still speaking in tongues in a tremulous voice he reached into his pocket and produced a vile of anointed oil. This he poured into his palm and used the same palm to slap the boy's cheeks. First the left one, then the right one, then the left one again. He continued to do this and when the oil ran out he went back to striking the boy on the shoulders and head.

Once the Elder was riled up he did not let up. His earnestness turned to anger as he fought the demon that was refusing to come out of the poor boy. No battle in the Bible was easily won but won it was, in the end. The elder shouted obscenities at the demon and spoke in tongues till spittle flew into the boy's face and the ushers' faces who were holding him up. He mopped his own brow with his handkerchief but did not once, in the thirty minutes that followed, let up. It was only when he noticed the one cameraman sneaking out the room that he seized his striking and turned to confront him, "And where, in God's name are you going?"

The cameraman looked back, alarmed that the man who had been so physically and emotionally invested in the attack of a demon would take issue with his silent departure. He stuttered, "The memory is full in this one," he pointed at the camera, "I'm going to the media booth to get a new card."

The man of God wiped the trickling sweat off his brow and turned back to the boy as suddenly as he had turned on the camera man. He stood there silently scrutinising the crying host of the stubborn demon and then he noticed it. He figured out why the demon was refusing to leave. It was not because he was not strong enough in the power to cast it out, it was, he noticed with horror and disgust, because the boy was wasting his time. "And where, in God's name is your healing power wrist band?" he boomed. "Let him go," he commanded the ushers who were only too happy to oblige him.

The whimpering boy sunk to his knees in pain without the support of the ushers. He was determined to receive his healing and so he found courage and spoke up for himself. "I, I no afford at this time. But God can heal me still?".

Elder Shiri spat on the ground in disbelief. He was incredulous and taken aback. He was angry too, that this boy had wasted his time. He began to jog around the room. "The devil is a liar," he declared. He pointed a finger to the floor and jumped up and down on the same spot whilst saying, "Satan, you have tried to make a fool out of me today, but I have caught you red handed, ha, ha."

Elder Shiri began to laugh. He began to laugh uncontrollably until he was clutching his pot belly and leaning against the wall for support. The lone cameraman moved closer to where he was for a better shot. Still laughing Elder Shiri shoved the camera away from his face and gesturing with his thumb toward the door he commanded, "Take the boy out of here. Be gone!" The boy was too weak to protest or beg for his healing, even though he knew that this growth that the nurses called a cancer would kill him.

* * *

Chishamiso was a petite, light-skinned congregant who often caught Divine staring in her general direction before looking away, but she did not mind at all. One Sunday, a demon that was within her decided that it needed to be cast out but, it vocalised in a gruff voice from the depths of her body whilst she was writhing on the floor when the prophet began to cast it out with holy water, it could only be cast out by Divine, which it addressed as the Mighty Prophet Divine. The prophet was taken aback but did not hesitate to beckon Divine to his calling. Within a minute, Divine had cast that demon, and as it revealed, its twin, out of Chishamiso who was left heavy breathing and quivering on the church floor for an hour afterwards. The congregation was amazed as there had never been a twin exorcism before and began to address Divine as Mighty Prophet even when he blushed and held his head to the side and insisted that he was still just Divine, a servant of the Lord. The congregants told their families about what had happened and the families told friends and soon the church had doubled in size and all huddled around Divine after services.

The Prophet and the Prophetess were, however, not among those that huddled around Divine. They were grateful to God that the twin demons had been cast out and that the church had grown, of course, but they felt that Divine was now intentionally distracting people from what was truly important – the Lord. One Sunday, with a heavy heart, the Prophet stood in front of the congregation and told them that God had given him a vision during the night. In the vision, it was revealed that Divine was in fact, himself, a demon, who had been sent to distract God's people. The prophet finished by saying that Divine was henceforth banished from the church and that he was ashamed of failing to notice the horns atop Divine's head for the past two months. The congregation was outraged. The younger of them shouted and jumped around screaming their disbelief in tongues. It was hard to understand whether they were shouting at the prophet for his vision or at Divine for being a demon. Divine maintained his composure and asked to say a few words. In his address he revealed that he too had had a vision the previous night in which he was Joseph and the prophet and prophetess were among his brothers who sold him into slavery. When he awoke from his vision the Lord had whispered in his ear that he was to become the leader of a new church which he was to name The Church of the Immaculate Holy Harvest of the Lord God on High. He said too that the Lord had also whispered secrets about the Prophet and how that very day the prophet was to spread lies about him out of jealousy. Before a guard roughly escorted him out and locked the door, he managed to warn the congregation about the prophet, saying solemnly, that the Lord had whispered to him that the prophet and his wife the prophetess were being used as puppets of the underworld. "I'll pray for you, let me pray for you!" he had called in their direction as the guard carried him out over his shoulder. The congregation was silent as the prophet stood behind the podium and began his sermon entitled 'You Reap What You Sow' but the following Sunday there were only a handful of congregants and no demons were cast out that day.

* * *

The prayer cloths came from Israel- the Man of God said so. Zviko was not sure where Israel was on a map but she was certain that the miracle cloths worked because it had worked for her soon to be husband and she was overjoyed. Zviko's soon to be husband did not know that he was her soon to be husband yet. He did not even know her, but she had faith. The man of God had said that you must declare what you want in the physical in the spirit and Zviko bound Nathanial in the spirit very hard every night with the blood and name of Jesus.

Nathaniel was a banker as far as Zviko could tell. She first noticed him after paying her ZESA bill at Megawatt House in town. Just as she was leaving the building she saw a man in a shiny grey suit walking into the bank opposite her. She also saw that he had a beard and she

associated beards with success so she walked after the man into the bank. Just as she got through the door she caught a glimpse of the back of him walk into the back section behind the teller counters and that is how she came to know that he worked there. She decided to wait for him in the waiting area, not knowing what she would do if she came face to face with him, but after an hour of her sitting there the guard saw that she had no banking business and asked her to leave. Zviko worked in a nearby hair salon so she knew she was able to observe her soon to be husband's coming and going easily and that is what she had done for the past month. From his interactions with the guard she learnt his first name. She learned that he liked shiny suits and African print ties. He got to work just after eight o'clock and left just before five o'clock. Some lunch times he would get a pie from the OK along First Street but, much to Zviko's concern, he did not have a car. One day she saw him leave the bank with a woman and a small boy and she had heart palpitations for the rest of the evening. She concluded the next day, after an extensive discussion with her fellow hair dressers Molly and Precious, that it was not his wife as the two had not, in the time that she had followed them to the kombi rank in Fourth Street, exchanged any affectionate physical contact or even terms of endearment. Even if, concluded Molly, it had been his wife, their body language – or there lack of- obviously showed that their marriage was in its final dying stages. Zviko's concern over his relationship status ebbed but her worry about the fact that he did not have a car grew. She was trying to rise up in the world, she had told Molly and Precious, thus it would not make sense for her to marry a man who wore a suit to work yet had no car. She could not be a banker's wife and still use public transport. It would not do.

Zviko did not always attend the Man of God's church at the sport stadium because it was expensive and most times she only ever got as far as to stand in the overflow section, but she did like to go at least once a month to keep her spirit levels up. Last month, when she went the ushers were holding out squares of plain white cloth. Some people already had their cloths and were waving them around during praise and worship. Zviko hated to feel left out but she had not brought any money with her to church save for her fifty-cent bond coin for transport back home, her fifty-cent bond coin for the offering and the twelve dollars her grandmother had sent her to pay Mbuya vaKuku back for the two chickens she had borrowed on her way home. Aside from having no money, Zviko the miser thought that ten dollars was too much to pay for a piece of plain white cloth the size of a pillow case, especially if that amount of material could be bought in the down town material shops for less than a dollar. In fact, she would go down town near Kaguvi street on her lunch break tomorrow and buy herself a piece of cloth and wave it in church the following Sunday.

It was only after the Man of God explained that the cloth was from Israel and had been hand woven on a blessed loom did she start to think that perhaps the pieces of cloth that the ushers were holding up were perhaps worth more than a dollar. When the man of God admitted that he had personally prayed and laid hands on each and every one of the one thousand – and there were only one thousand- cloths, Zviko felt the spirit compelling her to buy one. The man of God said this cloth was so spirit filled and powerful that it was an extension of himself almost. He said that if you saw something you wanted or needed and believed that by faith you would get that thing and then rubbed that thing you saw and wanted or needed with your prayer cloth- he called it a prayer cloth- then, in Jesus name, it would be yours. When he said this, that is when Zviko was convinced that she absolutely needed to purchase the prayer cloth. She could see it already, a life of luxury filled with everything she needed and wanted. With no hesitation she purchased a prayer cloth and immediately felt blessed beyond measure. Her grandmother was not happy about her expenditure, but Zviko assured her that she would earn the money back the following day as she had two clients booked at the salon and both of them wanted thin twist braids.

Zviko put her prayer cloth to work the very next day. There was one thing she wanted above all else in her life, and that was a man with a car, or more specifically, Nathanial with a car. On her lunch break, she left her client with her braids half done excusing herself for an important duty, and walked around town looking for her dream car. She walked down Samora Machel all the way down to Eighth Street and then down Eighth Street back up until she came to Mazowe Road. By this time her lunch hour was almost over so she turned left into Mazowe Road back towards the salon. And then, when she emerged on the road beside the National Gallery, she saw it- her dream car. It a matte-black Range Rover Sport, although she did not know it. All she knew was that Nathaniel would look great in it driving her to work and their children to school. She walked around it and peered inside, yes, she thought, it was big enough for at least six children. Hurriedly, because her client was phoning her on her cell phone now, she untied her prayer cloth from around her waist underneath her shirt and began to use it to wipe every single inch of the car. She was only half done when a man in a dashiki walked out and shouted at her for touching his car. She ignored him, only wiping faster, but when he came down the steps leading out of the gallery with a guard with a baton behind him she ran away, she ran all the way back to the salon with the prayer cloth in her hand. She finished her client's braids whilst recounting her adventures to Molly and Precious and even Zuka the barber who came in twice a week.

For a week after that Zviko travelled everywhere with her prayer cloth tied around her waist, hoping to spot her dream car somewhere so she could finish wiping it and declaring it and binding it in the spirit. She went to the gallery every morning before work and on her lunch breaks and on her way home too but she never saw the car again. One Wednesday, on her way out at the end of the day when she was just deciding that she needed to find another car that she could wipe down, she saw God's hand at work. There was Nathanial getting into the driver's seat of a car. It was not the matte-black Range Rover Sport, in fact it was a little golf, but it was black and besides, Zviko concluded to herself, wasn't a car a car. She praised God. Zviko also praised the Man of God and then went to look for one of those shops with wedding dresses in their display window.

* * *

The Church of the Immaculate Holy Harvest of the Lord God on High started off in the spacious Borrowdale yard of one of the congregants who had volunteered it to Divine, now known simply as Prophet. The prophet prophesied more wealth and prosperity over this congregant's life and it was revealed to him in a dream that he, Prophet Divine, should anoint this Borrowdale congregant as an Apostle in his church. Within a couple of months however, the spacious yard became too small, so the services moved to the Harare Conference Centre where Divine held double the amount of sermons and got double the amount of tithes and offering money. On God's instruction, of course, he anointed several more men, who coincidentally were the top financial contributors to the upkeep of the church, as apostles and it was these men he spent most of his time with and these men that helped him run the church, prophecy and cast out demons.

One Sunday during a particularly riveting sermon on prosperity and claiming victory in the spirit, the small light-skinned Chishamiso was rolled up to him on the stage in a wheel chair. "Heal me, Man of God," she had said, looking up at him from where she sat in her wheel chair. "Heal me," she repeated, never breaking eye contact. Prophet Divine the Man of God remembered the young woman from which he had extracted twin demons, but he did not remember her in a wheel chair. Taken aback and unsure of what to do he looked down into her imploring yet confident eyes. She reached out and touched his moist hand and it was then he felt a powerful surge as the spirit soured within him. As he looked into her glittering eyes he felt confident that he could heal her, with the power of the blood of Jesus, of course.

"My brothers and sisters, *hama neshamwari*," he boomed into the microphone turning to address the silent congregation now sitting at the edge of their seat. "Which of you has faith that this young girl will walk again?" The church erupted into noise and all shouted, cheered and clapped to demonstrate the great faith that they each possessed. Energized by their positive responses and his own faith in himself, Prophet Divine raced up and down the stage chanting in tongues into the microphone as spittle flew out of the sides of his mouth. After a minute he came to a stop in front of the disabled Chishamiso who smiled up at him with a twinkle in her eye and lay his left hand heavily upon her braided head. "I demand you to get up and walk in the name of Jesus!" he boomed into the microphone, shaking her head from side to side as she sat there. Chishamiso fell out of her wheel chair sideways and began writhing on the floor screaming and cursing. Prophet Divine, elated, took a step backwards and turned to address the excited congregation. "My brothers and sister it is a demon which has been causing her not to walk, as you can see." He turned back to Chishamiso. "Demon of disability, come out!" Chishamiso sat up, threw her head back and screamed a blood curdling scream, or rather, the demon screamed a blood curdling scream from within her, before throwing her back and causing her to writhe again. "Come out I say!" The demon caused Chishamiso to open her legs, and her open legs caused her tight pencil skirt to ride up her thighs. Mrs Shiri took off her coat and laid it over the writhing girl so that she may not be disgraced as the prophet was about to disgrace the demon by casting it out. "Come out!" Prophet Divine commanded again, taking a few steps backwards and mopping his forehead with his handkerchief. He did not expect it to be this hard to heal a disabled woman in a wheelchair, especially one who had looked up at him so imploringly confident with the prettiest brown eyes. "Wha, what do you want demon?" he managed to stutter after a while. The congregation was silent.

The girl stopped writhing and sat up, staring straight into the prophet's eyes. She threw her head back, or her head was thrown back, and her mouth was opened and from it came a gruff manly voice. "I am the demon of disability. I am hard to cast out but I know that soon I must leave this house that I have for the past many several years inhabited." The girl's mouth shut. She stared into the prophet's eyes but he, just like the congregation, was silent. Her head was thrown back again and from her throat the same gruff voice spoke again, "You are wondering how I entered her. It was in an accident. The motor vehicle collided with a tree. It was a tree that I was perching in looking for a house. I entered her whilst she was unconscious before an ambulance came and for the past fifteen years here I have stayed." Chishamiso's head snapped back up and she stared at the prophet who looked confused. Her head was snapped back again and the gruff voice, now in a panicked tone, said, "Oh mighty man of God do not make me leave this house for I have nowhere else to go, please!" Divine felt powerful as the demon begged for its life before him. He walked towards Chishamiso and she used her hands to push herself backwards away from his approach.

"Get out demon, in the name of Jesus, so this poor girl can walk again!" Prophet Divine, the Man of God, demanded. Chishamiso went limp for a few seconds before meekly coming to and looking around as if one just out of a deep sleep. She reached out her hand and Prophet Divine helped her get up and walk. The congregation went wild and a week later the Harare International Conference Centre was too small a venue for them and so the prophet moved his church to the bigger sports stadium, but still there had to be an overflow section.

It was at that same sports stadium with an overflow section that three months later Prophet Divine wed Chishamiso, the woman he had twice delivered from the jaws of the evil one. Chishamiso, according to the stickers, posters, T-shirts and other merchandise with the healing power of God that the church sold to its congregation, had since plumped out to nearly three times the size that she had been when she was in the devil's jaws and all praised God that the Prophet was taking care of his fragile and soft spoken wife well enough in their triple story house in the Grange which had a landing pad on the roof for his helicopter. It was also at the sports stadium that many miracles were performed. At first the healing and miracles were performed to new members of the congregation whom were only seen on that one day of their healing. They would appear when it was time for healing and prophecy and either leave with a prophecy of success and prosperity over their lives and holding their crutches, wheelchairs, back braces, hearing aids, bandages, growths and tumours in cooler boxes and sometimes a nondescript brown envelope, but after they left through the gates of the stadium having given their elated testimonies to a camera crew they were seldom seen again at the church. When more permanent congregation members came forward for prophecy and more specifically healing of an ailment or disability they were not so easily or miraculously healed by the prophet and his apostles. It was, the prophet said to the church at large and into the camera through which he was being broadcast live, because they lacked in faith. Healing and miracles could not take place in the absence of faith, thus, the congregation members who needed healing and prophecies needed to complete a rigorous course to strengthen their faith and prepare them emotionally and mentally for their miracle. The faith course was not for the faint hearted or the doubters or those who could not afford to pay for the course, buy the healing power wrist band, the holy water to spray on your bed every night and the bumper sticker with the prophet and his chubby wife's faces to stick on your car or over your front door for spiritual protection. Those that went through the faith strengthening course certainly had their faith strengthened.

The Church of the Immaculate Holy Harvest of the Lord God on High, the Man of God and his Apostles never ran out of fresh and innovative ways to help people who believed in the blood of Jesus. One Sunday it was prayer cloths, the following Sunday was a truck load of oranges which the Prophet and apostles had climbed on top of, praying and spraying with holy water and anointing oil as the congregation looked on before selling the blessed oranges at five US dollars each. The mediums which the power of God worked through were numerous and new and often unorthodox and not to be analysed too deeply. "My brothers and sisters, *hama neshamwari*," Apostle Patrick had announced one Sunday during the announcements, "The Man of God, Papa, Daddy, wants to be with you everywhere you go, in your homes, in your cars, so that you are blessed and protected every day of the week and not only during Sunday and Wednesday services." From his pocket he pulled out a plastic doll in the shape of a man which was thirty centimetres high and whose face vaguely resembled that of Prophet Divine. The oversized ken doll was clothed in a shiny red suit and leather slip on shoes. "That is why," Apostle Patrick continued, "it is imperative for each one of you to have one of these statues of the powerful man of God. Husband and wife, you are one in the Lord yes, but you cannot share. You each need your own as you are not always physically together every day of..." He continued to speak but Thandiwe no longer heard him as a crowd of ushers began walking through the aisles holding up trays of Prophet Divine dolls, their red suits glittering in the afternoon sun, and exchanging each doll for fifty-dollar bills. Thandiwe grabbed one and as the usher stood in front of her with his palm outstretched expectantly she turned the doll over in her hands. "*Izvi hazvizi zvechikwambo here izvi*? Witchcraft..." she inquired quietly to nobody in particular. She gave the doll back and clicked her voice recorder off and walking towards the stadium's exit.

* * *

Banele lay down on the dusty ground outside the sports stadium in pain listening to the sermon go on until early evening. He was in the very same spot that the two ushers had left him after his failed healing session. He thought about whether that failed healing session was his fault. He thought it was, even though from his diagnosis he had always had faith that God would heal him miraculously although he could not afford any sort of treatment save for the couple of painkillers his mother brought him every week. His and his mother's faith was what made him travel all the way to Harare from Bulawayo on his uncle's suggestion. He had seen the Man of God's church on ZBC every Saturday night and Sunday and he had witness every one of the miracles and healings that the MOG and his apostles performed. Fleetingly he wished that it had been the MOG and not this elder which he had never seen on TV that prayed for his healing. Still, he knew that God could use anyone and the enthusiasm of the elder showed that he was a powerful man of God himself, besides, he could speak in tongues and Banele had learnt from one of the MOG's preaching on TV that that was one of the signs of the presence of the Holy Spirit.

At seven p.m., the church service finally ended. The MOG and his apostles were ushered out of the venue and then everyone started swarming out of the sports stadium. Banele painfully moved himself behind the panels of the stadium wall so as not to be seen, and there he remained until half past eight when he was sure that everybody had left. He got up and hobbled into the stadium, down the steps and towards the stage, shots of pain now shooting in all directions of his body with every step he took. He was not sure why he was going back in, perhaps he was in denial that he had come all this way and suffered for so long for no reason. He did not have a plan but, even though he could not articulate it, he was determined not to leave this place and time without his happily ever after.

And then he saw it. On the floor near the stage in front of him. He saw, sitting there in its red garb and dirtied white letters amidst the dust and litter, a healing power wrist band. He could not believe his eyes which started to water with tears of joy. Bending over and doing his best to ignore the excruciating pain, he reached out his left hand and closed his trembling fingers around the cool plastic band. He read the words 'Healing Power!'. The pain was too much for him now, it had gotten to his head and was causing one of the bad migraines which he knew made him faint. Already on his knees he let himself fall over gently and curled up on his left side and closed his eyes. He knew his happily ever after was near. He could feel the power coming in waves from the wrist band. Carefully and slowly he slipped the band onto the thin wrist of his right arm which he then pressed against his chest. In the darkness, a light rain began to fall, settling the dust that thousands of feet had trodden up during the day. Banele did not mind. He curled up, closed his eyes and waited for his new life.

"Come Lord, heal me. I am ready, I am waiting," he whispered, and then all was darkness.

* * *

Prophet Divine, the Man of God himself, hopped out of his Robinson R22 before it had landed and stopped its propellers as per the safety instructions. His two guards and his armour bearer ran up to him from the stadium entrance and fell into formation in step behind him. Once he entered the stadium from his private back entrance his apostles also joined in the entourage.

As the Man of God climbed the stairs onto the stage, a guard beside him holding onto his arm to make sure he got up safely, the crowd of thousands erupted into a deafening roar as they all simultaneously began to chant out his name, "Man of God, Man of God, Man of God." Prophet Divine Emmanuel, the Man of God, walked onto the centre of the stage and gazed at the sea of people which spanned out as far as his eye could see.

From his place of elevation, the God of Man looked out and saw all the kingdoms of the world and their splendour- and they were his.

THE INTERVIEW

Could I have a copy when this is done?

Sure

Do you mind shifting seats, Sweetheart? You are blocking my clients. Thanks. So, what do you want to know?

Let's see, how about you start with...

Where I was born?

...Sure

I was born in Harare Hospital in 1978. I was six days overdue and I weighed 4.7 kilograms... I grew up in High Fields, the location. You know it?

Sure... how, uh, how did you get to where...

I loved school. It was my escape. I mean everyone in the country had it tough but my family was so poor that poor people felt compelled to pray for us. Anyway, yes, school was my escape. I was great at mathematics. In grade seven I won the award for the best maths student and in form four I got an A for both mathematics and statistics.

I don't mean to interrupt but I really just want to know...

How I got here?

Yes, exactly, sure.

That's what I'm trying to tell you. It all started with Maths. Like I said, I really loved school as it was my escape. I just felt that if I do well in school then I could become whatever I wanted to become and I wanted to become a doctor or a professor of mathematics. You look shocked, ha! People have always been shocked by my ambitions. I didn't only want to be those things because I was more than capable, and not only because I would make a lot of money and be free of financial constraints, but also to help people. I wanted to be a doctor for kids.

Oh, a paediatrician?

You know, in my heart I believe that I still can be.

You laugh, but I do want to get a higher education. I'm not going to be, this, forever. I started eight months ago, just after Christmas, and I plan to stop exactly a year from when I started.

Why?

What do you mean why? Do you think this is nice?

No, I just thought...

I have two children, Tinotenda and Kundai. Kundai is the older one, my sweetheart. She's at university in South Africa. She's studying law. Though she's not too much into the sciences she does love school, just like me. Tinotenda, he's in boarding school in Mutare. He's good in school but he sometimes finds it hard to concentrate and apply himself, you know how boys can be. He's on the rugby team, my big strong boy. This is what is paying for their school fees. But I have a business project I want to implement. If I start now, by the time I stop this work I'll be making enough to support me and kids.

Do your kids know?

No, they can never know! I was the eldest of three kids so from a very young age I had a lot of responsibilities, more so because we were poor. I mean, I was forced to mature fast and had adult responsibilities long before any child should. I mean, it's good for children to be aware of reality and all that, especially in this country with all its hardships, but children should never ever be burdened with the knowledge of how low their parent is willing to stoop to provide for them. I mean, this is my struggle, not theirs. I need to protect them so they need never know. It's hard I will not deny that. In the April school holidays Tinotenda stayed with some relatives there in Mutare because I did not have the ten dollars for his bus fare home and another ten to send him back when school started. I figured that I'd rather stay working and earn money for his school fees for second term. In June, though, at Kundai's university they kick the students out. In fact, they say that students have to have moved out of their residences forty-eight hours after their last exam. I don't understand that because when we pay fees we pay for the whole year, but anyway, that's how it is. So she had to come home. I tried to encourage her to look for a job for the holidays but she said that it is hard for foreigners to get work even in the restaurants, and anyway she still would not have anywhere to stay. Luckily though she had saved up enough money for the bus fare home from this campus job she said she got, I think she said its signing books in and out of the library.

It's hard you know, going so long without seeing your children. Don't think that this keeping them away is out of malice. It's not. I miss them every day, but as a mother you come to a point where you know you have to use logic in terms of what is best for your children, and at this point what is best for them is to get a good education, because despite how Zimbabwe makes it seem, I still think that someone with a good education is in a better place than someone without, even if a graduate and a *dofo* are both selling tomatoes on the side of the road at the moment. There will come a time when Zim is good again and it's the graduates who will lift it up. We used to spend so much time together, me and the kids. You know they say sibling rivalry what not? But my kids never fought, we all loved each other. I was a house wife back then so I had the luxury of getting to really raise my children, you know? So even though they are away from me right now, I am confident that I have instilled strong morals and values in them to see them through life.

So... what happened in June?

Oh yes, in June. So Kundai was coming for the June holiday and of course Tinotenda wanted to see his sister so I organised for him to come on his half term break, short though it was. He got tonsillitis during that half term so I kept him with us for an additional week. I knew that a good mother would not let her kids see truth that was this ugly, and I am a good mother, so I had to organise. Obviously, I have my own little room here which I live in and I pay about fifteen dollars a night. So I had to find somewhere for my kids to call home. Last they knew I was staying with my friend Kayla in Arcadia so I had to find something. Biggie said if he ever saw me again he'd kill my children and myself, so I could not go back to him. I prayed, I prayed hard. By some stroke of luck Kayla said she had found me a job as a house girl in Glen Lorne. Kayla is a good friend and she doesn't like me doing this. So I took the job because it provided me accommodation. A decent little cottage at the back of the garden. It was a couple of weeks before the kids came. It was a lovely little cottage come to think of it. I'll tell you now though, Tinotenda and Kundai were distressed. Not because I was a house girl - they never learnt of that - but because we went from living in a house in Greendale to a cottage at the back of somebody's garden. I mean, of course they knew about the situation with their father but they were still shocked.

You know I wish life wasn't like that. I made my mistakes, yes, with their father and many others, but those two children are my gifts from God. I wish that even though things between their father and I didn't work out that he'd at least be man enough to take care of his children. How do men do that? To just throw away their own offspring just because of the inconvenience of who their mother is. How can you just throw away your own children?

Anyway, as God would have it, my bosses left for a holiday or something just as my children arrived, and only came back several weeks after they were gone. I honestly thought about moving into the main house whilst they were away but they had locked the bedrooms and how would I explain that to the kids? So, my story was that I had of course moved out of Kayla's house and was temporarily renting this cottage whilst I looked for a proper house to buy. What did I do for a living? I sold African print material- which I got from the boss's sewing room- to tourists, which was, I convinced them, a very lucrative business.

It was hard for them, the shift in standards of living. But they are so loving those children. They never complained. I obviously did not do any cleaning of the main house whilst they were there and I took them out the cottage as often as possible. We went many places, Mukuvisi Woodlands, Lake Chivero and just to small restaurants and the likes just to have fresh chips and coke. Kundai even convinced me to let her taste her first alcohol since she is over eighteen and I was reluctant at first but after a while I thought, better she try it with me than with the peer pressures in university. She hated the taste, thank God. Funny enough, I've only just realized now that we were in the same place- Crown Plaza- as I was when I had my first taste of alcohol. Ha ha, would you imagine that? Only difference is I was with my sugar daddy and she was with her loving mother and brother.

So why didn't you keep the maid job?

A house girl earns about two hundred dollars a month if they are working for a wealthy and generous family. When I lived in Greendale I had Biggie pay my helper three hundred dollars, plus from my own pocket her children's school fees and uniforms. Don't look so shocked, her kids learnt in the rural areas so the fees and uniform only came up to about three hundred dollars a year so it wasn't too much. Look, my mother worked as a maid for the greater part of her life when I was a kid. She worked so hard yet still barely had money to provide for all of us. I know the struggle, that's why I was so willing to help my helper. So, the average house girl makes less than two hundred dollars a month, before food and transport and tithes that's two thousand four hundred and you and I both know that that is not enough to send two children to good schools where the teachers don't strike then demand your kids pay them for private lesson. Currently, I can make two hundred dollars in a day. Don't open your eyes so wide, Sweetheart, it's certainly not admirable work, and besides, that money goes so fast. But because I work alone and not under someone else as some of the other girls do I am able to pay school fees with not much left after that. That's why I didn't keep the maid job. Look, I know people say make an honest living and suffer but still keep your soul but the way I see it, there's nothing dishonest about the way I make money. Everyone sees who and what I am and they can judge if they want to but at the end of the day I am providing for the children that God gave me to take care of and I am sure he sees my efforts and knows my struggles and he shall bless the fruits of my labour.

God?

Yes, dear.

Are you... ah... a Christian?

Ha ha, oh I see. You assume that I can't be Christian and still do what I do? Ask Mai Ino, that lady that referred you to me? I go to church with her, we sit next to each other. Honestly, I wouldn't have agreed to do this interview with you if it wasn't for her. I don't need the judgement and I could have made money from at least two clients in the time that it is taking to talk to you, but she mentioned that this is a youth camp program or something. What is it called?

Renewal. Really, we aren't judging you though.

That's fine. People think that just because I do this I am far from God. People hear my story, look at my life and think, no this woman cannot possibly be godly, she has sinned too much and what not. Let me tell you, I'm a born again Christian. I got saved during a scripture union revival at school when I was in form three, yes, before I got into the mess with Biggie, who I only knew as Daddy back then. I was a devout *Mai weRuwadzano* back when I lived in a big house in Greendale, and just because I am suffering now it does not mean that I have to throw away God. People judge me but God sees my heart, and I dare say He is the one who provided me with this job- because that is what it is, a job, and not who I am- to be able to stay alive and to be able to provide for my precious children.

But then...

It's alright, you can ask me anything.

I just want to ask, and I mean no offense...

Okay?

Would you be happy if your daughter was in the exact same position that you are in right now?

No. To answer your question as simple and as honestly as possible whilst staring you dead in the eyes as I am right now, my answer is no. Never, of course not.

Okay but then isn't that quite hypocritical?

Look, from the start I told you that desperation is what led me to where I am right now. It's not a walk in the park, it takes a lot out of you. But you know what, I'd rather I go through this, and I'm constantly in danger, and I'm ridiculed and shunned, just so that my daughter is never in this position, ever.

So, okay well this is a weird question, but like do you somehow wish your mother would have gone to the great extent that you are going for your children so you would never have had to be in this position?

Ah, that's a complicated one. Look, my parents were not the best parents and they left much to be desired, but everything happens for a reason. They did what they knew how to. I've tried to forgive them, my father in particular, but yes, well, I have to admit that even though I do not expect them to have gone to as great lengths for me as I do for Kundai and Tinotenda, I just wish they had supported me in my own pursuits to success. At least cheered me on regardless of if they would have help me or not.

How did they hold you back?

Academically. Which hurts because I loved school. Kids that love school and do so without encouragement are rare. Instead of seeing this rarity as a blessing and seeing that through education I could have been the one to delivery my family from poverty, my father saw me and my sister's education as unnecessary.

Why?

Because we were girls.

Oh my gosh!

I don't know, I think the only reason I made it to my O'levels whilst I was still at home was because my brother was only born when I was in form one after which the bulk of the meagre family funds went to his upbringing. That and there was a loose law in the country about children having a right to an education and some U.N. led NGO did pass by every couple of years to make sure that we were indeed being sent to school.
I remember telling my parents that I wanted to go to Arundel school...

I go to Arundel school-

They laughed so hard- I can count the number of times that there was laughter in that house- they laughed so hard, and the thought of me going to one of the best schools in the country amused them so much and uplifted their spirits that they slept together that night. It's disturbing but that is the only time I ever heard my father and mother getting along.

I mean, the house, if you could call it that, the house was small enough to hear absolutely everything, but for my parents that was the first I heard that, and the last time.

At least. No one should ever hear their parents.

No I mean, there were other times. Plenty other times I heard sounds in our house. But they were always when my mother had gone on a church trip or to visit relatives. Don't look so shocked, Darling. What do you expect from a man who thinks that girls shouldn't even go to school, loyalty? No, such sounds were common place in our house as my mother did travel a lot to find money to provide for her unemployed husband and her kids. I never questioned it, didn't even realise it was bad and the thought of telling on my father to my mother never crossed my mind. I just thought, I don't know. I just thought it was an arrangement, just normal family dynamics. It's all I knew so I never questioned it. It was only after I found out that Biggie had a wife that I found out first-hand how painful and wrong cheating was. I guess I was quite naïve when it came to relationship issues.

After that did you tell your mother?

No, it was much too late for all that and besides, something tells me that she knew. In my experience women almost always know but they choose to ignore it for the sake of peace, or because they are dependent on their husbands, or in my case for the sake of the children, because if they leave just because their husband isn't satisfied with just them, then where will they go? Back to their father's house? The same father who also mistreats their mother and teaches his son how to mistreat women in turn? The father would laugh and say that at least you have a roof over your head. Heck, some women would say the same thing. I even said it to myself.

I'm sorry.

I'm not looking for pity.

Okay, sorry. So, was Biggie your husband?

Ha ha, no, Honey, he was my sugar daddy. I'm so scared to ruin your innocence, Mai Ino will kill me. You know a sugar daddy, right?

Yes. Oh, yes you did mention earlier.

I was a very ugly child and to make it worse I was

shapely, which was not in fashion back then. Well, to be fair, I was only ugly because we were poor and did not have money for fancy acne lotions or even Vaseline half the time. Anyway, after puberty boys liked everyone else except for me and plus I always found boys at school very immature and one track minded. I mean, if I had opened my legs or advertised my privates as well as some of the other girls I could have had one or two suiters in high school but I was just focusing on my maths. That's until I met this dreamy mature man in an air-conditioned car one day.

I know people think that girls that get sugar daddies are usually greedy children who are willing to sell their souls and virginities to the devil in any form just for a few nice things, but this was different. I honestly can say even to this day after everything he did to me, that I genuinely felt loved and wanted initially. The monetary gain only then came into fruition after I'd been with him for about a year. In fact, God works in amazing ways, I think he gave me Daddy – I called him Daddy for the longest time because he asked me to and I honestly didn't know his name for the longest time- right when I needed him most.

How come?

Short answer would be to say that I was depressed, well not depressed so to speak, depressed is a state of mind and poor people don't have such luxuries, but I was at one of the lowest points in my life. Even with school as an escape it's still important to have a life which is at least half full of love. Daddy provided the extracurricular part of my life. I had never felt so wanted and cherished as those times after school when he would roll down his tinted windows and coax me into his car where a hot pizza or hamburger would be waiting for me.

Would you like it if your daughter had a sugar daddy?

Aren't you getting what I am telling you at all? I went through all that so that she would never have to.

Oh, sorry, sorry…

This is my story. Please, do not involve my children, okay? In fact, I expect you to change their names and my name and everyone's names I have said if you are to retell this story. You hear me?

Yes.

I am serious. I'll ask you to leave right now, Mai

Ino or no Mai Ino.

No, no, I'm so sorry.

This has nothing to do with my children, I am telling you about my life, me and Daddy.

Look, Daddy happened just before my O'level exams and even though he was a welcome and refreshing part of my life I never allowed him to distract me from my exams as school always came first in my life as it was an out for me and my family. We met after school on my way home and rarely on the weekends in that first year and because I knew never to let boys distract me from my goals, Daddy was no exception. I could even say his presence benefitted my studies because it's hard to study on an empty stomach but when he arrived in my life my stomach was never as empty as often as it used to be pre-Daddy era. I passed my O'levels with flying colours but as I said, my father did not see the necessity of me continuing my schooling and my mother obeyed him even though she was the breadwinner so they never gave me the money to even register myself in school for my A'levels. To make it worse, my mother got sick so I became the woman of the house, doing odd jobs to provide for both my parents and my younger siblings. It was a hard year but Daddy made it bearable. Even during the periods when

I would not see him for months on end because he was travelling, I would communicate with him using the smart phone he had bought for me. And when we did see each other? My, my, life was sweet. He would spoil me, love me and I would love him back to thank him for everything he had done for me. Besides the first time when I was sixteen I can never say he was forceful with me, I guess because I was always willing. Why wouldn't I be? He was the only person on this earth, until my kids were born, that loved me unconditionally. So I learnt to enjoy it for his sake.

Like I said, he made life bearable, but still, life was going nowhere for me and I hated that. And then God again, I guess. It just so happened that some distant relative saw me in Daddy's car and took it upon himself to inform my father. I remember that day well because it was a day full of so much malice. The distant relation came to my house and instead of saying, "Oh, I saw your daughter in a wealthy man's car," they said, "Why didn't you tell us your first born was married?" as they extended the congratulatory gift of a chicken they had brought knowing full well that this was not the case. They brought a whole entire chicken. A chicken! They brought it as a prop to fuel the embarrassment, not as a sincere gift. I know this because after my father informed them through his embarrassment that

I was not, in fact married to a wealthy man, they left with their chicken. Had there been no hint of malice, they would have said, "Sorry for the mistake, here is the chicken anyway seeing as you are poor and probably hungry," and then gone on their way. I got a beating worse than I have ever had that day. My mother and father both took it in turns to whip me with a hose pipe- a small piece borrowed from one of my father's friend's yards. I had welts and bruises all over my body but part of me was happy because they knew and now I had nothing to hide. It was not fun sneaking around. I called Daddy and exaggerated my pain and anguish hoping he would come and take me away from that terrible place but he said he had a family emergency and then switched his phone off.

My mother and father seldom acted like a married couple, like a team, but that night they put their heads together and the next evening I walked into the house to find my mother and father and in addition my father's younger brother who had travelled from Ruwa and my father's cousin who I don't remember hearing about or meeting ever before. They sat me down and after the introductions and *sadza nederere* which my mother had borrowed from her neighbour friend, my father's cousin said, "We heard that you have a man who is wanting to marry you."

I usually remain mute in the presence of elders as children should be seen and not heard was a rule I had learnt the hard way. However, it was so ridiculous what these elders had contrived out of thin air that I could not help but ask them indignantly who said that I was thinking about marriage. "You did, when you sat in his big car and opened your legs," that is what my father said.

His younger brother said, "Let Sekuru speak, Mukoma." So my father's cousin repeated what my father had said. Because I couldn't help but giggle, all the males got angry and because they're words failed to hurt me they began to insult my mother, telling them what a poor job she had done of raising me. If I was judge and jury I would say my father was the cause of our troubles, but I did not entirely excuse my mother because she always caved to my father's demands, never standing up for herself or her children, but as is our culture my mother got all the blame for the short comings of both of their children. My mother was a tough woman and it is unlikely that the half-brained words of three malnourished men sincerely affected her, but to appease their male egos she began to sob and weep on queue.

My father's cousin said, "That man has deflowered you, has he not?" My amusement turned to indignation because I felt like it was none of their business. None of them had contributed anything to my life so it really was none of their business. My father's cousin ordered my mother to go and check and so my mother and I went to the bedroom which I shared with my two younger siblings and ordered me to undress. Thinking back now I don't think she had the skill to tell, medically, whether or not I had lost my virginity but she examined me quietly whilst ignoring my protests and concluded that, and as she related to my father and his male relatives, I had, "Been deflowered like someone's personal whore of five years." Ironic, isn't it?

Anyway, to cut a long story short, my father's male relatives, half of which I had never met before in my life, decided that since I was already playing house with Daddy that he might as well marry me. You know, the thought of marriage had never crossed my mind because I wanted to have a degree and a good job before committing myself to anyone, but at that time my education had been stunted and the future looked so bleak that I willingly gave up Daddy's number to my father's cousin when he asked for it. When they phoned him – with borrowed airtime- I had to go and wait in the bedroom with my mother because, they said, it was men's talk. Both my mother and I kept as quiet as possible to eavesdrop better and from what we gathered Daddy had hung up the phone as soon as he heard who was calling and why. Well, we were let out the room and my father and his relatives decided to go let off steam at the local bar and I honestly thought that I had heard the end of that. I did notice though, that Daddy became more and more aloof, even though I apologised to him for my father's tomfoolery. We met up two weeks after that I remember, I remember that day well because he could hardly keep his hands off of me. When he finished, I broached the subject of marriage. I had never seen him so angry. He stopped his car and told me to get out and I didn't hear from him again after that. That is, until I walked into my house and there was Daddy sitting on one of two of our old tattered brown sofas along with my father, his younger brother and their cousin again. I couldn't believe my eye and I was immediately protective because I was sure that the only way Daddy was in our run-down rack sack part of town was if he'd been forced.

Oh my gosh!

Oh my gosh, yes, oh my gosh is all I could think and, "what?" is all I could say. I wanted to go over to him and hug him and envelope him with myself to protect him from the ugliness of poverty but between me and him was my father, his younger brother and his cousin. I knew there and then that my life wasn't ever going to be the same again and I was both nervous and excited. I was excited because I loved him and I was under the impression that he loved me and also the impression that love could overcome all things.

Looking back, do you still think it was love?

I think so. I mean, it was love as I knew it back then. I believe that love is different for everybody at different stages of life and at that time I did believe that I was in love with him. I had reached a stage where I had gradually released my inhibitions and I knew that I would do anything for him, even die for him. I mean, I know that these sound like very radical words but you've got to understand that at that stage in my life Daddy was my saviour, my safe haven, my hope, because even in the months where we had basically no contact and communication the mere thought of him or the hope of eventually seeing him kept me going. It kept me positive and light and if it hadn't been for him I would have kill myself many times because life was tough.

Do you think that he felt the same way about you?

You know, knowing what I know now that which I didn't know then, I'd have to say of course he didn't love me. The thing is, back then I though he did and that was enough for me. In my very naïve head I was like, why else would he spend so much time and money on me? Why would he buy me cellphones and Chicken Inn and Pizza and give me pocket money? It all sounds very trivial now, but to someone with nothing, even a little bit is a lot. The way he made love to me, he was my first and only for a long, long time so even though I know now that his performance wasn't great I thought then that it was passionate and I equated passion with love. Obviously, I know better now.

That he never loved you?

That men are creatures to be weary of. Of course, he had a wife- the same one he had told me a year earlier that he had divorced- though I only learnt that way too late though everyone else seemed to know. Business men like Biggie, the typical African man, are never satisfied with just a wife. In their circle, I've come to learn that for such men, love is a game. You have your wife who is a social raincoat to shut relatives up and bear your offspring to continue your bloodline and the family name. A wife is also useful for everyday things like cleaning, cooking and planning but for them life would be boring with just a wife. You need a pursuit that makes your blood rush, that brings your youth back. That's where small houses come in. I also found out that Daddy has a small house, but that's beside the point. There is no rule as to how many small houses one can have, but there comes a point where it's no longer about number but also about how young a girl you can legally or illegally have sex with. The more tender the meat the better. It's apparently harder than most people think you know, getting and maintaining a young girl to have sex with whenever you want, but men like Daddy enjoy the thrill and the danger. They use you and take, take, take until you have nothing left to give of yourself, and then they throw you away like a dirty rag for the men in your own age group who will wine and dine you hardly, just enough for you to commit to the role of wife. Mind you, by that time, you have probably lost all hope and self-respect so you will accept this poor excuse of courtship in return for wife duties, stability and security.

Anyway, on that day I knew none of this and though life was tough, it was worth it because I had him. It turns out that my family had gotten over the embarrassment and decided to use the situation to their advantage. They decided to marry me off to the man who had spoilt me to alleviate some of their poverty. A big important businessman like Daddy with government connections would not usually have fallen into such a trap but my father, who was only intelligent when it came to illegal or immoral goings on, had managed to hook him by investigating which people would violently disapprove of my and Daddy's relationship and threatening to tell them that not only was I his lover, but that I was pregnant and that I he had infected me. However, I only found out this trap mechanism later, at the moment I walked in the door, saw Daddy on the sofa and realized what was happening, I thought he was there because he loved me.

That day my father, his younger brother and my father's cousin made the first crack in my wall that would lead to my eventual downfall. My father's cousin told Daddy that he had ruined me for other men, but since I was a hard-working girl, and, as he did not hesitate to point out, albeit not attractive, he would have no qualms in marrying me off. Daddy hesitated and my world slowly and inconspicuously began to fall apart because this was the very first time that I began to doubt that he loved me, but I swallowed the lump that had formed in my throat and sat obediently on the floor with my eyes downcast as is necessary in our tradition.

Is your phone ringing?

It's just a message from my group leader notifying me of time. It doesn't matter, carry on, please.

Where was I?

Daddy in your house...

Oh, yes...

Are you okay?

Look, to cut a long story short, Daddy made a deal with my father and his relatives which traditionally is not honourable but which my father and his relatives agreed to because they were not honourable men. Daddy agreed to pay them a monthly sum, not much but to poor men's ears, enough. He would pay them in return for their silence. He went out and returned with beers and meat and my father and his relatives were so happy with these short-term pleasures that before Daddy left, my father's cousin whilst picking pieces of meat from between his teeth with a piece of straw, admitted that this arrangement had pleased him so much that it was only the honourable thing to do to throw me into the deal as Daddy's wife.

Oh my word.

Daddy had nothing to lose so he thanked them and left. I was to be his wife but stay in my father's house.

Did this arrangement work?

It depends on whose angle you look at it from. From my family's point of view, it worked well. Every month my father and his relatives looked forward to spending my bride price, if you can call it that, on cheap beer and questionable meat. My mother made sure to black mail my father for enough of the money to take care of their precious son. For me though, I didn't see Daddy for more than a year after that. He must have blocked my number because I could never get through to him. I continued with my odd jobs to sustain my family for the remaining twenty days of the month which the money did not last for. I got into a sort of listless routine of working for peanuts and finding creative ways to sustain my family. Life was dull and worthless in that year but I never stopped calling Daddy's number until the phone itself gave up one day and refused to turn on and that was that.

Then one day in the one apartment in the block of flats that I used to clean I noticed one of the children of the house struggling with their homework. The little boy was struggling with form one mathematics and he had tried to ask his father who was just about to leave to go back to the office as lunch time was over, for help. As the dad went to his bedroom to get something for work I couldn't help but point out the error the boy was making in his homework and he was very grateful, and apparently so was his father because he told me that I was wasting my brains cleaning apartments. He told me this in the kitchen whilst I was cooking, with his hand on the small of my back. That changed my life, there and then I decided that I needed to further my education no matter how long it took. I removed his hand from my back, finished my work and marched out of that apartment block so purposefully one would think I had a plan already. I sure as hell didn't have a plan but God did because I marched right out of that apartment block right into Daddy's pot belly. He had found out where I was from my mother and come looking for me. I should have been angry with him for his year long silence, I should have made it hard for him to undress me that night but I don't feel bad for being so easy because in his drunken mirth at our reunion in that cheap motel I managed to convince him to pay my way through my A'levels and college.

I was overjoyed. I attended evening classes after my work on weekdays in town and got fourteen points for M.B.C. I'd see Daddy at least once a week and life was so great that I grew careless and on the day I received the good news of my results I also realized that I had missed three months of my period. The first month I brushed it off as exam stress but the two months after my exams it still hadn't come so I used some of my pocket money to buy a pregnancy test and that is how I discovered Kundai.

Oh no, what about college?

What about it indeed. Sometimes life has other

plans for you that are different from the plans you have for yourself. I wish I had gotten that degree, I think my life would be a bit different right now, but I don't regret what happened. When my parents saw that I was pregnant after a few more months they called Daddy and kicked me out of the house. Daddy picked me up, asked me if it was too late for an abortion and then put me up in a motel for a week. He paid damages to my family upon their request after which they said they would take me back as well but demanded an increase to the monthly bride price so absurd – by this time my little brother was enrolled in an expensive school- that Daddy said no, he'd rather take me to live with him as a proper wife. I was thrilled. Me and my first love and our baby were going to be a real family. Daddy had a new car and he was more cheerful than usual, seeing me more often. I felt loved and cared for. Then one day, reality struck and it nearly destroyed me.

I had been living in the motel. Every Saturday Daddy would take me shopping for groceries and things I needed and often we would stop to have lunch. That day we stopped to have lunch at Sam Levy's Village and we were just about done when I heard a shriek. I looked up as the shriek came again from a rotund woman who was looking down at our table at where Daddy's hand was placed over mine. He quickly snatched his hand away from mine. He got up and reached towards the woman and said, "Cynthia!" but she backed away, nearly tripping over the waiter behind her. I got up, only to be met with another shriek as the lady looked down at my pregnant belly. Daddy said, "Cynthia, I can explain!"

Then the Cynthia in question walked over to me and slapped me. She said, "So it's true. You are the whore, gold-digger sleeping with my husband." She made to slap me again but I managed to back away and walk away quickly from the small, mostly white, crowd that had gathered to watch the commotion. Daddy didn't follow me. He stayed behind and tried to comfort his wife.

I manged to get back to my motel in town with blurry vision. Daddy didn't contact me for another week but when he did he was stern, not apologetic or guilty. He told me that he could no longer pay for my accommodation in the motel and told me to pack my things and get into the car. I did. I suspected that he was going to take me back to my family but he didn't. After driving for some time, I said, "How could you?" He didn't answer me. I cried hot, bitter tears all the way to Nyanga. He had taken me to his rural home where he told me I'd be staying with his blind mother from there on out. I protested feebly because I knew that I was and had nothing without him and that this rural situation would be better than a street situation.

I'm so sorry.

It's alright. I made good friends with his mother. She said I was harder working than the *musalad* of his first wife. In fact, everyone there came to love me, and I them. They loved Kundai too, when she was born, and Tinotenda too when he came along several years later as a result of one of Daddy's rather rare visits to Nyanga. I adapted and even became comfortable with life in Nyanga. My only worry was that my children, mostly Kundai who would soon be starting grade one, would not get as good an education as I had dreamed my kids would have. My mother-in-law spoke to her son and thanks to her constant nagging five months later Daddy came to Nyanga. His intentions were to take my children and put them in a boarding school in Harare. "My kids go nowhere without me" I had declared. So, he took me along. I guess life had been good for Daddy. He put me and my kids in a lovely little house in Greendale and we were a family again even though he only visited every other weekend. Kundai started grade one at Highlands Primary School, Daddy took care of us, I joined a church and life was great.

What about his wife?

After moving into the Greendale house, I got threatening phone calls from her at least three times a week but I told Daddy and they stopped.

It's funny how she was angry at you and not him.

That's how life works I guess. To be angry at him would mean leaving him and all his money. Meaning I would win and probably move into their house to literally take her place. Maybe she loved him. I know exactly how she felt though because years later when Daddy's visits were a thing of the past and it was a chore to get money from him I actually saw him with another woman. It's funny actually. I saw them walking away from his car in town into a fancy restaurant. My heart sank and I felt betrayed, even though I had no right to be. She was very young and very slim and light and beautiful.

Which is probably why, when she got pregnant Daddy didn't send her to his rural home like he did me but instead moved her into my house.

With you still in it?

Well, yes. For a while.

So, would he come and visit you both, plus the kids?

Well, his visits certainly increased but it was painfully obvious they were just for her and not for me or our kids. He would give all our money to her and even though I was at least ten years older than her I'd have to beg her for my share of the money. What hurt most though, was hearing them at night from mine and the kids' room. On days he visited I'd always force the kids to go to bed unreasonably early.

She was a vindictive little girl and me and my children did not get along with her at all. My mother-in-law told me that I needed to make way for her just as Daddy's first wife had graciously made way for me. I swallowed my pride, ignored my pain and tried to be cordial with her. I thought we were getting along fine until one day Tinotenda accidentally broke one of her perfume bottles when I wasn't watching. She scolded me, in her best British accent, for being a careless mother and I apologised. She smiled and said it was fine. The next morning she was more cheerful than usual, even offering to pack my children's school lunches. I had been praying about our relationship so I thought this was an answered prayer, but I walked into the kitchen whilst she was making the lunches and saw her pouring bleach into Tinotenda's juice bottle.

What?

I took the kids to school without lunch and I came home and beat her up badly. She tried to fight back but she was a slight little thing. I phoned Daddy and he came and took her to the hospital. They returned two days later. She had lost the baby.

Oh my gosh!

I told him about the bleach but it was her word against mine and of course he took her side. She said she didn't feel safe with me anymore so he kicked me out. He said she'd take care of my kids for me but I had to leave.

Oh no.

He beat me right in front of her and my children, telling me to get out. So I took my children and left. No way I was going to leave them with that witch. I'd rather they go hungry till I found my feet than they get killed by that girl. That's what happened. I moved in with friends but after a couple of weeks they would tell me that they could not continue supporting me and my children so I'd move on to anyone else who would take me. Daddy wanted nothing to do with me or his kids and I was scared that if I approached a lawyer to help me to try force him to pay child support he'd build up a case against me and he'd win and have the children taken away and I'd probably never see them again. He's also threatened to kill me on the occasions that I've contacted him or gone to his home or the Greendale home. I've done a lot to get my kids to be at decent schools, but mostly I had to borrow, even from those notorious money sharks. You'd think good A'level results would be enough to get a decent job, but in a country where even graduates are sitting around there is nothing for people like me.

When my last friend told me that I needed to do something other than try and sell vegetables and that I could no longer live with her that's when I decided to do this. It was my very last resort. I owed the sharks close to a thousand dollars and my kids were about to be kicked out of school. This is way more lucrative than what people think of as an honest living. All that matters is that my kids are provided for. I don't care about the friends I lost, even when the church told me to stop coming I didn't care.

It's all about my kids. I'm now even able to send my children to college in South Africa and I'm proud of that. I'm proud of them. I love them.

I won't be here forever, like I told you. I'm planning to stop in several months if my project takes off...

It looks like I've got a client, Sweetheart. I'll have to get going. Sorry, Darling.

Okay...

You are really fortunate, you know? Don't forget that.

I won't.

Thank you

No, thank you, for your time.

Bye, Sweetie. God bless.

Oh, wait, one more thing.

Yes?

For the article I'm writing which term do you prefer for the work you do?

Sex worker, Sweetheart.

ACKNOWLEDGE-MENTS

I have so many people to thank, family and friends, that to attempt to name you all would require many more pages. I will however take this opportunity to thank the people who particularly nurtured my love and passion for writing:

To start off with, my family and other animals. Dad you planted the seed of literature in me and nurtured it. I love you endlessly for all you did to water my seed, like forcing me to go to the library during the holidays and write book reports, and making me look up the same word in three different dictionaries, and making me memorize two books of idioms. Thanks for listening and reading all my stories and poems when I was little, and sorry for skipping pages when I had to do my reading homework in the car whilst you drove us home from school. I know you are proud of me.

Mama, thank you for your love, sometimes tough, sometimes tender, and your endless support and encouragement.

Sisters, Abi, Tongie, Tanda, I appreciate all your

individual types of love and support, and all the crazy. Baby Hannah Ru, thanks for being cute... and weird.

Also, the women who once taught me and encouraged my love for creativity and writing: Jess, Sarah, Rebekah, Lara, I may never have the courage to call you by you first names to your face even after you insist, but I hope you always remember that you have impacted mine and many other students' lives so beautifully, and you still do. In a country which cannot yet fully appreciate art, you encouraged and inspired me and helped me grow. I cherish you all. Thank you.

Last but not least, thank you to my Friend who'll never leave me nor forsake me. And thank goodness that my Birth Place is one which provides me with an endless number of stories to tell.

Made in the USA
Middletown, DE
27 March 2019